MARRED

FALLING FROM HELL
BOOK THREE

SUSAN PERSON

PERSON PUBLISHING, LLC

For all those who faced the darkest storms for love

AUTHOR'S NOTE

Dear Reader - Please be advised that this book series contains content that may be upsetting for some readers. Should you wish to learn more information for your best reading experience, please scan the QR code below for additional details and content notes.

MARRED

CHAPTER I

RENA

My family was awkward, but we were loyal, as loyal as demons, vampires, and archangels could be to each other. My Aunt Barachiel's disappearance was bad timing—self-imposed, or so she said, to the Library for unrevealed archangel research. She came back to Hell right away to help us find Uriel. My uncle was not as fortunate. He'd been taken right in front of me and the rest of the family. The one thing I knew with absolute certainty was that I wasn't letting Typhon hurt relatives. Any of them. Especially not the uncle I'd grown close to since his two-hundred-year slumber ended.

The crystal spun of its own accord on the chain and dropped like a weight to the map in front of me. It was low magic, like a witch would use, some would say unbecoming a demon especially in Hell and by Lucifer's heir, but it worked. I successfully scried for Uriel. I marched into the meeting room we'd turned into a command center in Hell. We weren't any safer here than in Gothica, but at least we had a demon army here if Typhon dared to enter my father's realm. Vampire numbers were still depleted from the attack on Gothica while Uriel's Ascendant was out in the world. Those same events cost Mother her second-in-command, Alessia, to the horrible grey-wing Nephilim Adam had created. I shuddered at the memory of how she'd turned into fiery ash on the table in front of us.

There were limitations to Typhon's abilities even though everyone feared him, but there was no denying he was the most powerful being in all the realms we traversed. My fear had long since gone—left on the floor of this very room at the thought of losing even one of my family members. My anger at his intrusion into our lives replaced it. He would see the error of his ways, and I would be the one to show him. *Show him right to his demise.*

"He's here." I pointed to the map of the human realm, one of several maps on the table Jax, Father, Michael, and Gabriel had gathered around to strategize. Michael was in his warrior attire minus his helmet, but Gabriel was in modern clothes. He stood tall, his white wings in contrast to his ruffled dark hair. "Uriel is here."

"Rena, you're sure?" Jax studied me, but my mask was up so I could focus on the task of retrieving my uncle.

"Positive as of about a minute ago." Typhon's power prevented us from summoning Uriel, or so we assumed after several failed attempts. Uriel was a master at denying a summons unlike anyone else. I didn't believe he would willingly be taken though. Either way, nothing warded off the low magic because beings this powerful didn't consider it a threat. Typhon could breathe fire capable of mortally wounding an angel. Scrying would be inconsequential to him.

"How quickly can Typhon move?" Jax glanced at my father.

Father met Jax's stare with determination. "Fast, but we could portal there."

"Typhon won't be able to tell we came through a portal?" Even less powerful demons could sense the ripple of a portal and then there were the demons, like Jax, who could even read the lines of a portal like a map.

Gabriel ceased pacing the floor and pushed his dark hair back out of his face. "I'll tell the others."

"No." Father held up his hand. "Typhon's fire can injure any of you."

My uncle scanned between Father, Jax, and me. "You three are not immune."

"My fire is more powerful than his," Father said, tracing a finger along the map where I'd indicated Uriel was being held. "Rena has my fire."

"But I don't." Jax gripped my hand in his.

I peered down at our hands, dropping my shielding down just enough to glimpse our connection and feel its warmth. His rich earthy scent washed over me like a hug. Then I slipped the mask back into place to focus on Uriel.

Jax's portal would provide the element of surprise Father counted on.

"I've got you," I whispered. Typhon would not get close to Jax. Not if I was there.

"This is not a good idea, Lucifer," Michael said, placing a hand on Father's chest. Father swiped it away.

"And we can't risk the balance and the scale," Gabriel said, his tone pleading. "They are bound for eternity because fate requires them to work together."

It was a risk without our replacements having entered the world yet, but their arrival could be centuries still. Uriel didn't have that kind of time. Snippets of his tortured thoughts broke through the archangels' mental connection to each other. Jophiel, my aunt who was my teacher for so many subjects, had called it an overwhelming sense of agony. That was enough to tell me we needed to get him out.

"This is literally what we were meant to do, Uncle. Trust us to save him," I said, shifting toward Jax and my father, determination visible on both their faces. "Jax, portal please."

Father nodded to me. Jax made the symbols and the blue light shimmered as the portal opened. The other side was shrouded in haze, which meant there were protections in place. We would need to move as fast as possible. *In and out like lightning.*

"I'll go through first," Father said, stepping through without hesitation. He wasn't a risk-taker, at least not in my lifetime, so I knew he'd done the math on our chances. He wouldn't put himself and me, the heir, in peril without believing our odds of success were solid.

Jax still had a death grip on my hand, and together we followed Father through the blue light and into the haze. The room was dark, but the vastness was betrayed by the hollowness of the space. Even in the dim lighting, I could see Jax and Father clearly with my demon vision.

"Warehouse," I whispered.

"And they've already gone," Father said. His words bit through the air as if meant to be a curse.

Something called to me in the room. Like a rope tugging me to it. I couldn't ignore it, but it was different than a call for the balance. "Do you feel that?"

"Yes," Jax said. "The heaviness of torture hangs in this room like poison."

"No, there is something else." I walked toward the pull, confused by the familiarity of the vibration. Jax stayed on one side and Father on the other.

"What is it?" Father's tone was reserved. His voice was full of concern.

"I'm not sure." I stopped where it was the strongest. A silver shimmer glinted up from the floor. I knelt and picked it up by the end. A metal tang filled my nostrils and coated my tongue. Heat flashed over me and then a chill skated down my body. I shivered. *So cold.* "Uriel's feather. Can I use it like Gabriel's?" I asked Father, laying the metal feather across the palm of my hand.

"No, Gabriel is a messenger. Uriel's are not imbued with the same power."

Fuck. No matter how quickly we made it to a location,

Typhon had already moved on and taken Uriel with him. *How are we supposed to get a step ahead of him?*

Jax squatted down where the feather had been and ran his fingers across the floor. An unreadable expression passed over his face before he stood and looked at Father. "What do you think he wants with your brother?"

"Uriel carries a lot of knowledge," Father said, shrugging but it was not a casual move. "I suspect he needs him for a specific piece of information he thinks Uriel possesses."

I inspected the metal feather. Although light like the other archangels', Uriel's feathers were made of a unique substance. "Do you think it's these?" I held the feather out to Father, but he didn't take it.

"No, I think Uriel left this one for us to know he was here." The despair in Father's voice nearly broke me. He had his differences with his siblings, but he loved them. Uriel's suffering was a burden all the siblings shared.

"Lucifer, we will find him." Jax grasped Father's shoulder, reaching for the feather.

The metal warmed in my palm, and I pulled back closing my hand around it. Jax was the scale to my balance, but after how Gabriel's sword had nearly taken his existence, I wasn't willing to risk an injury to him with Uriel's feather. Like anything with the angels, it was never just a feather. A sting emanated over my fingers, and I realized how tightly I'd gripped the metal quill. I opened my hand, and a thin line of crimson beaded along the fate line. The corners of my vision blurred. Haze crowded in around me, and although I couldn't see, my body twisted as if it was spinning.

As the vapor cleared, Uriel came into view a few feet away. My mind raced at the sight of him, but relief mixed with worry as I closed the distance and assessed his condition. Restraints imprisoned him on a device eerily similar to a rack or some other medieval torture contraption. A roar like a wind tunnel raged around me. Uriel's head hung low, chin pointed down toward his chest. Gusts whipped around him, lashing at his body. Streaks of gold angel blood lined his skin. *Too many to count.* My stomach folded in at the sight. I grabbed at the knots around his wrists, but my hand went right through. His malty, cinnamon-and-honey scent wafted around me, tinged with the metallic smell of his blood. I was allowed to be here in sight and smell but not touch — an apparition only able to view but not affect. *What fucking shit is this?* It certainly wasn't low magic.

"Can you hear me?" I whispered near Uriel's ear. His head jerked up, and his eyes flew open. When I met him, I'd thought him the most beautiful and feared of his kind, even above Michael. He was still frighteningly handsome with his chiseled features, but his skin was marred from the violence he'd endured at Typhon's hands. "Are you alone?"

He peered ahead, straining forward, and I followed the direction.

A huge being unlike anything I'd ever encountered came into my view. My gaze traveled up his body for what seemed like an endless number of seconds, and I shivered. He had wings like an angel and a humanlike upper body, but that was where the similarity ended. His unkempt hair trailed behind him past his shoulders. I stared into his eyes. They were black pools with no white, but fire flashed in them like it waited to lash out. Dark tendrils wrapped around his legs, and as I focused on the tendrils, snakes appeared. Massive snakes. Dozens of them. I gagged. Not only was it disgusting, but I hated snakes more than anything in all the realms. What terrified me most about him was his sheer size. He made Uriel look like a toy figurine in comparison. *Typhon.*

When my gaze went back to Uriel, his was locked on Typhon. Defiance in his eyes mixed with hatred. Uriel hadn't lost his fight. *Thanks to all that is Hell. He hasn't given up.*

"You have a visitor." Typhon's voice boomed from all directions like dozens of megaphones were pointed at me.

I snapped my head toward him but didn't speak.

"I can't see you, daughter of Lucifer, but I can smell you. Your scent carries your father's treachery as well as your own."

What the fuck? My lip curled up. I was disgusted and furious. *Who is this creature to speak of my family? I can talk shit about us all day, but I won't let him do it.*

"Go," Uriel whispered. "Go."

"Not a chance," I said, keeping my voice low and my eyes on the massive monster in front of us. Typhon's leer slid from Uriel to me. The snake-legged fucker couldn't see me, but he could hear me.

Uriel's hand contorted in the restraint. "Now. Go."

Typhon sneered in my direction as if he did see me.

I didn't know how I got to the torture chamber much less how to leave. It didn't matter. A force sucked me away, and I landed where I started the day. In Hell.

CHAPTER 2

JAX

A portal opened in front of me and Lucifer. The lines were as familiar as my own name. The lines appeared to me as they always did, and they were directed to Hell. I couldn't see her, but Rena's presence passed through. The gateway slammed closed. The balance and scale were drawn to each other in the brief second she'd been here. I turned to Lucifer. He grimaced, his brows knitting together.

"You felt that, right? We need to go back to Hell."

He rubbed his chin. "I did. Call the portal but be ready to fight when we step through. We don't know if Typhon was with her."

I nodded, replaying the events in my head and forming the symbols as fast as I could. If Rena was hurt, I'd kill Typhon and Uriel both.

Gabriel and Michael greeted us in Hell with swords drawn. Lucifer growled, and his brothers lowered their weapons. Rena's father towered over most of us, and his black leathers made him appear more menacing.

Rena sidestepped her uncles. "I told you it was them."

She appeared unharmed, but I grasped her shoulders and patted her down for wounds to be sure. I wanted to wrap her up in my arms and carry her away, but she'd probably kick my ass if I did. "Are you okay, my love?"

"I'm fine," she said, but her voice shook. "I saw Typhon. He couldn't see me, but he knew I was there." She looked at her father. "Was that because of Uriel's feather?"

"Maybe an enchantment he put on the feather," Lucifer answered, uttering a curse under his breath. "Tell us what you noticed."

Rena recounted the things she saw in detail. Uriel was alive, but I supposed the archangels would have known if he'd been ended.

"How did you get there? You disappeared in front of us." The worst outcomes played through my head. *What if Typhon had taken her too? What if she'd been hurt or worse?* I swallowed my fear of what could have been.

"I don't know. It wasn't a portal but similar." Rena peered off into the distance as if the answer was there. "It was like I moved in the time it took to take a breath."

"It was Typhon," Gabriel said, his tone grim.

Lucifer nodded. "He allowed you to ride the wind. His wind."

"Any idea what he was using Uriel for?" I asked instead of if it could happen again. The latter was what I really wanted to know but couldn't find the courage to voice.

Rena shook her head. "No, but Uriel was bleeding and in that … device. He was clearly in pain." She looked at her father. "None of you could tell what he was thinking while I was there? None of it came through?"

"Our connection to him has been far too limited since he was taken for that kind of detail," Michael said. "I was on my way to the human realm when Rena arrived here. Keep me posted." He focused on Rena. "Stay safe." The archangel shot upward and disappeared in a bright flash of light.

"Typhon is strong enough to limit the connection?" I asked, not able to reconcile there was a being with the kind of power it would take to disrupt the psychic archangel network. Their bond was forged in their creation and had been in place for millennia.

"Possibly," Lucifer said. "But I suspect Uriel has chosen to shut us out. That could be the pain Rena saw on his face. It takes great strength to obstruct out the collective group."

"Why would he block his family?" Rena asked. "What would be the point of shutting out the very people who could help him?"

"He doesn't want his siblings to suffer. It's love. I'd do the same." Lucifer's tone was bleak.

Rena nodded as if she accepted the answer, but she chewed on her thumbnail. The nervous habit was a tell she was still thinking about the issue. That beautiful mind was working on an answer to what she perceived to be a problem, but it was in those desperate times I worried most about her. She was willing to sacrifice herself so easily to save her family.

"Why now though?" I asked. "Why take Uriel now when they could have taken him while he slumbered? It would have been easier."

"If Typhon's children brought him back, they might have sensed Uriel's return. When an archangel crosses realms, there is a ripple not all that different from a portal." Lucifer watched Rena, and it was obvious in the way he opened his mouth slightly and closed it there was more he thought hadn't been said.

"He knew I was there," Rena said. "Even though I wasn't whole. He still knew I was there. What did he want me to see?"

"He allowed you through in a way you couldn't be a threat to him."

Rena's eyes widened, and she threw her arms up in the air. "What in all that is Hell could be a threat to a being so powerful?"

"You, daughter," Lucifer said, turning to me. "And you. The balance and the scale."

Fuck. "He wasn't wanting her to see anything in particular except his power. He set her up to see if she would come for Uriel. If he mattered." And it was a fucking coward's power move to psych Rena out. I should be used to those tactics since Nephilim liked to work the same way, but it pissed me off. Rena didn't psych out so easily, and I wasn't worried about her determination. I was worried about her fear for her family overriding her good sense.

Lucifer nodded. "I think so."

"What makes him so different from the archangels?" I asked. "Besides his terrifying size."

"Nothing really," Gabriel said. "He's another celestial."

Lucifer sighed. "Because his power is vast, and he spawned all monsters. We vanquished him but spared his children. It appears they found a way to bring him back."

"His children…" Rena's voice trailed off as she hadn't heard it before. I was concerned she might be in shock and moved closer.

Gabriel crossed his arms over his chest. "The monsters who haunt human children's nightmares. They were left powerless when Typhon was defeated. Nothing more than phantoms. But that might not be the case with his return." Things would get messy if we were fighting multiple creatures like Typhon. All of us against one monster gave us the numbers, but if our numbers were equally matched, the power might be too.

"Were there others with him, Rena?" I asked.

She shook her head. "No, not that I saw. It was just him and Uriel."

The question on the tip of my tongue had to be asked, but I didn't want to hear the answer. I knew it as sure as I knew my name. "Where was Typhon banished to when he was vanquished?"

Lucifer studied me as if he didn't want to answer any

more than I wanted to hear it. "First to the opposite side of Eden and finally, to the dream realm."

Rena let out a small gasp.

"We let him out..." Dreamwalking had to be what gave him a path out, but which time? It didn't matter if it was my entrance or Rena's. It had to be fixed. We had to put him back in his cell. "How do we capture him? At Megiddo?"

Everything came back to the intersection at Mount Megiddo. The sandy gravel in front where Lucifer and Lilith met as the people they are today. The tunnels and chambers there were a constant reminder of the great sacrifices Rena and her family had already made to keep the balance intact for all realms.

Lucifer's eyes widened a little. "It was Uriel's plan last time, but Michael led the execution of it."

"This is revenge," I said.

"Where's Michael now?" Rena rested her hand on Lucifer's arm. "Can you hear him?"

"He was at Gothica with your mother," Lucifer said, panic lacing his words. "Portal, Jax. To Gothica."

I formed the symbols as fast as my hands could move. Lucifer and Gabriel went first. Rena followed, and I went through last. The familiar rug and couch I wanted to burn greeted me. Light shown through the stained glass window depicting Lilith and Lucifer and cast vibrant colors across the room. I'd sent us to Lilith's apartment instead of the command center. It wasn't intentional, but the apartment had occupied my thoughts from my time as a vampire and when my leaky soul was plugged by Uriel's angel juju.

Rena hunched over and clutched her collarbone where the pentagram birthmark was. "Nephilim," she gritted out.

I clenched my jaw and reached for her. "Where?"

My question died in the sounds of struggle from the lower floors. I dashed into the hallway and down the stairs with Lucifer and Rena behind me.

I skidded to a stop at the bottom. A creature with the head of a lion, the body of a goat, and a scaly backend and tail filled the vast hallway of the inner sanctum. The backend reminded me of a Komodo dragon only bigger. A scent drifted to me, and I resisted pinching my nose. It smelled like a barnyard. "What the fuck is that?"

Gabriel let out a whistling sound. "That is Chimera. One of Typhon's children."

"Guess we have the answer if they have power again." But what I saw surprised me. Nephilim fought beside vampires and demons against the beast. *The enemy of my enemy is my friend.* None of them struck the beast though. They kept Chimera confined in the space. Typhon's child looked wide-eyed. I scanned the crowd until I found Rena's mother.

"She can breathe fire. Watch her mouth," Lucifer said, as he leapt toward Lilith.

"Her?" Rena glanced at me. "How did *she* get in here?"

I shrugged and pulled my double-fighting swords from their sheaths. "Maybe she can portal?" I took a giant step and flipped into the middle of the fight. Rena and I were long past me asking her to sit a fight out. Neither of us could abstain.

I spared a brief look behind me to see Rena jump right toward the monster. *Of course, she is.* Her feet planted in the monster's side, but Chimera didn't even seem to notice. Lucifer had taken up the space in front of Lilith, who didn't appear to be the beast's primary target.

Chimera looked around as if searching for something specific. The warrior archangel was missing. She was looking for... Michael. I scanned the crowd, but I didn't see him among those fighting. He should stand out at his height. *So, where the fuck is he?*

Rena landed next to me. Her eyes glowed demon red, but she hadn't invoked her devil's face.

She tilted her head toward Chimera and winked at me. "Together?"

My dick twitched at her fierceness and how brave she was when faced with such danger. *Damn, I love her.* "Together."

"You go for the throat," she said. "I'm going for right between the eyes."

"On three," I said. "One...two...three..." Rena and I leaped into the air in practiced synchronization. Rena went high, and I went low. I crossed my dual swords and readied myself. Chimera's neck moved, but I was still on track to deliver my blow. I scanned up to see the lionlike mouth open in a terrible scream. I couldn't cover my ears, but I guessed what would come next. *Fire.* And Rena was right in the line of it. *Fuck.*

I flung one of my swords at the gigantic head. Chimera turned in my direction. My sword was inches away from burying into her neck, but my body slammed into the floor.

A thud hit beside me. "Ouch."

I rose to see Rena next to me. She was alive and not burned. Relief loosened the tension in my neck. I wanted to pull her into my arms, but we were both covered in a substance I didn't recognize. "Where did Chimera go?"

The chaos around us quieted.

Lucifer knelt down next to us with Lilith at his side. He ran his fingers through a yellow goo. "My guess would be her nest."

Rena gulped. "Nest?"

"She's had a litter recently?" I looked at the liquid covering the floor.

"Litter?" Rena's eyes widened a little. "There are more of them?"

There wasn't fear in her eyes but shock and amazement. She was fearless.

"Yes, she's given birth recently," Lilith said. "She is definitely lactating."

I dry-heaved and rolled out of the sticky liquid. Looking over my shoulder at the vast number of Nephilim present, I extended my hand to help Rena up from the floor.

The half-angel, half-humans began to file out without

so much as a peek toward us. One very pale tall one stopped in front of Lilith. "Our truce will remain intact as long as Typhon and his children roam free."

Lilith gave him a half nod.

Lucifer didn't look surprised. Rena was caught off guard by the way her mouth gaped open. At least I wasn't the only one who didn't know. "When did we make this truce?"

CHAPTER 3

RENA

A *truce with Nephilim? What in all that is Hell are they thinking?* I narrowed my eyes at my parents. "Monsters are walking in the human realm, and you're making peace with our enemies? The same ones who believe we are abominations?"

"I made the truce." Mother leveled her gaze at me with unflinching resolution in her eyes. She didn't look the least bit repentant in her choice. Her black hair was coifed into a soft glamorous style from what she usually wore, but it didn't hide the grey streak at her temple, darker than my silver tint. She had on a pantsuit, and I couldn't recall the last time I'd seen her in one. "You didn't think Michael followed me here for another reason, did you?"

"No, I didn't know why," I stammered. I hadn't had time to think about it, but they hadn't exactly been open with their plans either. Something in how harsh her look was told me this wasn't open for discussion, at least not in front of Father.

"Speaking of Michael. Where is he?" Jax moved the subject on, saving me from the sarcasm about to erupt from me.

"He left just as we finished the truce agreement. The Nephilim didn't even have time to leave before Chimera arrived."

"My brother left you alone with the Nephilim?" Father roared. His anger was palpable in the air around us, charging it in what promised to be punishment.

I took a step back into Jax, and he rested a protective hand on my hip.

"They are far less concerned with my people than they are with yours, Lucifer," she said like she hadn't just been alone with several dozen of the half-angel beings. Well, not completely alone. There were a couple dozen or so vampires still at Gothica. "He got a call. You know how hard it is to ignore a summons."

"It can still be done." Father growled, but Mother had done what she did best, calm Father's temper. He relaxed some, and he wouldn't be completely until he confronted his brother. He needed to hear why from Michael.

"Call out to him," I said, twisting my hand into the air. "See if he returns."

Father closed his eyes. He didn't need to sing the angel's song like I did. *Or do I? Now that I'm the balance and Jax is the scale, can we reach them like Father?* I didn't want them in my head though.

The warm light of Heaven flashed and filled the room. Vampires dashed away for darker spaces, making so little noise it was almost like mice scurrying away. Michael stood in front of us. Mother opened her mouth, but before she could speak, Father was moving. Michael, for his part, didn't even try to move out of the way.

Father slammed him into the wall. "You were to remain with my wife in case she needed to be evacuated to safety, and not only did you abandon her, but you also left her with the enemy."

Jax put a hand on Father's shoulder as if to push him away from Michael, but he didn't force it. Father narrowed his focus to Jax's hand and lifted his head until they were eye to eye. Jax impressed me by not budging.

"I'm well, Jax. He will not hurt me," Michael said, his voice low and calm. "This is just what you might call a sibling spat."

Jax backed away with his hands up like he needed to show he wasn't a threat. A wise move because standing between two archangels wasn't a place a half-human should be, especially when we were in the human realm.

Father gripped Michael's shirt and launched him into the hall wall. The wall caved in from the impact as Father caught him and held him in place.

"Hope that's not load-bearing," Jax mumbled.

Mother stepped forward. "Luc—"

I threw my arm out in front of her. While she was typically his source of calmness, he was only going to get angrier if she interfered. It was her safety and that of his family triggering this. It had to be me to intervene.

I positioned my hands between them. While I worried about Jax, the odds were far less likely I'd be severely injured. Father was huffing and didn't look at me. Michael cut a look in my direction and winked, so he was fine for the moment. "Father, no one was injured."

"Morena, step away. This is between my brother and me." He snarled at Michael.

"I don't think your anger is really at him. I think you are upset Typhon has made us all vulnerable." No one had dared say it out loud, but any of us would be fools not to realize how unshielded we were from a threat like Typhon. He came in and snatched Uriel like he'd picked a flower from the garden.

Father didn't release my uncle but inched closer. His devil face was on full display, and he stood almost nose-to-nose with my uncle. Father shoved Michael harder into the damaged wall.

"Stop," I yelled, and my tone was the strange voice I'd first invoked on the battlefield when I'd claimed the throne. The sound reverberated off the walls, and I sensed all eyes on me. I forced myself to focus my voice into the normal range. "We are stronger together. Being divided makes us easy targets. We're playing into Typhon's hand."

"I'm fine, Morena," Michael said, and he was. There wasn't a scratch on him. "He has not hurt me."

"The wall you are embedded in would differ," I countered. "Let him go, Father. Focus your anger on Typhon."

Father's face returned to normal. He looked at me. I relaxed, my shoulders dropping from the release of tension.

"When did you get so wise?"

I smiled, and he released Michael. I let out a breath. "I've had two very good examples. Do you think we should call everyone to Hell and regroup?"

He nodded. "Why don't you give the order?"

I worried the fight might resurface later, but he was calm for now.

"Jax, take us home. We'll summon the rest once we are there."

Jax made the symbols that came so easily to him now, and Jax, Michael, and I moved toward the portal. Father held out a hand to Mother, but she hesitated. He shook his head and walked on through behind Jax and Michael.

I studied Mother, expecting to see alarm or fear, but she only wore a mask of determination. "What's wrong?"

"My people need me here, Morena," she said. "There are so few left now."

Worry soured my stomach. "You don't have enough protection here."

Mother motioned for one of the vampires I didn't know to clean up the mess in the hallway. He dashed off for what I assumed were supplies. "I know there is much to do." Mother's tone was soft and even, missing the notable cadence that was her. "Your wedding needs my time too—"

"Mom, the wedding can wait. What is going on?" I reached for her arm.

"Go back to Hell, Morena. We'll talk later." The harshness in her expression told me not to push on this.

I dropped my hand and stepped back into the portal.

CHAPTER 4
JAX

Panic snaked up my spine. Rena wasn't right behind Lucifer, Michael, and me. I started to step back through, but reversing direction through a portal can cause it to become unstable, so I waited.

It seemed like a long time passed, but it was probably seconds in reality. Rena stepped through and I sighed with relief. My relief disappeared when I saw the concern on my love's face.

"Where's your mother?" Lucifer asked.

"Jax close the portal," Rena said before turning to her father. "She's staying for a while to take care of Night Children business."

"Night Children business…" Lucifer muttered. He was pissed, but he didn't push it further, to my relief, and I was sure to the others as well.

I held out my hand to Rena. "Maybe we should get cleaned up. This yellow stuff is sticky and smells like—"

"Like something regurgitated on you." Gabriel pinched his nose. "Multiple times."

Rena looked down at the residue on her clothes from Chimera and scrunched her nose. "Gross." She slid her hand into mine. "We'll be back as quick as we can."

Lucifer's brows lowered as his gaze met mine. I wasn't trying to get on his target list after that display with Michael, so I turned and led my love away.

Our room was dark and quiet, but the lamps came to life when we entered, lighting the way as we moved deeper into the room. We were home and safe if only for a brief time, but these were the moments that occupied my thoughts, being alone with my love. Caring for her. Adoring her. I turned the shower on and began removing Rena's clothes. I peeled off her leather jacket, taking in how stunning she was even covered in funk. She looked up at me with deep affection in her eyes, and my chest expanded.

"I can undress myself," she said softly.

"I know, but I want to do this for you," I said, dropping her jacket to the floor. My gaze drifted over the soft skin at the base of her neck. I lifted her shirt, and she raised her arms. "Want to talk about what happened with your mom?"

"I don't know what to say there. She was just..." Rena frowned. "Different."

The tiny scar on her chest was the only reminder she'd died not too long ago. I pressed a gentle kiss to the jagged, raised skin. Steam billowed out from the shower, casting a haze in the room. She braced her hands on my shoulders as I removed her boots and socks. "Different how?"

"I think something is going on with her and Father. Like when Gabriel was under the influence of the Ascendant and hid it from everyone. Only she's the angry one, and Father's oblivious except to be mad he's out of the loop for once."

I slid her pants down, taking her underwear with them, and I stared at her core, tempted to taste. The topic stopped me. I wanted to give her space to talk if she needed it. "They go through ups and downs like in most relationships."

"Mmm hmm." She ran her fingers through my hair and gripped it until my head tilted back. Her look was heated, telling me she needed the same thing I did. The warm scent of her arousal lapped over me. Blood rushed to my cock, always ready at the slightest touch from her.

"Unless you have a new fetish for this goo on our clothes, get in the shower." My voice came out husky and thick with desire.

"No, I'd prefer your clothes shredded in the corner." She smirked and sauntered into the shower swaying her hips. She looked like a goddess, and I watched the path of the clear liquid as it ran down her body until it reached her center.

I yanked my clothes off in a blur and joined her under the water. Steam filled the space around us. I pressed Rena against the shower wall and devoured her mouth with mine, ready to show her my devotion by giving all I had to her. Her lips were soft and parted to let me in. She pulled back.

"I love you, Jax."

Her wet hair draped across her face, and I pushed it back so I could look her in the eyes. She was my life, and hearing those words was the sweetest symphony. "Love isn't enough to describe what I feel for you, Rena, but I guess it will have to do. I love you."

There was only one way I knew to show her how much more this was. *Worship at her shrine.* I dropped to my knees in front of her and lifted one of her legs, hooking it over my shoulder. "And I'm going to show you just how much."

She dug her nails into my shoulders. "Show me then."

I licked the entire length of her slit to her clit and circled my tongue around the bundle of nerves. Rena moaned, and she thrust against me. My dick hardened and twitched in a painful response. I resisted the urge to rise and thrust inside her. This was about me glorifying her as the goddess she was.

She fisted her fingers in my hair. "I want you."

"Patience, my queen." I clamped down and sucked on her nub.

She arched her back, tilting her hips up toward me. "Jax."

The way my name crossed her lips in a breathy moan stirred my desire to see her come undone. I worked my tongue on her and inserted two fingers inside her.

"So wet." I growled against her.

"Faster," she said, her voice raspy with need.

I obliged, moving in quick strokes with both my tongue and fingers. She moaned and her core clenched around me. She was a drug I couldn't get enough of on my face, on my fingers, and on my cock.

"Give it to me." I circled my tongue and sucked harder on her.

Rena moaned and rode my fingers in a wild dance as her walls contracted. I smiled against her center and continued to work to ease the pressure as her body jerked. Her head fell forward, and her body relaxed. She unwound her hands from my hair. I loved the blissful expression on her face as if this was a drug for her too. Precum dripped from my dick. I needed her, but first, I slipped my fingers out, sucking her juices off as I stood in front of her. Her lips parted as she tracked my movements, eyes still filled with desire.

I claimed her mouth and positioned my hands under her thighs, my need to meld our bodies into one taking over. I lifted her and thrust into her hard. My cock slid in with ease, and she was soft against my throbbing shaft. I held her still, fighting to not let my release go.

Rena's breath came out in little pants. "Jax..."

"I know," I said. "You'll get another one."

She wrapped her arms around my neck, and I thrust deep inside her, hitting the spot that made her eyes roll back in her head. My blood burned through my veins and straight to where we were joined. I loved seeing her in a blissful state. She was beautiful. I leaned her back so I could kiss her breasts. I licked her nipple, unable to control myself and bit down on it gently. Her pussy contracted around my cock, and I planted my hand against the wall to keep us upright. Rena moaned and dropped her forehead to my shoulder. She sank her teeth into my flesh.

"Fuck, Rena." She drove me mad in the best way. One more thrust and my seed spilled inside her.

Rena screamed my name.

I held her against the wall under the water for several minutes, not wanting to lose this moment. Our connection was strong, and I never felt closer to her than I did after I worshiped her.

She raised her head from my shoulder and captured my lips with hers. "You are all the realms to me."

I let her slide down my body, coveting the feel of her skin against mine. She was my everything, and I wanted her to know what that meant. "When our world seems too big and our enemies too great, remember this. This moment. This connection. Us. That is what matters."

CHAPTER 5

RENA

Mother was in the meeting room with Father and Michael when Jax and I joined them. I didn't think the two of us had been gone all that long, but maybe her Night Children business hadn't been time-consuming. Her forehead creased as if stressed, but otherwise, she appeared as she always did.

Father stood apart from her, looking over a map, and I suspected he was ignoring Mother from the way he had his back to her. To be as old as they were and considering how they pushed Jax and me to communicate, they were doing a poor job of being a unit.

"Where's Gabriel?" I asked.

"He hasn't returned from his rounds yet," Michael said. "But we expect him soon."

"And the others are safe?"

"Gabriel has connected with most and they are."

"Good," I said. Jax placed his hand on my lower back.

It was a small gesture, but I relished the strength his connection gave me. We'd been through so much, and we would survive this too.

Light flashed just outside the door, and Gabriel's figure darkened the doorway. My shoulders eased down, thankful he'd returned safely. After seeing Typhon and Chimera, I'd worried if we had the numbers to stand against them.

"What news do you bring, Brother?" Father asked.

"They have all been awakened by his return, and they all have their powers," Gabriel said.

"Who? His children? How many are there?" I asked. Panic gripped my gut, but I tamped it down.

Jax shifted closer to me. He didn't try to shield me anymore. He supported me.

"You met Chimera earlier," Father said.

I cringed at the memory of the goop and the terrifying part goat, part lion, and maybe dragon-at-the-tail creature. "Yes, and you said she had a nest."

"She'd given birth recently," Mother said. "Their offspring don't always survive, but one or more likely did from this litter."

"And the others?" Jax asked. "Are they like Chimera?"

"No, they are all as different as they are all alike," Michael said.

Sweet angel's ass. How do we prepare for that? If we needed a battle plan for each one, the additional time needed put us at risk. It wasn't like fighting the Nephilim where we knew what their tricks were and how they all trained to fight mostly the same way.

"Hydra is the oldest and probably the one who should be most feared," Gabriel said. I didn't know much about these creatures, but I wasn't looking forward to meeting more of them.

Jax swallowed hard next to me. "As in the mythological nine-headed monster?"

"The same, but she is not a myth," Father said. "She is fierce, and the myth was correct in that two heads will grow back where one was. When the extra head is no longer needed, she sheds it."

A shiver ran through me. "Eww."

Jax's hip brushed against mine. "And the others?"

"Orthus is a massive, dog-like creature," Gabriel said.

"I take it not like a cute puppy," I said.

"Not at all," Michael said. "She's vicious and her drool works like an acid."

Hell have mercy. It's like Typhon mixed one of his storms with his DNA to create a creature made of chaos and the results yielded were different every time.

Jax's face wrinkled in disgust. "Is that all of them?"

"No, there is Typhon's only male child," Mother said.

"Cerberus," Father supplied.

"The giant three-headed dog?" I asked.

"The very same," Michael said.

"He really is the father of monsters," I whispered.

"From Typhon's chaos came forth his children, and they are as terrible as he is," Michael said.

My body shook with a tremor, and Jax tucked me against his side. "But we don't have to defeat all of them, right? Just Typhon and then the children lose their power."

"He can't be killed," Gabriel said. "We can only vanquish him. If we are successful, his children, indeed, become powerless."

The task of locking Typhon away overwhelmed my thoughts, and I wondered if we were up to the task. The archangels had done it once before, but it was many life-times ago. *Can we do it again?*

"His children will make it harder this time. They've lived lifetimes as phantoms. They will not be eager to go back to such," Father said.

I couldn't blame them for that, but we couldn't let them exist in this world either. The destruction to the humans would be devastating and probably start a war. Some would seek to destroy them, and some would seek to use them to gain power and control. "So, they are going to defend Typhon with everything they have."

"And if Chimera has reproduced, the others may have as well," Mother said.

"They are building their own army," Jax said, making small soothing circles on my back.

"They might be monsters, but they are smart to raise an army any way they can." The discussions around fighting Typhon were daunting. Add four, maybe more if they were reproducing, powerful monsters who didn't seem to be able to communicate in human-like form, and our task became disconcerting. Plus, we had Uriel to rescue. Nothing about the days ahead would be easy, and the nervous pit in my stomach grew. I inhaled and let out the breath as Jax and I had done together many times. *One... Two... Three...* Jax squeezed my hip.

"How did you fight the children last time?" Jax asked.

"We didn't. We lured them away while we forced Typhon through a series of portals." Father ran his hand through his hair.

"And Typhon didn't have Uriel that time," Gabriel said.

"But if we were to separate Uriel from Typhon, is that our only way to vanquish him?" I asked. "Could we trap him in a cell in Hell?"

Father shook his head. "No, Cerberus was the original guardian of Hell before me. His time was brief in comparison, but his ties to the Underworld are still intact."

"So, Cerberus can enter Hell anytime he wants without setting off any alarms?" I asked.

Michael stiffened next to me as if the realization hit him at the same time.

"Theoretically, but his entry would be noticed," Father said.

"But would he bother if Typhon stopped time as soon as they entered?" Gabriel asked.

"That's how he did it," I said. "They entered the Underworld, immediately stopped time in the room, and took Uriel."

Gabriel leaned back against the wall. "But why not stop it for all of the Underworld?"

"He wanted us to know he could get inside at will," Michael said.

"And fuck with us on demand," Jax added.

"Language, Jax," Mother said.

I cut my gaze toward her. *That's what she's focused on?* Jax's language was cleaner than most demons and the vast majority of her remaining Night Children. Besides, I liked it when Jax cursed. Like when he was buried inside me in the shower and moaned *fuck* along with my name.

"And Gothica is apparently not an option since Chimera was able to get in there," I said. "Where can we go where we are fortified?"

"Not the dream realm. Our bodies would be vulnerable here while we walked there," Jax said.

"The Library of Knowledge," Gabriel said. "Barachiel and Jophiel are there combing through books for passages predicting Typhon's return."

The Library was both salvation and damnation in my eyes, both home and not. It was a place where truths could be found but sometimes it was an unexpected force.

I regarded Mother. She wrung her hands and tilted her head down, preventing me from reading her face. She still didn't believe she had a soul, even though she believed I did. My heart ached for the turmoil that must be raging in her thinking she was the only one standing here who couldn't enter. But she could. Gabriel had told me she had a soul too. I smiled up at Jax and untangled myself from his firm hold.

I faced Mother and rubbed her upper arms. She jerked like I'd startled her, but she met my eyes. There was more than fear in her expression. I saw terror there.

"You have a soul. You can enter too."

"No, Morena. I don't think I can." She peered over my shoulder, and I followed her line of sight to Father. Was she worried he couldn't? "Father?"

I inclined my head toward Mother. He rushed over, looking Mother over as if she might be physically injured. "Are you hurt, Lilith?"

Whatever strangeness had been between them earlier disappeared. Father's worry for Mother's safety outweighed any residual anger he had for her. Mother's hand rested against his cheek. "I'm fine, Luce."

She tried to mask her fear and use his nickname to make him believe she was fine, but I saw through it. Father's eyes narrowed a fraction, so I knew he must too.

"You can still enter the Library, can't you?" I asked Father. There were stories of those refused entry being turned into dust and others being able to see into it but never allowed through the doors.

"Yes. It responds differently to me but does not deny me." He turned back to Mother. "Is that your concern? You're afraid you cannot enter?"

Mother was unusually timid. I'd never seen trepidation like that from her. "Yes," she said, her voice so quiet I barely heard her. "I don't think I'll be welcome there."

"I don't know if I'm welcome there, Lilith, but I'm allowed entry." Father cupped her face in his hands. "You will be too."

Her eyes reddened, and she nodded. "I trust you."

Father kissed her forehead with a gentleness he never showed in front of others. He let his tough exterior break for her, for Mother's need to know she wasn't excluded. That she was safe. That was love. The unbroken kind, like the circle of a wedding ring.

CHAPTER 6

JAX

The scent hit me as soon as we dropped through the portal onto the steps of the white marble building. Everything about the massive structure welcomed visitors yet we never saw anyone but us here. Embellished gold doors stood before me. A musky mix of amber and florals blanketed me with a soft invitation to enter. The Library might not be in Heaven, but I couldn't imagine Heaven smelled better. The aroma lapped at my senses as if it was the most important thing in the realm requiring my attention.

I walked to the top of the stairs, but Rena wasn't with me. I glanced at Michael and Gabriel. They had turned, looking down the way we came. Lilith took the steps in slow motion. She surveyed, taking in everything. Rena was on one side of her and Lucifer on the other as they reached the top.

Lilith lowered to her knees in front of the doors, and

her body shook with sobs. My heart lurched. Lucifer knelt in front of Lilith and wrapped his arms around her. I made my way to them, unsure what happened to make her stop. Was she rejected? We hadn't even tried to enter. Rena wiped at her mother's tear-stained cheeks.

"I didn't think I'd ever step foot on these grounds," Lilith choked out.

Rena stroked her mother's back. "We wouldn't have brought you here if we weren't certain."

Lilith wept and stretched her arm out to pull Rena to her so Rena, Lucifer, and Lilith's heads all touched. It was like she'd created a shelter for the three of them.

A knot formed in my throat, because despite how strong Lilith was, even she didn't feel worthy to be here. I understood, because the few times I'd entered the building, I never thought I deserved to be. Yet, she'd made the trip anyway, willing to make a sacrifice if it was necessary. I'd been willing to offer my way up for Rena more than once, and I would do so if my existence allowed. *Maybe I have more in common with the Mother of Night Children than the brief shared past of when I was vampire.*

Lucifer lifted Lilith from the ground and pulled her against his chest. He rested a hand on her cheek. "You are here. You are flesh. You have a soul."

I'd never seen Lilith cry openly before, but she did against Lucifer's chest. Her body molded to his, and Rena wrapped herself around Lilith's back. It was a vulnerability the Mother of Night Children rarely showed, and it was so intimate between her and her family that I shuffled awkwardly away.

The Library door opened with the scraping sound of stone against stone, and Michael gestured inside. I debated staying, but I followed him to give Rena and her parents some privacy. They didn't have much time for just the three of them anymore, and I knew from chats with Lucifer that, he at least, looked forward to the days when the threats were minimized and when they could spend time together. I wanted to be a part of their future as the family unit I never had, but this didn't feel like the right time or place.

I fell in stride with Gabriel and Michael.

"Was there a chance she might have not been allowed here?" I asked Gabriel although I doubted they would lead her here to end her existence.

"None. The only reason she has never visited is her own belief she was not deserving," Gabriel answered, his voice solemn. Relief in that knowledge unwound the tension in my gut.

The others knew all along Lilith was deserving to enter, that she still had her soul, but she'd never even tried or believed it herself. *Why hadn't she tried to visit before?* The answer came so easily to me. She didn't believe the risk of being separated from Lucifer and then Rena was worth the chance. Lucifer and Rena were more important to her than any of the knowledge the Library held, like reversing her vampirism. But perhaps it was presumptuous of me to think she would want to reverse it. Being a vampire was a curse to cure when I had it, but being the Mother of Night Children had given her a life with Lucifer and their daughter. The biggest reason she would have to visit was the judgment of decency the Library gave by granting us entry.

Maybe I could be worthy to be Rena's scale one day. *Worthy to be with her.* Above all else, I wanted Rena to know how deep my love was for her. She deserved someone devoted to her in the same way her parents were to each other, and I would be that person. If I succeeded at nothing else in this existence, she would understand she was the only altar I would ever worship.

"And all these years she could have visited," I said more to myself than to the two archangels by my side.

"None of us are immune to our ignorance," Gabriel said.

Michael bumped his shoulder against Gabriel's. "We all carry fears that shape our choices as much as our hope."

"Even the warrior archangel?" I raised an eyebrow at Michael. He was right, but the air had become heavy between Lilith's overwhelming emotions, the two archangels being philosophical and my own contemplation.

Michael scowled at me. "I am a healer too, Jax. We all have many parts making up the whole. Even you as the scale. You have pieces of yourself you are yet to discover."

I chewed on his word choice. My soul had been shredded through my sacrifice and was patched by Uriel's essence while I found the separated parts of myself. *What other pieces were left for me to find?* The thought that I was still incomplete after what I'd had to go through... what Rena had to go through. I swallowed down rising bile.

"Fear not. Your soul is intact," Michael said, pausing to face me, as if he knew my thoughts.

Gabriel stopped just ahead of us. "That doesn't mean there is no more room to grow."

I inhaled a breath and let it out.

Lucifer, Lilith, and Rena emerged into the entryway where I waited with the two archangels. Rena came to my other side, and I brushed my shoulder against hers. She smiled up at me, but tears stained her cheeks. The sadness on her face loomed between us, and I wanted to make it better, so I lifted her chin and kissed the dampness away.

"Barachiel and Jophiel are this way." Michael gestured down a long hall. Except for Lilith, we'd all been here before—using the Library as a base of operations safe away from danger. But that didn't protect the humans, and as a half-human, I saw the danger there probably better than anyone. We needed to get answers and get back in the fight before Typhon wiped out the human race to get our attention.

As we wound through the corridors, the heaviness from earlier dissipated. Rena hooked her pinky finger with mine in a gentle reminder of our connection. Our life wasn't simple, nor would it ever be. That wasn't our destiny. But our trust in our love for each other held a promise of a future together whether in this domain or Hell or the human realm.

The Library had seemed to grow, and the extended walk left time to think about old grudges. I'd spent too much time hating Uriel for setting all these events in motion, but my anger had been misplaced. The chances of me ever being friends with him weren't great. However, it was time to forgive him, and I wanted to be a big enough person to do it… if I got the chance.

CHAPTER 7

RENA

Mother and Father stood on one side of the large table. Father had stayed within two steps of Mother since we entered the Library. Jophiel's long strawberry-blonde hair cascaded down her back, but the mass of hair couldn't hide her beauty. She and Aunt B were next to my parents going over their findings. Jax, Gabriel, and Michael were on the same side as me, but I paced behind them. The scene was reminiscent of where we were not all that long ago preparing to take Adam down, and my grandmother, Eve, was the casualty. She gave her time on Earth to save me, and it was my responsibility to make sure her legacy lived on in my choices. Her example inspired me but also overwhelmed because I knew I'd never possess the same honorableness as Eve.

Michael's large frame blocked the view of me and more importantly the door. If I was going to step away unnoticed, this was the time. I stared at the back of Jax's head for a long moment, but the pull to the room Uriel had taken me to was something I couldn't ignore. The hum singing to me like a siren's song was meant for me alone. If not, the Library would have made sure the others heard it in the same way. Whatever the message and whether from the Library or Uriel, it was only summoning me. I slipped out the door when no one was paying attention and hurried down the hall. It was hard not to run to the powerful draw. The drive to be in the golden room overruled any other thought. I navigated the hallways as if I had them memorized, but I didn't. The same hum from last time buzzed in my veins and led me to the gilded door I'd been amazed by on that trip with Uriel... when Jax had left after ending Adam. I'd forgiven my love, and although I of all people understood, it still soured my stomach to think he left to deal with the burden on his own. Apart from our solo calls as the balance and the scale, we were doing better about leaning on each other. I hoped we had both learned our lessons on that topic.

I gawked at the center of the door where Uriel had placed one of his feathers. It was required to open the grand door. I sighed. The feather Typhon used to bring me to where he held Uriel wasn't meant to be used as a trick. Uriel, proving once again how smart he was, had left it as a key for me to this room. I'd tucked it into the sheath of the dagger, the dagger Father had gifted me, and that's where it had been. I unhooked the sheath and drew out the blade, exposing the metal feather.

My shaky hand withdrew it and placed the metal quill in the center of the door just as I'd seen Uriel do. The feather turned molten shades of gold and orange as it melded into the door. I relaxed seeing the success. Whether the entrance was for me or Uriel, it was granted, but the strength of the pull told me it was my presence required. The scent of leather from the bound books mixed with the amber and floral notes around the Library welcomed me in as if it were home.

The same desk from last time sat in the dimness, but I remembered how to turn the lights up from my previous visit. I snapped my fingers, and the vast space was illuminated. Books with golden spines shelved along the walls came into view as well as the circular couch that framed the sitting area. The pull that had led me here was gone, so I had no clue which book I was supposed to see. I ventured toward the reading nook Uriel and I had sat at when he had me read the passage about the balance and the scale existing together. Being alone in the room was odd but comforting because I sensed my uncle here as if he were guiding me, not the Library. I pulled out the same chair and closed my eyes. I held out my hands and imagined Uriel handing me the book. Warmth spread over my fingers and palms. A weight settled in them. When I opened my eyes, I gasped. A book with a golden spine and golden edges sat in my hands.

The leatherbound book had no title and was unmarked. I sat it on the table and opened the volume to the middle. "Show me what I need to see."

The pages flipped back and forth, and my stomach flopped in time with the motion until the tome finally settled. I read each word with careful precision, consuming it with intent. The passages didn't seem relevant. Nothing told me how to save Uriel or my family.

"It's really interesting how you have grown on your own to accommodate new books, Library, but you aren't being very helpful to me right now." *And I'm talking to an inanimate building. No, it's not because it grows and changes. But is it?* I wasn't sure anymore. Maybe it was just some form of enchanted power that didn't really understand anything. I flipped the page and a sting lanced across my finger. "Ouch." I sighed. *A paper cut. Why do they hurt so bad? Apparently, I pissed off the Library.* I let my head fall back and mustered as much sarcasm as I could. "Message received, your divineness."

I lifted my head and shoved the damn book away. Red dotted the page. "Well, I guess I left my mark in the Library."

Gold light encapsulated my blood, and the words began to swirl and rearrange on the page. I jerked the book back toward me and read through the new message meant for me. "For she was never made for him, he claimed her as his, and she loved him despite the way he possessed her. Echidna fell from the heavens to live with him. Their family grew and blossomed, but he wanted more. She was his only weakness and the only one who could protect him from himself. Once Typhon was defeated and their children were at peace,

Echidna found her rest with the Mother of Life until fate called on her."

Tears burned my eyes. My grandmother had helped Typhon's wife in the end as only she could and had given us a way to defeat him. Eve was the epitome of goodness until her end, and I was sure wherever she was, she still carried that goodness. This was a gift I wasn't even sure I deserved, but the rest of the world did. "Thank you, Grandmother."

Typhon had a weakness. A big one, and she rested at a place I wish I didn't know so well. *Megiddo.* There was no detail in the passage as to where exactly, but Jax and I could open the mountain together to reach the crossroads. Grandmother had put Echidna in stasis there for a reason. Typhon couldn't get to her. She would be safe there until it was time for her to share in our destiny. *And we need her now.*

"Thank you, Uriel," I said. "I don't know if you can hear me, but if you can, message received."

The space around me shimmered and distorted, and a force yanked me through a path like an unstable portal. *Sweet angel's ass.* My apprehension briefly retreated when I saw him alive. Uriel was in the same place he was before, and his head fell to the side to look at me. His wounds were worse like they weren't healing. I skimmed my hand in this weird ghostly form over his cuts and bruises, but even if I could touch him, I didn't have the kind of healing power he needed. That was his gift. *Why are his wounds worse? Typhon will pay for this.*

"You shouldn't be here," he whispered.

At least his chastising me was a good sign. "I don't even know how I'm here. I thought you brought me here after I found your —"

"Don't say it," he said. The cinnamon aroma that was him mixed with the metallic scent of blood in the air.

"Is he here?" I whispered back. I couldn't fight him in this odd form, here but not here, and I didn't think he could touch me. My concern was my uncle getting some respite to heal.

"No, but he's never gone long. He's waiting for you." His voice was weaker than last time. His suffering at Typhon's hands went beyond this physical contraption he was stuck in, and I had to get him out of there quickly. Before Typhon could do anything else to him.

I reached for the strap despite the last experience, but my hand passed right through it like a ghost. *Fuck.* My hands formed fists. *Think, Rena.* I didn't know what to do when I couldn't physically touch his bindings. "How do I get you out of here?"

"You don't," he said, his voice firm even if it was hoarse. I couldn't allow myself to think about what caused it or I'd lose focus. "You need to go and use what you found."

"Did you miss the part where I don't know how I got here?"

His eyes closed. "Our blood is mixed. Spilled together on the feather." His eyes opened, and there was a clarity in them that hadn't been there before. "I didn't realize my own was on there. I thought Typhon had summoned you last time."

I leaned closer, not that it mattered since I wasn't physically sharing space with him. "What are you talking about?"

"One of the traits of my blood is it allows my family to find me."

"But you have the collective conscience." The archangels could hear each other's thoughts, which was creepy to me, but it never seemed to bother them.

"Not my siblings." The pain in his eyes wasn't the physical pain. It was for his family lost centuries ago.

"Oh," I said.

"You need to think of your scale. Think of Jax, and your attachment should pull you back." His voice cracked. He must have had memories flood back. I knew how agonizing that could be, and the parallels in my own life to my uncle's. But there wasn't time for me to go there.

I nodded and reached for his hand.

He jerked away even though I couldn't make contact.

"I'm not leaving until we figure out a way to take you with me, Uriel." Being the balance should give me the power to stay with him, but this wasn't a call for the balance. I'd will my damn self to remain here until he was free.

"No, I need to stay. As long as I am here, he will think you will come for me. It's your best defense right now."

The argument I was ready to use died. He'd thought

this out, and his plan did give us a better chance. *Fuck. I hate when his stubborn angel's ass is right.*

"He's coming back. I sense him nearby. You need to go now. Think of Jax, Rena."

He used my nickname from Jax, and tears spilled down my cheeks. I closed my eyes and thought of my love. The gentleness Jax showed. The strength he gave to me with a touch. A portal yanked me through. When I opened my eyes, I was back in the room I started in. I needed to see Jax, put my arms around him and feel something, but I had to get myself together first.

I swiped the dampness on my cheeks away. My blood dried on the pages and disappeared. The words faded back to the text about the Library's expansion. I exhaled and tried to commit to memory everything I'd read in the hidden passage.

CHAPTER 8

JAX

The energy in the room dipped in a wave of emptiness like I was swallowed into a pit. It was the feeling of being alone that came when Rena and I were a distance away from each other. I surveyed the room, and everyone was still there except...

"Where's Rena?" She'd been pacing by the shelves near the door, but she was gone. Panic skated down my spine.

The four archangels all turned to me. *They knew.*

"She left?" Concerned lined Lilith's face.

"She's fine." Lucifer slipped a hand around Lilith's waist.

A growl rumbled in my chest. The urge to rip the archangels apart until they told me where Rena was snaked into my head. I wouldn't act on it, but I narrowed my eyes, focusing my anger on them.

Lilith shifted away from Lucifer. Her brows bunched together, and I knew she was about as mad as I was. She was just better at controlling it. "I can tell the angels know the answer, so tell me where my daughter is."

Michael, Gabriel, Barachiel, and Jophiel all exchanged looks like they were having a conversation in their heads where they could exclude me and Lilith. They communicated daily in this way, but it was rude to do it in front of beings who couldn't. And it pissed me off. Their gazes settled on Lucifer.

"You suck at poker faces. Where is she?" I asked, trying to keep the anger out of my voice and failing.

"Answer him," Lucifer said. "You hear the message clearer than me, and nothing good comes at keeping her whereabouts a secret."

"Keeping what a secret?" Rena called from behind me.

My chest loosened at the sight of my love. I closed the distance between us and looked her over. "You're not hurt?"

"Why would I be hurt?" Her face twisted in confusion.

"Because you weren't where you were." I shook my head, knowing I sounded like a fool. "Were you pulled to the place Typhon is keeping Uriel again?"

She stiffened, and that gave me the answer. "Yes." She looked over my shoulder at the archangels in the room. "Uriel refused to be rescued. I could have found a way and brought him back with me this time. I know it. If I'd just had more space to think while I was there, but he said it would give us more time if he stayed."

"More time for what?" I asked.

"To use the knowledge he gave me on Typhon's weakness. His only real weakness."

"Echidna," Michael said.

"Is she no longer in stasis?" Barachiel asked. Her green robes wished as she moved.

"She is still in stasis, and she's in Megiddo," Rena said.

"How do you know?" I asked, not clear on how we would have missed a chamber with Typhon's wife.

"Because she can feel her energy," Barachiel said.

"And you can, too, if you focus Jax," Jophiel said.

"You can all feel her there? Why didn't anyone say anything while we were in that place for …" My voice trailed off. Eve's death was still painful for all of us despite the revenge I inflicted on Adam. I met Michael's stare. He and Uriel had been with me. They helped me torture and end Adam. Michael didn't flinch. I looked away first and found Rena. I had to live with that decision for revenge every day. A death blow and torture like I dealt to Adam never went away, no matter how justified. I'd do it all over again to protect Rena. The consequences were worth her safety, and I'd fight for her until my end.

Her eyes locked on mine with concern. She gave one shake of her head. Lilith had the strongest bond as Eve's daughter and the hardest time with her death. She still grieved. We all did, but not with the depth she mourned.

I cleared my throat and rephrased. "What I mean is, why did no one mention this ancient being when we were at Megiddo before?"

"As long as she is undisturbed, Typhon cannot reach his full power," Jophiel said.

Maybe it is better to leave her. If Typhon doesn't have all his strength, we would have a better chance of defeating him.

"He's not at his full power now?" Rena asked.

"No," Gabriel said. "You would see more destruction around the world if he was.

"That's what the text Uriel guided me to meant," Rena said. "Echidna makes him stronger in some ways, but she nullifies his power in others, so she is his biggest weakness."

"Uriel guided you? While he's imprisoned?" I asked.

"It's a long story. I'll tell you later," Rena said, keeping her voice light. Too light. I was grateful for Uriel being there for Rena while I was dealing with my shit after I ended Adam, but I still didn't like her uncle.

"I believe we have the time," I said. There was a period when I might cower as the lowest-ranking person in the room, but that moment had passed. I was the scale to Rena's balance, and as such, I was named her equal. I had no delusions I was actually her equal, but in name and rank and by a prophecy written here in the ultimate library, I was.

"Maybe we should give the balance and the scale a moment," Michael said.

It surprised me Michael would suggest that. Of course, it would take more than a brief interaction to decouple this complication. The door closed behind the group, and Rena looked anywhere but at me. She twisted her fingers together in a nervous tell.

"I don't want to make you mad, Jax," she said, trying to manage me when what I needed was honesty.

The rug suddenly became interesting while I chose my words to let her know I was always her safe space, even when she knew I'd disagree or dislike something. We'd been down the road of keeping things from each other, and it nearly broke both of us. Our love was too big to let that happen again. "I'm not mad. I want to hear the truth from you, and I don't want you to ever feel like you have to hide it from me. Remember, we made a promise to each other to always talk to each other."

She crossed her arms over her chest so tightly they looked like a straitjacket. I took her hands in mine and unwound the tautness. "Just talk to me, my love."

"The feather," she said, biting down on her lower lip as if she were wary to tell me the rest.

"Uriel's?" We knew it was his by the unique material it was made of and where we found it.

Her words tumbled out in a rush. "It had Uriel's blood on it. He didn't know, and I didn't know. That's how I found him the first time."

"And you kept the feather?" That's what was bothering her. She'd kept the feather in hopes of rescuing her uncle. She honestly thought I was going to be angry about the feather? I swiped my hand down my face.

"Yes," she said, her cadence returning to normal. "It led me to a room Uriel had brought me to while you"—she swallowed hard—"when you were finding yourself."

That stung. I couldn't be angry for it either, but damn, it hurt. I'd fucked up shutting her out, and I'd asked Uriel to be there for her when I couldn't. She trusted him more than the other archangels. I still thought he was a dick, but he did care about her safety.

"It's okay, my love. I know he was there at my request." I urged her on.

The tension in her shoulders eased and her jaw relaxed. "The feather gave me entrance to the room, and my blood was the key to a text with the answers."

"But you saw Uriel again?"

"I got frustrated and somewhere in there, a portal was activated to take me to Uriel. Once I was there in my limited form, we realized our blood had mixed on the feather."

"And it bonded," I said, understanding the ramifications. She could find him and he could find her as long as they shared blood. Uriel's blood was more potent than the other angels. "I'm aware of the properties of his blood."

"He told me how to get back here, and the key was to think of you," Rena said, her voice softening into a melodic tone that sunk in under my skin in the sweetest burn. "I thought of you. Our love."

Uriel's feather might have been the key to a room, but I was the key to her home. She'd chosen me again and again, and I needed to touch her. To let her feel my heartbeat for her. I yanked her into my arms and crushed her against me. "Our bond will always be stronger, Rena. The bond with him will fade. If you want it to."

She nodded against my chest. "You are the only one I wanted to be bonded to, Jax. In any way."

I kissed the top of her head. The only thing I didn't like was the rest of the fuckers, except maybe Lilith, knew exactly what was going on and didn't say a damn word. They probably would claim the 'no interference' rule, but they had done plenty of that. *Assholes.* "I know, my love. I know."

Rena held onto me. Her worry about my reaction was what overwhelmed her. I felt it in her rapid heartbeat and shallow breath. *Fuck.* This was my fault.

"I'm sorry, Rena." I leaned away and tilted her head up. "My past reactions made you think I'd react a certain way to this news. I've been angry when he's around or at the mention of his name, but I never meant any of my frustration to be directed at you, my love. I want you to know that will not happen again. I am letting the grudge go."

She searched my eyes as if she wasn't sure that was a promise I could keep.

It hurt seeing the unspoken question in her eyes. She needed more, and I could give her that today and always. I was her scale for a reason. "You have my word."

She nodded, and I pressed my lips to her forehead in a

gentle caress. She didn't need me to ravage her in this room with her family just outside the door. She needed reassurance, and that was what I would give her. Her trust in me was equally as important as her love. In my mind, one could not exist without the other like the passage she read about the scale and the balance.

CHAPTER 9
RENA

The map was creased. My frustration got the better of me a few minutes earlier. Everything had to fall in place almost perfectly for us to defeat Typhon, and failure was a real possibility I refused to accept. Jax tried to smooth the crinkles in the paper out. He'd been so calm when I told him about Uriel and the room. *Why do I feel guilty? I did nothing wrong. It's because you didn't tell him until you had to, dum-dum.* I didn't want to hurt Jax, but keeping where I'd been from him was foolish. I refocused on the plan we were making to enter Megiddo and rescue Echidna. *Rescue. Lie.* We planned to kidnap her. No need to sugarcoat the truth. We'd devised yet another trip to pull a celestial being out of stasis. *I should question why I don't feel the least bit guilty about it. Am I becoming numb to these actions?* I pushed self-examination to the back of my mind and tucked it away for later.

"Let's go over it one more time," I said.

"Starting with when we portal to Megiddo." Jax ran his hands over Aunt Jophiel's still-creased map, but the evidence of my exasperation was impossible to erase.

"Jax, Gabriel, Jophiel, and Mother will all enter with me. We only have one entry point." I tapped my finger on the spot.

Michael pointed to the map. "Lucifer, Barachiel, and I will guard the entrance. Me here. Lucifer there, and Barachiel on the other side."

"If anything happens inside, Gabriel will set off the angel alert system," I said, amused by my nickname for their telepathic communication.

Jax snickered, and I fought a smirk.

"We don't call it that," Gabriel said flatly.

"I know, but I like the sound of it." I let my smile spread.

"Not funny," he said, using the unblinking angel glare on me. I was long past the time where he intimidated me.

"If there is any activity out front, Barachiel will bring down the lightning, and you should feel it inside the mount," Lucifer said, drawing us back to the plan. "And I do expect activity."

"Agreed," Michael said. "I think the chance Typhon would leave Echidna's place of rest unguarded is nonexistent."

"He doesn't know." Eve had made sure her place of rest was hidden.

All eyes fell on me.

"How do you know?" Mother asked.

"It was in the text. Although she wasn't seen for a decade before, she didn't go into stasis until after you vanquished him. Her grief over him and her children's lack of physical state sent her to Eve for help. Eve helped her by placing her somewhere Typhon couldn't go."

"Mother..." My mother's voice was thick with unshed tears. I reached for her, rubbing her upper arm. Mother grieved her mother so deeply, but Eve's gifts were everywhere. Her love as the Mother of Life was a legacy that never ended.

"Yes, her compassion knew no limits," I said. "Even to the Mother of Monsters."

"We will be leading him to her then," Barachiel said, her tone thoughtful. She'd cut her wavy dark hair above her shoulders when she returned after her disappearance as if it was a liability in the coming days. I wondered if it was a silent signal to us, and she'd declined to answer me directly when I'd asked. "I'm not sure exposing her without knowing if she will agree to help us is a good idea. We should rethink the plan."

"I, too, think we should reassess," Jophiel said. "We might be giving him exactly what he wants."

I'd considered that, but it was a risk worth taking. Especially, if I could reason with Echidna to reach Typhon and save Uriel.

"My thoughts are different. I believe Echidna does not want the world destroyed by Typhon and her children. She and Eve were close in the end from what I deduced in the passages, and I think she will help us."

"Whatever you choose, I will follow. You are the balance." Gabriel kneeled in front of me.

I held in a sigh. They were my family. None of them should be bowing to me, and it saddened me to see any of them lower themselves.

Michael followed. Jophiel was next, and Barachiel was hesitant but did the same.

"Rise," I said. "It pains me you make me say that before you get up or that you even kneel at all."

"It's respect," Father said.

I raised an eyebrow toward him. "You didn't."

"You have my respect, but I take a knee to no one," he said. "I'm still the king of the realm you are heir to."

I smiled that he was still him despite the heavy burden destiny placed on our family. Father kept it real, and I'd rather have him pushing me than have a blanket following just because I was the balance.

"Does anyone have any questions?" I asked. The silence was almost too much. I thought of those we fought for across the realms and of my friend, Stassi. She had befriended me when Jax left to train for the guard, and she made me forget the pain of his absence. Despite a few hookups, we were able to remain friends.

Stassi was to marry soon. I would be at her wedding, and she would be at Jax's and my ceremony. A memory of something she said before we took a road trip with some of her friends tickled me. A smile crossed my face. "Anyone need to use the bathroom before we go?"

That earned a chuckle from Jax, but it was lost on the rest.

"Rena." Mother scoffed, shaking her head. "Really."

I inhaled and took in the face of each member of my family. Battling Adam was like swimming with the current compared to the clash with Typhon upon us. We would all be marred by the coming events, and there would be no escaping it. I'd defend every one of them with my life, but this war was more than us...it was for everything. "If everyone is ready, make us a portal, Jax."

I watched his hands form the symbols and inhaled a cleansing breath. My nerves were on high alert, prickling up my spine. This was either going to go stellar or extremely bad, and there wouldn't be an in-between. Either our assumption he didn't know would pan out and this would be a quick in and out with Echidna, or Typhon anticipated our moves, which would be a fight for our lives. I hadn't experienced many things the easy way since becoming the balance. That made me second-guess this choice. It had to be done though. Echidna was our best option to defeat Typhon, but if we had to fight through him to succeed, could we succeed? *Only one way to find out.* I let out a well-practiced breath. *One... Two... Three...*

CHAPTER 10

JAX

Portals came easier, and this one grew large enough to accommodate our team to pass through all together. Each time I called one, it required less and less thought or energy from me. I was getting stronger and could call them at longer distances. The opening was at full height, and I motioned for the others to walk through. *No turning back now.* I'd chosen a place on the path about a quarter of a mile from the actual entrance. If Typhon was watching Megiddo and happened to know Echidna was here, I wanted to give us some space to react.

I stepped through to find everyone crouched down and against the short stone wall. No one had a sword drawn, but they were in a defensive posture. I scanned the area but didn't see Typhon or anything else threatening. Rena grabbed my hand and jerked me down beside her. Sandy gravel rustled as I shuffled my feet to get low.

"What's happening?" I whispered against her ear.

She pressed her finger to her lips in a hush gesture and pointed to a shadowed space several yards in front of us. There were no noises. No birds or animals. No wind. A shadow came into view. Three heads. Dog-like body. *Cerberus.* Typhon's only male child and the guardian of their family. *He must believe Echidna is here.*

I glanced around trying to make eye contact with anyone in the group, but they were all glued to the shadow of the giant dog. He didn't have wings. *How the fuck did he get here?*

Cerberus sniffed the air with all three heads. All three looked in different directions. If his sense of smell was half as good as the hounds of Hell, he already knew we were here. Panic turned my demon blood to ice in my veins. We were trapped. I scooted around Rena, putting myself between her and the creature. She'd make me pay later, and I would welcome the punishment if we survived the day. *Was he toying with us? Did he enjoy the hunt?*

Fuck it. We hadn't planned for this, and I refused to play hide and seek with a giant dog. I formed the portal symbols and willed it to land in front of the massive three-headed beast. I'd never thrown a portal that size before. To my surprise and fascination, the portal obeyed. The blue light opened in front of Cerberus. All three heads looked around it as if he was curious. They sniffed it. He tried to bat it with a paw, but it didn't move. If he didn't go through, I might have tipped our hand, and a hasty exit could be needed. I perched on the balls of my feet ready to act one way or the other. I didn't know whether he would take the bait and do it. Until he did. To my relief, Cerberus walked through the portal like he was being led on a leash. *No fucking way. It can't be this easy.*

I rose from the crouched position and slammed my hands together closing the portal. Taking a few steps closer, I examined the area to make sure he was really gone. *Un-fucking-believable.*

"Did you just drop Cerberus through a portal?" Rena asked, her voice full of amazement.

"I did." Pride swelled in my chest even though I still didn't quite believe what I'd just watched. "At least I think I did."

"Quite impressive thinking, Jax," Jophiel said.

"Thank you." I nodded my head toward her.

"Where did you send him?" Gabriel arched a brow.

"Antarctica," I said. "As part of our training, we rode the Drake Passage during a full-on Drake Shake with twenty-three-foot waves and landed in a remote area before hiking inland a couple hundred miles. It was brutal, and I thought it might keep Cerberus busy for a while."

"Excellent work." Michael clapped me on the shoulder. "Impressive even by archangel standards."

"Not sure that's a compliment, but I'll take it," I said.

"Any praise from Michael is a compliment," Lucifer said. "Well done, Jax."

Lucifer's praise was hard to come by, and my chest swelled a little from it. The approval I wanted most was from my love. Hers was what mattered the most to me.

Rena leaned up close to my ear. Her breath tickled my lobe. "That was incredible. The things I want to do to you right now are unspeakable." She kissed my cheek and stepped back.

I was on a high from the feat before she whispered to me, and my thoughts went straight to what she'd look like if I dropped her through a portal and buried myself deep inside her. The things I wanted to do to her were a mix of wickedness and worship, and I tucked them back for when we were alone. Me with a hard-on wasn't what anyone needed to see at Megiddo.

"Was he the only monster here?" I asked, looking around and feeling vulnerable for exposing us. I didn't see any other shadows lurking near the mountain or the remains of the ancient city that once stood here, now not more than paths and low stone walls marking where buildings once stood.

"Yes, it appears so," Gabriel said, his tone confident.

"It's odd how the children are never paired up isn't it?"

"I noticed that too," Rena said, her voice distant. She shielded her eyes with her hands and looked up.

A shadow cast down over us, and I tilted my head back to peer up to see the clouds swirling above us. *Shit. Did I miscalculate? Is Cerberus about to drop on us?* The circulation looked like a hurricane was brewing, but we were in the desert. The sight unnerved me, and panic seeped in around my chest causing my heart to beat faster. *Typhon.* He must have sensed when I portaled Cerberus away. Or maybe they could communicate like the angels did. Either way, I'd led him straight to us and given away our advantage. *Fuck.*

Typhon hovered near the mountain as if he scanned around Megiddo, but he didn't get too close. Neither did he make a move toward us. I was confused as to why he wouldn't attack. He could stir up a tornado in the dust and carry us away, but he just studied Megiddo. It appeared he couldn't sense us here. Maybe the protections of Megiddo provided some barrier between us and him. Or maybe it was Echidna. *His weakness.*

CHAPTER 11

RENA

Light grey swirled around Typhon's waist and legs. It looked like the dust ahead of a storm with a lot of wind in it. The mass slithered from the literal Father of Monsters, and disgust twisted in my belly. *Snakes. Fucking Snakes.*

I resisted the urge to shove someone in front of me and cower. But damn I wanted to put anything and everything I could between me and those fucking slithering serpents. I inhaled and let it out in the rhythm to calm the pounding sound of blood in my ears. *One... Two... Three...* Unfortunately, the effect wasn't quite the same, especially when I tried to use it while staring at snakes the width of a big tree. They were massive, their length at least three times the height of Jax. *Maybe longer. Probably definitely longer.* The color was an utterly uninspired medium grey. They used the flexibility in their long spines and muscles to propel them forward, and the weird, scale-like surface on their wide bellies to grip the surfaces. Nothing about them looked friendly. They were vile to see, and their hisses were unnerving. *And they were fucking snakes.*

"Why did no one mention the damn snakes?" I whisper-yelled, my words coming out in a hiss that rivaled the snakes. I'd seen them in the torture chamber Typhon had Uriel in, but I wasn't whole in that form. Typhon couldn't touch me then. Here, I was, and those were big-ass, fucking snakes, and I was pissed no one had ever thought to share that fact.

"We should portal out," Jax said. "We were not prepared for this."

I stood firm. This was the closest I'd gotten to Typhon without him knowing. He was consumed with something else, and I wanted the element of surprise. "We might not get another chance."

"You might freeze if history is indicative of how you react to snakes."

"Says the demon who screamed in a way the guards thought it was me when you saw a python someone had brought to Hell as a pet," I said. "And we're staying. We lose our leverage if we leave." We might never be able to find whatever blind spot of Typhon's we happened on again.

"I have to agree with Jax," Michael said. "We can't take Typhon head-on in a fight, and we can't risk you both in that type of battle."

Michael's argument made sense, and damn it, I didn't want it to. I wanted to end this.

"He will not be able to open the door," Mother said. "He'll need you and Jax or Lucifer and me."

My stomach soured with fear. I'd take Typhon on one-on-one before I'd allow him close enough to use my parents for entrance into Megiddo.

"It's a bigger risk with the four of us here," Father added.

I looked up at the storm Typhon hovered in and at the hideous creatures slithering down the mountain toward us. *Sweet angel's ass.* My family was right, but that didn't mean I liked it.

"Jax, portal us back to the Library," I said, not hiding the defeat from my voice. It was our only safe haven left. Typhon wasn't granted access there, and the archangels had confirmed it. The Library of all libraries was our only haven against our latest enemy. Flashbacks from my death at Adam's hand in Eve's chamber at Megiddo repeated in my head, but they weren't debilitating anymore. While those memories were irritating to the point I got light-headed, they didn't stop me in my tracks. My only regret about the end of his existence was that it was at Jax's, Michael's, and Uriel's hands. The blow was as much Jax's to deal as mine, but I would rather carry the weight of it.

Our group huddled behind the ancient masonry and hurried through the portal like a bunch of mice running from prey. We were not prey, and Typhon would meet his end. I spared one backward glance, and an alertness came to him. I stepped through the portal before he connected the ripple to me.

I PACED the length of the expansive room where we'd made our latest command center. It was smaller than the one at Gothica but was bigger than the previous room here. The wooden table was large enough to lay out our various maps. Wearing a path in the floor seemed to be the only thing I could do. Typhon had been one step ahead of us since he appeared and took Uriel from us in Hell to my unplanned visit with Uriel to Megiddo. I found it was easy to understand how. He'd had centuries to plan his revenge or whatever he was doing. I'd had days to plan a counteroffensive. *How can I hope to defeat him when he's had so much time to consider how and where we could come after him?*

"We need a plan Typhon hasn't anticipated, and I'm out of ideas."

My frustration peaked, and I rolled my shoulders to lessen the tension. The images of the snakes still haunted my mind. *That's not going away anytime soon.*

"Let's take a walk." Jax came to stand in front of me. He looked tired, but even as the corners of his eyes drooped, the concern was obvious. "Some fresh air will clear our heads and give us a better perspective."

Jax needed a break, and I knew he wouldn't take one if I didn't. A change of scenery and a break from the energy in this room might help me come up with an idea. I looked over his shoulder at the archangels. "Are we allowed to do that? Walk around?"

Michael smirked. "Are you really asking for permission?"

"Not really," I said. "I just want to make sure we're not going to turn to dust if we do."

"You will not turn to dust, Morena," he said, smirking and shaking his head.

"You are welcome here," Aunt B added. "Anyone who is welcomed has free rein."

Aunt B's statement wasn't entirely true. Entry was selective, but I knew what she meant. We were free to roam the grounds.

"And you are the balance and scale," Aunt Jophiel said. "You are meant to be here. Part of the Library."

She was trying to reassure me, but the last portion of Jophiel's statement was stomach-churning. Being a piece of the Library sounded like a prison.

Jax held his hand out to me. I slipped mine in his and let him lead me out of the room.

"Anywhere in particular we are going?" I asked as Jax guided us toward the entrance.

"I thought we'd check out the garden you've been eyeing out the window."

Garden seemed wholly inadequate to describe the space in the same way love wasn't a strong enough word to describe how I felt about Jax. I'd never seen anything that was half as beautiful. Not even the Garden of Eden.

The amber and floral scents mixed with the aroma of

fresh apples as we walked under the canopy of trees to the gazebo built around a rather large tree. The sight and fragrances intoxicated the air, and I inhaled deeply, letting them penetrate every inch of me. The part of me that felt guilty for taking a moment was overpowered by the gratitude for how Jax understood me and what I needed so well. He pulled me into an embrace and held me close. I never was safer than when his arms were around me. No matter where we were, this was home.

He kissed me under the limbs of the tree. Our lips mingled, and I welcomed him in, hungry to be reminded of how fierce our love was. The only thing that kept me from ripping his clothes off was knowing my family might be able to see us. Although, we were deep in the garden, I weighed whether the potential for embarrassment was worth the risk. I parted my lips and his mouth opened, letting me in to explore. *Safe. Home.*

CHAPTER 12

JAX

I mustered all my will, and it took everything I had to pull myself away from Rena. I wanted her, and my blue balls from the situation were the physical manifestation of what it cost me when I broke off the moment under the tree. I imagined fucking her up against the tree and at the base of it in the pink blossoms that covered the ground. They were soft like her pussy. I couldn't take her there in the garden. She wouldn't have stopped me, but I loved her too much to expose her to who knew what in this place. I might feel the peace as she did, but it was eerie how the Library seemed to know everything. It was like someone was looking over my shoulder constantly, taking note of my deeds both honorable and not so honorable. Fucking her there where anyone who was at the Library could see would expose her in a way I wasn't willing to do. Not that we'd seen anyone other than our group,

I looked down into her crystal blue eyes. "How do you feel now?"

Her eyes danced with electricity. "Do you really want me to answer that question?"

"Hmm... maybe not." I chuckled and pinned her against the tree with my hardness.

Rena made a soft, murmured noise, and I closed my eyes.

"We better get back before I fuck you right here."

She buried her head in the sensitive spot on my throat, and a whistle escaped through my teeth. Her intention was clear. She wanted to drive me as mad as she was, but I was already there. I'd give her everything I had if she wanted it.

"If I don't step away from you right now, I'm not sure I will."

She pressed a kiss on my neck and loosened her hold on me. "Later then. When it doesn't feel like a dozen eyes are watching our every move."

"Yes, my love." Relieved she understood the desire and the weirdness, I leaned forward and placed a chaste kiss against her lips, afraid my need would take over if I did more.

"Thank you for bringing me out here. I finally stopped thinking about the snakes slithering around Typhon." She shuddered. "It's so unnerving."

My stomach curdled at the thought of those serpents and soured further at the abandoned plan to retrieve Echidna. I wrapped my arm around her shoulder as we walked back the way we came. "Everything about him is meant to be disarming."

"True," Rena said, her tone distant. She'd retreated into thought, and since we were close to the door of the room, I didn't try to distract her any longer.

Rena and I entered the room where neither her family's expressions nor the smothering energy of the room had changed much. They were still working through our various ideas.

"I have a proposition," Michael said. "I think it's the way Uriel would approach it."

"Let's hear it." Rena leaned her shoulder against mine.

"I think it could work, but that leaves you and all the other archangels exposed," Rena said, chewing on her lip. "I'm not willing to take that chance with my family unless there is a guarantee no one will get hurt."

"You would take the risk if it was only you in danger," Barachiel said. She was right. Rena wouldn't hesitate to put herself in the line of fire to protect her family.

Lilith stiffened but remained silent. Her composure slipped as her gaze slid to Rena. I followed and Rena's jaw tightened. She didn't look at her mother or me but focused on Barachiel as if she was prepared to accept her statement as a challenge.

"We've been in danger our entire lives," Jophiel said,

drawing Rena's attention. "Someone or some creature has had issue with us as long as we have existed."

Rena's aunt spoke the truth. I'd never known a time when, at least as a demon, I didn't have a constant sense of danger. Risk came with being a demon as I'm sure it did with being an archangel. Rena squeezed my hand. I squeezed back to give her my strength if that was what she needed. I'd trade anything to see her happy—for us to live in a time when we weren't constantly fending off celestial beings just to exist. Once we defeated Typhon, I'd spend my days doing whatever it took for her to have the happiness she deserved.

I examined the plan Michael had laid out. I agreed with Rena's assessment. It had the potential to get the job done. There were a few things I'd do differently, but overall, it was a pretty sound plan. The risk Rena saw was accurate too, but we risked our existence every time we stepped into a fight whether that was with Nephilim or Typhon.

"If our timing is off, then..." Gabriel's voice trailed off.

"Uriel will die," Barachiel answered him. "But we will not fail."

My confidence wasn't as unwavering as hers, but I thought we stood a chance this way. "Do you believe it is possible to make the silent room a cell?"

"That was what it was originally used for," Michael answered.

"But it will cut off the mirror side of the garden," I said, a statement, not a question. We'd imprisoned some of the traitors who unleased Uriel's Ascendant in there until Lucifer saw fit to release them—if ever. But they would be stuck there as long as Typhon was in the silent room.

"Which is currently being used as a prison." Rena let out an exasperated sigh. I wasn't sure if her energy was bleeding into me or if my frustration matched hers, but it vibrated my insides.

"You would think this library could tell us if we are on the right path," I said.

"The Library doesn't work like that. It gives us our freedom while providing knowledge to make sure our decisions are informed," Jophiel said.

It wasn't new knowledge, but I hadn't thought of it in that way. Maybe we should be looking at the whole situation in a different way that analyzes our decisions. There was no way to know what Typhon had planned. He could destroy a city to get our attention, or he could sit and wait for us to come to him. The unpredictability made it more urgent for us to deal with him sooner rather than later. The biggest problem was there was no prescribed way for us to take him down, at least not without hurting his family. Even if his children were the monsters of nightmares, it felt wrong to make them pay for his mistakes by becoming phantoms again if it wasn't required. They couldn't stay in the human realm either way.

Rena stared down at the map of Eden, her head cocked to the side as if she were listening for the Library to give the answer she needed. "If there are other suggestions, let's discuss them, but I'm only hearing Michael's option. If we don't come up with another, the plan laid out here is what we will have to go with."

The room was quiet, and I looked at each face. The concern I saw in each of them told me they were unsure but not enough to speak up. "Silence is acceptance."

Rena's face was where my survey settled, and I noticed the dark shadows under her eyes. She was tired or hungry or both, and that wasn't normal for her. My love was giving too much of herself to everything and this cause and not saving strength for herself. I couldn't let that happen. As her scale and her future husband, my job was to weigh the cost to her, and this was more than I was willing to sacrifice. *Fuck Typhon and fuck the prophecies.* Rena was all that mattered.

I scanned the room. "Maybe we need a break to regroup our thoughts."

Rena winked at me. She leaned in so her mouth was close to my ear. "I like it when you take charge."

My dick strained against the zipper of my pants, and I turned, giving the group my back.

CHAPTER 13

RENA

Jax was coming into his own as a leader, and I'd never desired him more. The dampness between my thighs confirmed it. I wanted to crawl off into bed with him, but there wasn't time to hide in his arms from the inevitable, even to satiate the want building in me for Jax. If we took the battle to Typhon, there were no guarantees we would succeed. I didn't know if we got him back to his cell, would he be able to easily leave his old prison from the Jinn realm. We didn't have time to test that theory.

Typhon didn't attack us at Megiddo. The question was if he did that to protect Echidna or if he was trying to show us he could touch us anywhere. The answer was so clear. He'd known Echidna was there. *A cat and mouse game perhaps.* I wanted to understand what made him tick because if I did, maybe I could figure out a way to defeat him without bloodshed. But I would not get the answer to that question if we imprisoned him in the silent room or the mirror world.

"What made Typhon feel the need to have children with Echidna?" I asked.

"He wanted a family." Aunt B lifted one shoulder. "Isn't that what most beings want? To have someone they connect with and a piece of both of them to live on as a legacy?"

"And he had that with Echidna," I said, but my mind wandered to what it would be like for me and Jax to have a family of our own. A warm sensation started in my chest and bloomed outward. I tamped it down to think about later and refocused on our task. "So, what caused him to change?"

"What do you mean?" Father asked.

"Was there a war? Did he accidentally kill some folks?" I asked. "Or on purpose?"

"He, indeed, wanted a family," Gabriel said. "But his mortal children were made."

"Mortal children? I thought they were immortal monsters?" I asked. If he had mortal children, they would have passed on by now, but where to... No, I wouldn't disturb a soul's peace to stop Typhon.

"The ones you have seen or we've discussed, yes," Michael said. "Typhon's first family was all mortals. He took a piece of his essence and a piece of Echidna's and molded them into human form. They only lived for a brief time. Helena was the only one who survived to adulthood. There was something different with her."

First family? He had a family before the monsters. Something about Typhon's actions didn't work with the reports we had. Our expert opinions seemed stitched together on this topic, but we were missing something important. My gut nagged at the gap. The archangels were used to taking a hard line, but the details were scattered. *And made mortal children?* That seemed a little impossible, even for a being like Typhon. He was powerful, but making a human child? How would that have even been done?

Regardless, the monsters couldn't be left to destroy the human world now that they were no longer phantoms in dreams. That was the bottom line of it all. I needed to move past the feeling we were missing something in the story. It didn't matter if we were. The end result would be the same either way. *So, why am I hesitating?*

I sighed, and I didn't care the entire room heard me. "I think Jax is right. We need a break."

The archangels moved into a group and talked amongst themselves. They kept their voices low but weren't trying to hide what they were discussing either. If they had wanted to keep their conversation secret, they had their archangel mind thing they could have used.

"Your mother and I are going to take a walk. There is somewhere I've been wanting to show her," Father said, escorting Mother out the door. I smiled and waved them off, wondering if they ventured to the same garden Jax and I visited.

Jax came to my side, slipping his arm around my

waist. "Let's take a stroll down the hall." My body reacted with anticipation of what a trip down the hall might mean, even if we only had a few stolen moments of reprieve.

He led us a few steps away and turned to face me. Disquiet shadowed Jax's face. I didn't want him to be concerned for me. We needed to focus on our job, and that was eliminating the threat Typhon caused. He rested his hands on my hips. "If you do not think we are approaching the situation correctly, say the word. You are the balance, and this is your gift guiding us. Everyone here trusts you."

Jax had a way of saying things that gave me what I needed, but more moreover, his words held truth in them too. Not that our options were vast, but we at least had something. "I know we have to expel them from the human realm. I get it. There's this feeling in me that there is so much more to this story than what you and I know."

"And you're frustrated because you can't fit all the puzzle pieces together to figure it out," Jax said. "Like when you have a problem you can't solve."

I nodded. "Exactly."

"You are not always going to know how to deal with these ancient beings. Many of the texts were lost or edited when they were restored. We will never have all the answers. We do the best we can with what we have."

"I get it. I understand it. I just don't like it," I said. "My gut is on fire from not being able to interlock all the pieces."

"But…"

"But I can't let Typhon's children destroy something so precious and fragile as the human realm, so I might have to destroy them to prevent their destruction," I said. "Even if I'm not sure that's the right thing to do."

My powers as a demon had been kept secret. Perhaps the worst-kept secret in all of Hell, but this might be time to use them. Hell's fire responded to me in a way it didn't anyone else, maybe even better than my father. I didn't know if there were risks associated with using my abilities now that I was the balance. My powers were our best bet at this point, and I hadn't used them in so long that I wondered how hard the drain on me would be. I'd practiced up until my sixteenth birthday, but I hadn't practiced since. I swallowed hard against the memory of the lives I took when the humans summoned me six years ago. While he hadn't offered me absolution, Uriel had given me peace, and I would make sure he didn't fall at the hands of Typhon. Hell's fire had no match, and if that's what it took to defeat Typhon, I wouldn't hesitate to perform the same kind of sacrifice my grandmother had to save my family.

"You can't do this alone," Jax said, drawing me from my thoughts. His voice so low it was almost like he was afraid to say the words out loud. He pulled me to him. His warm, woodsy scent enveloped me, wrapping around me like a loving embrace. "I know that's what you're thinking."

It was. "I don't even know if there would be consequences for me using my powers in this situation."

Eve's death to let me live flashed through my mind.

Grief gripped my heart. I'd known her my entire life but didn't find out she was my grandmother until right before she died. Her death still covered me in a veil of regret and guilt. No matter who or how many times someone told me it was her choice, her time, or her gift, I blamed myself. I worked a swallow against the knot forming in my throat.

"If I use my power—" Someone would get hurt. Maybe someone I loved. Someone who was family, and my heart couldn't take losing another person important to me. The worst fear was that I would become like Adam or Typhon.

"You are unique, Rena." Jax rubbed my upper arms. "But you can neither do this alone nor can you judge the outcomes by what anyone else has done."

"But I am the balance, and the last balance we know of. Look how long Eve had to wait for me." I swallowed again, pausing to get control before I went on. "My grandmother sacrificed herself until there was nothing left to give. What if that is my fate too? What if we are separated for thousands of years? What if I can't stop Typhon?"

All of my fears tumbled out. I sounded irrational, but this was Jax. He'd seen me at my worst. It hurt to voice the weakness and admit the vulnerability, but there was a small amount of relief in saying the words out loud too.

"We don't know the future, my love," Jax said, his voice gentle as if the next words would break me. "My existence should have been over at least twice, and yet, here I am. Thanks to you."

I almost lost him, and I'd give up my eternity to never know that grief again. "It wasn't just me, Jax. Others—"

"Others helped at your behest," Jax said. "I would have just been a half-demon no one noticed if I hadn't met you."

"That's not true," I said, wrapping my arms around his neck. He'd always been different in the best way. Just as the electrical current humming between us was unique. "You've always been special. You were destined for greatness."

"Only because I love you," he said.

I studied him, and the sincerity and love overwhelmed the concern in his eyes. He was worried I was going to do something on my own. A deed he would call stupid but wouldn't hesitate to do himself. And I wasn't sure I wouldn't act in that way. I wanted to save the realms, but I wanted to save him more. If circumstances came to it, the choice would be mine to make and one I'd make easily.

JAX

Rena and I strolled the hall hand in hand toward the room where the others waited. She'd reassured me when I'd meant to do that for her. I'd wanted more time with her, but she needed to solve this puzzle. The power of the balance was playing into that drive I guessed, but Rena was driven on her own. I tucked back my frustration concerning not being able to help her more.

A tug yanked at me. Not hard enough to move me, but strong enough I couldn't ignore the sudden hard pull. Excitement for a calling of my own eased my discouragement over my failed attempt to lighten Rena's load. My palms slicked, and I released Rena's hand. A blueish tendril squirmed like a worm from my chest. The light wound through the hallway. *Uriel.* A piece of his essence was in me from when my soul was splintered across the realms, and he offered up a piece to plug the leak. He'd saved me, and this looked like he had a message for me. The last thing I wanted was to leave my love, but whatever Uriel had to share was my burden. I kissed Rena's cheek in haste.

"I'll be back," I said, glancing down the path. "There's something I need to do."

She scanned down the hall in the same direction and back to me. She locked her gaze with mine with understanding and trust. "Don't be long."

"You know the Library decides."

"I do." She gave me a small sad smile and cupped my cheek for a brief moment. "Come back as fast as you can."

"I will."

The trail led me down a twisted path, and I memorized the way. Not sure if the notation of the twists and turns did any good since the Library moved and changed as it grew. Strange how I never felt the motion. The blue tendril passed through a door...or maybe the thread ended there. I couldn't see the other side. As I approached the door, a symbol came into view. I ran my fingers over the emblem. The mark was an old language we'd worked on in my early teenage years. I tried to recall the letters in the alphabet for it. The last letter was an L. The first letter came to me in a rush. It was a U. The symbol was for Uriel. *Did the archangels have their own rooms here?*

I didn't have much knowledge about the Library beyond what I'd seen on my excursions with Rena and from what the archangels had shared of their experiences here. I ran my hand over the door feeling for a handle of some kind, but I found none. My shoulders tightened as did my neck. I was disheartened, and those old feelings of unworthiness closed in on me. *Asshole.* My hand rested over Uriel's name where the tendril touched the center. Blue radiated out between my fingertips.

The door groaned as if the hinges were rusty and had been sealed for a very long time. I jumped back but peered inside the darkness of the room, ready to fight if necessary. Lights came to life one after another until the room was entirely lit. Despite the way the door had protested, the space looked clean and free of dust, like most of the places here. There were no windows to the outside. The chamber was an internal room. *Fitting for the reclusive bastard.*

The blue string from my chest led to a stack of books on a desk toward the back. I walked past the floor-to-ceiling shelves filled with books. The urge to look in them for all of Uriel's secrets was strong, but the tug pulling to the stack of books on the desk was stronger. Apparently, there was something here Uriel wanted me to understand or wanted me to find for Rena.

The desk was black marble, a contrast to the pristine white marble that made up the majority of the Library. Uriel's actions were darker than the rest, and he was known for how intellectual he was. Like Rena, he internalized a lot. She was more like him than I'd ever admit out loud.

I sat in the giant gilded chair with black cushions. This chair did not suit the sparseness of the room nor Uriel's non-existent personality. The ornate piece of furniture contrasted with this place given Uriel seemed to be a minimalist, but maybe he wasn't always that way.

The tendril remained connected to the stack of books. I picked up the first one, but the tendril didn't end there, so I set that one aside. The second book was a tome from an ancient society on how to best live life. I chuckled. Even two thousand years ago, people were wondering about that secret. The tendril touched the third, and last, book. I lifted leather leather-bound volume, and the tendril remained attached. The worn cover was the one, and I braced myself for what the archangel had in store for me.

There was no title on the front. I opened the cover, and the handwritten entry told me this was private. This was Uriel's personal journal penned by him. I flipped the pages until the tendril stopped on one. Uriel had written this entry in the time after his human family had died. He was grief-stricken as one would have been expected to feel after losing his family. The entries were so personal, that wave after wave of guilt hit me with each one I read. The most shocking part was that Uriel had been in one of the darkest places I didn't think archangels could go, even as I considered him the most morose of their kind. He'd asked others to end him, and his two-hundred-plus years of sleep were a last resort to escape his pain and loss. According to the last entry, he prayed an angel's death would find him while he slept. The despair of losing a love so deep resonated with me. If Rena were lost, I imagined I would ask for a similar death. Knew I would want the same.

The next entry sang out to me. The tendril locked on the passage. With the surge, I realized I was about to read something I would not be able to turn away from once I knew. It gave me the urge to pull back. Uriel had sent this message for us to use, and I was the messenger the others couldn't be because of our unique bond.

I rolled my head on my shoulders and proceeded on through the archangel's text. Uriel created his own prison where he'd slept. A prison only he could open. This was his gift to us. Typhon could be sent there. The catch was we needed Uriel to lock the door. Uriel had to live. I could create a portal there for us to lure Typhon through, but I needed to see the place first. Luckily for me, Uriel left a guide to the space I could read like a map similar to the lines left behind after a portal was opened. The trip was still risky, never having seen the place, but it was a much better option than Rena expending all her energy. A quick trip should be fine if I left my path open, and there would be a viable alternative to our other plan.

I created the portal and recalled the coordinates Uriel had left. The only thing I could see in front of me was darkness. The disorientation reminded me of being stuck in the dream realm with Adam. Fear and disgust rose up in the form of bile. I shook that thought away and stepped through. *Smothered.* I couldn't catch my breath. There was no light. None. My breathing was labored, and I recognized the reaction was my anxiety leftover from my time in the dream realm. The breathing technique Rena and I used many times came to me. *One...Two...Three...* I reached out and patted around me. There were walls, and they were close. This was like a coffin more than a prison. Uriel had come here to die the only way he could at the time. An incredible sadness came over me at what he must have been feeling to put himself in this self-imposed prison. I formed the symbols back to the Library and focused myself just outside the door to the war room.

CHAPTER 15

RENA

Jax had been gone a long time, and I couldn't shake the feeling he wasn't in the Library any longer. It was the absence of his essence here that I keyed in on, but I couldn't bring a tracker into the Library. The Hellhounds were demonic and soulless creatures. They wouldn't be allowed entry. At the very least, Jax was some distance away, and he wouldn't leave the premises without a word. He'd promised after the way he disappeared upon ending Adam. My worry grew as I walked hurriedly in the direction he'd trekked earlier until I came to a branch with three choices. In front of me, the path went straight as far as I could see. To my right, the hall only went a short distance before the path veered left. I inspected the passage to the left. A shadow appeared, and I reached for the dagger at my waist. My adrenaline spiked with the anticipation of a fight. *Idiot. You're in the Library of Knowledge. The safest place you could*

be. Only those the Library granted entry to can enter. I inhaled, then let the breath out, but didn't re-sheath the dagger.

I flattened myself against the wall. There might not be a physical threat, but that didn't mean I wanted everyone who could enter to know I was there. The footsteps were quiet, the kind of practiced quiet of a soldier or the lightness of a celestial being. I listened to the cadence. The gait was familiar.

A male figure turned the corner without glancing my way. His earthy scent like an autumn campfire wafted toward me. *Jax.*

The sight of him brought me solace, and I found my voice. "Jax."

He faced me, his eyes alert with surprise. "Rena, what are you doing out in the hallway?"

"Looking for you. You were gone so long, and I was worried you got lost." It sounded stupid because I would totally get lost trying to find anyone in the maze of the Library.

"Uriel had a message for me." Jax's face softened as if I would break at hearing my uncle's name.

"He communicated with you? What did he say?" And why hadn't he sent me the message instead of Jax considering they weren't exactly friends?

"It's not like you think. The piece of him that is now a part of me allowed a connection," he said, taking my hand and placing it over his heart. Uriel's essence was still in Jax. I'd just assumed the link faded away like dissolving stitches when Jax put the strands of his soul back together.

"Your soul?" My voice barely came out louder than a whisper.

He brought my fingers to his lips and placed a soft kiss on the back of my knuckles. "Come on. Let's go find the others, and I'll explain."

"No," I said, emphasizing the word. My heart hammered in my chest. *How is he even considering something so stupid?* "You will have to get way too close to Typhon to create a portal that size to send him to Uriel's prison."

"This is our best chance, and I've been practicing throwing portals for a while. You saw what I did with Cerberus." He would have to get closer than that for the plan to work. "He's too prepared for us to use Echidna, and you had mixed feelings about utilizing her to begin with." Jax stepped closer to me.

"Mixed feelings, yes, but I would do it to save — "

"Your family," he finished for me. "This plan accomplishes the same."

"But this idea—"

"Puts me at more risk than you. I understand and accept the probability. I prefer that risk, and I think your family will too."

Even now, Jax doubted his place here with us, and my

heart cracked at the thought that through our nearly existence-ending experiences, he still didn't see himself as worthy to be part of this unit. I'd spend every minute after we finished with Typhon making him understand just how worthy he was.

"We're your family too, Jax." Mother's forehead creased with worry. "We are just as concerned for your safety.

The intent stare he shot my mother was clearly a shut-up look, and I would have laughed at his brazen reaction toward the Mother of Night Children if we were discussing any other topic than his life. *Fucking fuck.* His plan was good. Solid. Fully formed. It gave us the element of surprise we needed. *How can I stand between him and this choice? I can't, because if the plan was mine, no one could stop me either.*

"If we agree on this proposal"–I held up a finger, knowing we would be doing it despite how the idea conflicted with my gut reaction–"I will be using my demon powers as a distraction."

"No." Father splayed his hands out on the table. "You need to reserve yours. I'll summon some of the army of Hell to be the distraction."

"That's suicide." I shook my head.

Jax placed his hand on the small of my back. Warmth radiated out from his touch. "Better than you being dead."

"I agree," Mother said, her tone firm.

"We're not sending a demon army or anyone else to

fight this fight." I held Father's gaze and realized he and I were at an impasse. "This is our fight."

"It kind of is," Jax mumbled next to me.

"What?" Michael's head snapped toward Jax like he'd opened Pandora's box.

"Uriel and Typhon had a…" Jax paused as if he couldn't decide what word came next. "Disagreement."

My uncle has something personal with Typhon? If that was true, he hadn't mentioned a vendetta, and that doesn't seem like information one would withhold when threatened by a monster like Typhon.

"What do you mean?" Father's voice came out in a dull roar.

"He's right." Gabriel leaned his hip into the table.

Jophiel let out a long breath. "Yes, Jax speaks the truth."

Barachiel averted her eyes, and my favorite aunt was on my shit list for keeping secrets relevant to our current situation.

"What do my siblings know that I do not?" Father crossed his arms.

"The mortal Uriel fell in love with was Typhon's only human daughter, Helena. She was a made human much like Adam and Eve were in the beginning, but without the longevity of life the firsts were granted from the Garden of Eden," Jophiel said.

"So, for all intents and purposes, their made daughter was mortal and would live a human life," Barachiel said, tears thickening her voice.

Jophiel cleared her throat and continued. "Uriel hunted her expecting to find a monster, but instead he found love."

I gaped at my aunt, stunned that not only my uncle but the archangels kept important details from me.

"Typhon sent the Nephilim to retrieve her from the home Uriel had set up for his new family," Gabriel continued.

"But the Nephilim believed Typhon's daughter was an abomination even though she had no power other than Uriel's love," Michael said, the sadness in his voice wrenching at my heart.

"You all knew her?" I asked, my chest tightening.

The archangels nodded.

"But you didn't, Father?"

"I wasn't on speaking terms with most of my siblings then." Father landed a hard glare on Gabriel. "Except one."

"It was not my story to tell, Brother," Gabriel said. "Nor anyone's here."

Of course, my archangel side of the family would think that kind of information would fall under some code of honor. Nevermind the very relevant fact about why an incredibly angry monstrous being was terrorizing the human realm to get to us. Like what the actual fuck. I swallowed down my anger to try and be reasonable because regardless of when we heard the elements of the history there, we still had to defeat Typhon.

Father appeared to accept that answer, nodding his head. "I understand."

"Is there any chance Typhon would be willing to discuss this with us?" I asked, even though my gut said we'd already gone too far, and Typhon was too consumed by his grief. Still, if he could just see past his sorrow, we could stop the madness and possibly save some lives, including his and ours,

"Would you?" Mother said, raising an eyebrow.

No, I'd want revenge. If I were Uriel or Typhon, I'd channel my anguish into delivering the most horrible death I could think of... something along the lines of what Jax had done to Adam in scattering the pieces of him across multiple realms. "No, I guess that opportunity has been gone for lifetimes at this point because if it were me, I would want a very painful death for the person I held responsible."

CHAPTER 16

JAX

Uriel's sleeping arrangements over the last few hundred years were designed to keep everyone out and himself in. He set the seal up so only he could open the lock either on the inside or out. That was the tricky portion of the plan. Our group had to split up, and separating was the part that concerned me. Rena would lead her group to rescue Uriel. Her bond from the mixing of their blood would allow her to find him, and I hoped he would be strong enough to do the angel thing and swoosh them to his self-imposed prison. Michael and Lilith were to travel with Rena, and everyone else would be with me. The lopsided teams unnerved me, but Typhon's children would be by his side to defend him or so we had reasoned out. Gabriel's recon mission showed they were taking turns with their father at Megiddo. Perfect execution of the plan would take all of us to make this timing work, and this battle was not going to be an easy win. The one thing we had plenty of was hope despite our shitty option of a plan.

Gabriel had left to recon Megiddo one last time before we left, and both teams awaited his return in the foyer of the Library. Timing was everything for this mission, and we needed to be in sync on every level. I tugged Rena's elbow and led her around the corner, away from the group. Her soft scent like the peonies in the garden mixed with the warmth of fire in her spirit was the only heaven I needed.

"What—"

I crashed into her mouth with mine, shoving her up against the wall. Her lips parted and welcomed me. I needed a taste of her to carry me through the next few hours and remind me what was waiting for me when this was over. She slid her hands under my shirt and up my back with her own need. She urged me closer, and I obliged, pressing as much of my body against hers as I could. I wrapped my fingers at the base of her neck and ran my thumb over her throat. I captured her breathy moans and trapped them, not willing to give up anything from the moment.

Rena's nails dug in, and my dick nagged against my zipper. I had to break away before I took her right here regardless of who could hear. I leaned back and rested my head against her head. "Rena," My voice was rough with my aching need, and I wasn't entirely sure it was mine. "If I—"

"Don't you dare say it. We will see each other in a few hours."

I swallowed down my worry. "I love you with everything in me, Rena. Everything."

"It's so much more than love to explain what I feel for you, Jax. I don't think a word exists for what this is between us, and it scares me sometimes."

"What I have for you can only be described as devotion." It was. I was devoted to her with every fiber of my being and would bend to her will if she asked. I brushed my lips across hers and forced myself to step back. Letting her go wasn't what I wanted to do, and the thought I might have to, cracked open my chest as if my soul was bleeding out at her feet. "They'll wonder where we are."

"We're not parting on a goodbye." Rena slid her hand into my hair and pulled my head toward hers until our lips met again. Her kiss was a soft caress, reminding me of how our deep romantic affection could be intense, rough, and wild or gentle, malleable to whatever the other needed at the moment.

She looked into my eyes. Hers were full of adoration and a little fear. "Fuck the big wedding. When we are on the other side of this, we are getting married our way."

I smiled down at her, enamored even more if that was possible. Loving her for the way she would always be herself, wearing her very essence on her sleeve, and choosing us. "Deal, my love."

Rena studied me with intense scrutiny. "I won't ask for

a promise I know neither of us can give, but I promise my heart and soul are yours."

"And mine are infinitely yours." I threaded my fingers through hers and led us back to the command center for our mission.

Lilith looked us over and smirked. I ran a hand through my hair. Even though we were adults in both the Overworld and the Underworld, her scrutiny made me want to squirm. An urge I managed to ignore.

Bright, warm light flashed in front of us signaling Gabriel's return. A sinking feeling pitted my gut. His grim expression a clear indication his recon didn't yield good news for us.

"What did you find, Brother?" Michael asked.

"Cerberus and Orthus are both with Typhon at Megiddo. I didn't see Hydra or Chimera anywhere within a thousand miles."

"Does it make me crazy that I wish they were all four there?" I asked. "At least we would know where they were." My biggest concern was the two not with Typhon would be guarding Uriel and waiting for Rena, outnumbering them if not with bodies, then with heads and jaws for sure. "Anyone been able to use your angel juju to talk to Uriel?"

"No, he's still unreachable," Jophiel said. "Blocking us out by the haze in the connection."

"Should we rethink the team split?" Barachiel asked, fidgeting. She was uncharacteristically nervous, and that did nothing for my rising agitation. "Should I go with Rena?"

"We're not sure what it will do to her taking two additional people," I said. "It's already a risk as is."

"Our chances will be better if we sneak in and out, Aunt B," Rena said.

"Are you saying I can't be quiet?" Barachiel shot a brief grin.

Rena smiled. "Not at all. I just think your skills will be needed more at Megiddo."

Barachiel smiled, but there was sadness on her face. She and Rena teased each other often, and their relationship had grown stronger in the past few months. My future wife's family was important to her, and I thought of her aunts and uncles as that more often and less as archangels. Light flashed and Michael was in his battle armor. *Until they do something like that. Something only an archangel can or will do.*

"We should go while our intelligence is still somewhat current," Lucifer said.

"Agreed." I hated the plan more with every second, but Lucifer was right. The intel would grow cold the longer we waited. I leaned over and kissed Rena's temple. "I love you."

"I love you," she said, meeting my eyes. I saw a mix of fear and hope. I dwelled on the hope and used the resolve to stamp out my unease. We were better together. I knew it. She knew it. But the plan required us to be in different places, so I sucked up my insecurities. "See you soon."

Lucifer and Lilith embraced over her shoulder. The groups said a quick goodbye and divided up. I joined Lucifer, Barachiel, Jophiel, and Gabriel. Rena positioned herself between Lilith and Michael, holding out a hand to each of them. I formed the symbols to call the portal and watched the blue light, similar to the color of my essence, spin into existence. I looked up and met Rena's observant stare. The anxiousness on her face mirrored what jittered in my stomach. Rena, Lilith, and Michael faded away, and my team walked through the portal to Megiddo.

RENA

The warehouse came into view, and this room was too familiar to me after multiple visits where I was helpless to do anything. Uriel was strapped into the same tortuous position he had been the last two times I'd been here. His eyes were closed, and I feared the worst as my team approached him. He inhaled a deep breath, and his lids flew open. This time would be different. I was getting him the fuck out of this place.

"None of you should be here," he whispered.

"Stop being a martyr, Brother," Michael said. "You have duties to perform."

Uriel focused on me. Pain dulled his usually bright eyes. "Jax found his message."

I touched Uriel's arm, and I was grateful to connect with actual flesh this time. His skin was hot like fire, not the fires of Hell but much too warm. Probably from his body trying to heal after repetitive abuse. "He did, but we need to get you out of here to help."

"They don't leave me alone for long." His shirt was shredded, revealing marks in various states of healing. The freshness of some wounds was a clear indication of recent torture. *Are those...claw mark*s?

Mother and Michael worked on the bindings to free Uriel while I held him upright. He dropped into my arms, and his weight was almost too much to bear. A roar came from outside the door. A roar I recognized. *Chimera.* I fixated on the deep gashes healing on Uriel's chest. The monster had inflicted these. She'd attacked Gothica, forcing Mother into a truce with the Nephilim. Chimera would pay at my hands.

"We need to go," Mother said.

Chimera roared again, and the sound was closer to us this time.

"She sounds pissed." Disgust rolled over me, remembering the coating of sticky goop I was covered in after our last encounter.

"Chimera's nest is here?" I asked, reasoning she probably wouldn't venture far from her younglings if she had an ounce of mother's instinct in her. From what we saw at Gothica, I doubted she did. Chimera and her young could move after we rescued Uriel. There would be no reason to stay in this place.

"No, Rena. Do not deviate from the plan. We have a short window to make this happen." Michael advanced on me, but I was already backing toward the door. Timing was everything in our situation, and if there was a chance to eliminate one of the monsters, I had to take it.

"Take him, Michael. Take Uriel and Mother now," I said. "That is an order as the balance."

"It doesn't work like that, Rena," Uriel said. I inhaled at the use of Jax's nickname for me. "It's my blood that allows you to travel here."

Jax would be angry at my choice, but this was my decision. Both of us had to make hard choices whether using our best judgment or as the balance and scale. He might not be here to weigh my decision, but I had to take the risk if the act increased the odds for my family to survive. "I've got some of that, remember?"

"If we are successful, she will once again be powerless, and her children will be as well," Michael said.

"Morena, do not be foolish," Mother said.

"You should know I'm never foolish, Mother," I said. "And the monster hurt Uriel. She attacked you in your sanctuary. Michael, get them both out of here." I reached for the doorknob and ducked out. There was a wide hallway that looked like it had a catwalk over an open space— probably big enough to hold a monster the size of Chimera. I stuck close to the side of the wall as I slowly moved, listening. I heard yells that sounded human. A strong metallic scent drifted to me and burnt flesh mixed with odor. *Has she brought humans to feed her young?*

Chimera's roars turned into screams as I navigated closer to the sounds. She didn't appear to be moving toward me, so I didn't think she even knew I was there. I crossed a catwalk in the warehouse and froze. My birthmark roared to life. I clutched my shoulder, gripping the flesh where the spot sizzled. I gritted my teeth to keep from crying out. *Nephilim? Here?* The enchantments Typhon placed around the warehouse must have dampened my senses to them. I peered over the railing. Chimera was beside her nest. The nook was large and blankets were entwined with branches. I could have stood in the center and barely seen over the edge. The screams transitioned into gut-wrenching cries. There were three miniature creatures like her. Two were moving, and one lay in the nest without a head. The metallic tang in the air was from the little one. Something broke inside me at the sight of Chimera's newborn lying there dead, and I blinked back tears. *This is wrong. My thinking had been wrong. She was a mother protecting her children.* I scanned the area to locate the Nephilim. They were well hidden but still there. The aching burn of my birthmark confirmed it. I assumed the scorched piles were Nephilim at one time.

I was disgusted that the half-angels had decapitated the youngling, but I'd be lying to myself if I thought I hadn't planned to wipe out Chimera and her offspring myself. I regretted that plan. She was a mother protecting her children. Nephilim emerged from their hiding places, closing in on her. Chimera was frantic, herding her two remaining children behind her. The sight sickened me. This wasn't a fight. It was a slaughter. The same thing I'd planned to do, and the deed was despicable. The difference between me and the Nephilim is I could see how deplorable my actions would be and adjusted my course. They had zero intention of deviating from their butchering of this...family.

I climbed to the railing and dropped down to Chimera's side. She looked down at me, mouth opened to breathe fire. I put a hand up as if the appendage would protect me.

"I'm here to fight with you, Chimera," I said. "Against the Nephilim."

Mother's truce with the half-angels might be short-lived after this, but that was her agreement, not mine. I wasn't a vampire and didn't give two shits about the cessation of hostilities. They could all come for me and burn in the fires of Hell.

Chimera turned to the Nephilim and let out an ear-piercing screech— the kind only a mother in mourning could make. It was grief.

"I know," I said. "We'll not let them do the same thing to the others." I'd apparently lost my mind, not only reasoning with a monster but defending her and her offspring. The Nephilim crept closer. They were in range where I could use Hell's fire on them, but I unsheathed my dagger. I much preferred hand-to-hand. There must have been about a dozen of them based on the few charred spots and the nine of them surrounding us.

"You take the ones on the right. I've got the left," I said, hoping she understood me. She shifted her body to the right as if she did. I took that as confirmation. "Now."

I leaped into the air and landed my feet on the chest of

one, effectively knocking him into another one. They both went down. "If you wish to see another day, I suggest you make an exit now."

I wasn't feeling merciful, but the fewer of them here, the better our chances. They stood and faced me. Heat blasted from my side, causing a gust that blew my hair around me. I scanned to my right to see Chimera had taken care of her lot.

"Or stay if you want to end up like your friends." I lifted a shoulder and flipped my dagger in my hand, flashing my devil's face at the same time. "Or in Hell if I kill you with this particular dagger."

The four in front of me exchanged looks. A stain darkened the pant leg of one of the men. They turned and ran.

"Good choice."

Air rustled around my hair, and I turned to face Chimera, hoping I wouldn't have to kill her to get out of there after saving her children. Instead, I found her dropped down with a leg tucked under her. She'd bowed her head. Her position was unexpected, but I should have guessed she was intelligent. The tension in my shoulders relaxed, but I couldn't completely let the apprehensiveness go. I eased toward her and pressed my hand firmly on her head.

"You owe me nothing. No mother should have to see her children die, especially this way."

A tear slipped down her face and made a puddle on the floor. Her eyes opened and focused on me. "You are wise, princess of Hell. I am beholden to you. Whether you accept my pledge or not, I will be there to repay the debt."

I was surprised she spoke. I'd assumed the monsters were unable to form the complex constructs needed to verbalize much less in English. "Just take your children somewhere safe to raise them. Somewhere humans do not roam and will not find you."

She nodded. "As you wish. I assume you have freed your uncle."

There didn't seem to be a point in lying. "I have."

"He loved my sister, and she loved him. I bear no ill will toward him, but I am unable to ignore my father's commands. Should he call me to perform an act the mandate of my service will take over," she said, her remorseful tone tainted with bitterness.

"Your father controls you?"

"He does. He controls all of us, but he does not know we know. He can't hear our thoughts as we hear each other's."

The monster siblings communicated by thought like the archangels. *Impressive and useful.* "You can speak to each other?"

"Yes," she said. "We hate the things Father makes us do. Our only freedom was when he was sent away."

"But you were phantoms. You didn't mind that?"

"At first, we did, but then we realized we had freedom."

Typhon had forced his children to do his bidding. What he used wasn't even power by fear like Father had ruled with at one time. It was control, and I found that worse. At least ruling by fear left a choice, but control took away any hope of autonomy. They deserved more than to be their father's puppets.

"Are you able to help if he hasn't given an order?"

"Yes, but I'm not sure my siblings would. As soon as Father gives an order, we will be back to following his command."

"Very similar to my father's control of the demons," I said, understanding. "And there is no way to break his hold?"

"Not that I know of. We are of his blood and as such, he controls us."

But he had a weakness. *Echidna.* "What about your mother? Does she control you too?"

"No, she is our freedom, but she can control him," Chimera said, sadness in her voice as she spoke of her mother. "Not in the same way he controls us, but he cannot ignore her requests. She would not be pleased with the havoc he was causing."

That was a relief to hear. "He's not defending her to release her. He's defending her so he can accomplish his goal without her interference."

"Yes, if you could free her, you could stop him easily."

Freeing Echidna was even more important than I'd realized, and Jax's team had to succeed. "Thank you, Chimera. I need to go now."

"I can go with you and assist," she said. "Until..."

"No, stay here and take care of your children." I

surveyed the nest. The other two younglings were lying down near the dead one. They were mourning and needed their mother. "I've got this."

"I hope we meet again, princess of Hell."

"As do I," I said, using my connection to Uriel to pull me back to the Library.

CHAPTER 18

JAX

Orthus and Cerberus patrolled the area in shifts, but there was no sign of Typhon. He'd been here when Gabriel had done his recon, but he'd disappeared in the short time between then and our arrival. Michael and Lilith arrived with Uriel but without Rena, and the fury in my veins was replaced by ice-cold fear that Typhon had returned and snatched Rena. The plan was to take Uriel to the Library, but Uriel had insisted they come here. Michael had assured me Typhon was not in the warehouse, but Rena had gone to fight Chimera. *And she calls me an idiot.*

A thud landed behind me. I drew my dual-fighting swords and spun around. Rena stood, dusting herself off. The frigid anger and fear in my veins melted at the sight of her, relieved she appeared to be unharmed.

"That was an interesting arrival," I said, thinking maybe I should portal us somewhere to show her the kind of release I needed. She probably could use the same coming from a fight.

"It was not fun," she said, straightening her jacket.

The scent hit me hard—the light odor of angel mixed with the heavy scent of human. I forced calm through myself. "Were there Nephilim there?"

A surprised look on her face quickly turned serious. "There were, but they were inconsequential. Chimera gave me the key to defeating Typhon."

"What about the truce Lilith struck with them?" I shook my head. "I'm sorry. Did you say Chimera told you this?"

"The truce is with Mother, not me. So, I don't know, but yes, Chimera speaks. Apparently, they all can," Rena said as if it was no big deal that monsters were speaking. "We're demons and speak. Mother is a vampire and speaks. I'm not sure why we thought they couldn't."

She was babbling, and that only happened when something made her nervous. *What would she have to be so nervous about?* Maybe her reaction was shock. That happened to some of the best demons I knew after a skirmish. I looked for a place for her to sit. My gaze landed on her uncle. Uriel got to his feet, albeit in an unsteady non-archangel way. I thought they healed faster.

"Let's table the creatures who speak for later," Michael said, propping Uriel up.

"What did Chimera tell you, Morena?" Lucifer asked.

"A lot," Rena said, her eyes wide. She giggled.

Not normal. I reached for her hand, and the skin was

clammy. I rested my hand on her cheek, and it was cold, even though there was perspiration on her forehead. My throat plummeted into my stomach. We didn't get sick without outside interference, and the affliction was acting fast. That led me to my original conclusion.

"Barachiel," I called over my shoulder. "I think Rena is in shock."

"Don't be silly," Rena said, laughing. Her speech was slurred. "I'm a princess."

My hands trembled as I pulled her closer. She'd have never called herself a princess under normal circumstances. Something was seriously wrong, and she needed attention now.

"She's definitely not well," Barachiel said.

"It's me," Uriel said. "My blood mixed with hers."

I knew her blood had mixed with his on the feather, but she'd been fine. My disgust mixed with anger, and I hurled my words at him like a knife. "What do you mean your blood did this?"

"I'm sick, therefore she is sick. The barrier Typhon put on the warehouse is no longer in place to block the effects." Uriel's skin was pale and damp like Rena's. "It's the bond."

Dread drifted through my body mixing with desperation and making my limbs weak, but I held Rena up. Pretty certain my support was the only way she was upright. "What do we do? Do we need to fix you to fix her?"

Concern rippled through Michael's face as he

supported Uriel's weight. "What is wrong with Uriel has to run its course."

I slid an arm under her knees and hauled Rena into my arms. She nuzzled her face into my neck and sighed. "And Rena just suffers while he heals?"

The archangels exchanged looks as if they conferred in their mind talk, which annoyed the fuck out of me.

"The issue has to resolve on its own, but Morena will not be better until her system burns off the blood," Michael said, but I walked toward the door without acknowledging him.

She needed a safe place to recover while we stopped Typhon, but she would want to see the mission through. I would carry the load this time as she would do if the situation was reversed. "Then we need to get Rena to the Library while those of us remaining here finish the plan."

"We should all regroup," Lilith said. "Morena had information from Chimera."

"We have no way of knowing if that was part of this... sickness or if what Rena said was real. She would want us to finish our plan," I said, fighting concern that manifested in the tightness of my jaw.

"Are we playing a game?" Rena asked, her voice soft but at least an octave higher than normal. I caressed her cheek, wishing I could trade places with her or provide relief in any way.

"No, my love, but you will be better soon," I said.

She smiled and leaned her cheek into my hand. Then, she wiggled herself free and slid down my body. Lilith reached around Rena's waist and held her up. Lilith wrapped her other arm around Rena like a cage.

"I don't think it's a good idea in the state Uriel is in," Lucifer said. "My brother is strong, but he can't even stand on his own."

"I must agree," Jophiel said.

"Damn it," I said under my breath. "She would want the mission to succeed."

Lucifer clasped my shoulder. "She would, Jax. You're right, but she wouldn't move forward at the risk of you or the rest of her family."

I considered what he said. Most of the risks Rena put herself in were to protect others. She did it time and time again. He was right. I would not win this argument. "Yes, Lucifer."

"You are not doing this for me," he said. "You are doing this for her."

I backed away and formed the symbols to take us to the Library. Everyone was through except Lucifer and me. He turned to me. "Why don't you go first, Jax?"

I suspected he was afraid I was going to do something stupid, and I did want to stay, so he wasn't wrong. The decision tore at me as we debated because Rena was always my first choice. Putting her needs ahead of all else, I gestured toward the blue light. "After you."

He grabbed me by the collar and dragged me through with him.

We landed in the foyer of the Library. I resented him

taking my choice based on an assumption. "I wasn't going to stay." My words came out harsh.

"You tried to stay?" Lilith frowned.

"He did," Lucifer answered before I could.

"I wasn't going to. I was just thinking what I could do if I did," I said. "Where are the others?"

"They took Uriel to see if they could help him recover faster."

Rena came running up to me like she had when we were teenagers... before I'd entered the guard training. I reached out to steady her, but she jumped into my arms and wrapped her legs around my waist. "I can talk to monsters."

I almost bit through my lips in an unsuccessful attempt to hide a smile. She was going to be embarrassed by these memories when this was over, but I was thoroughly enjoying this side of her. In fact, I looked forward to teasing her when she was better. "Let's take a nap, my love."

She giggled. "Let's do something else."

I gaped at her parents who, to their credit, didn't look as mortified as I felt, and back to Rena. "I'm really tired. I need a nap. Don't you?"

She leaned back. The way she arched pushed her ass right against my cock which responded immediately. I glanced at Lilith and Lucifer. Lilith covered her mouth but was amused. Lucifer crossed his arms over his chest and looked like he wanted to burn me where I stood. "I'm taking her to rest. Nothing else. I wouldn't take advantage of her like that."

"You taking advantage of her is not what I'm worried about." Lilith smiled.

I turned away before they could see my dick didn't care they were there. Rena buried her head in my neck and licked from my collarbone to my chin. "Mmm, salty."

My dick was rock hard. I growled. "I was just going to tease you and wasn't going to remind you of every detail when you are better, but I've changed my mind."

I made my way down the hallway to an open room I'd seen with a big couch, assuming the space was still in the same place I spied earlier.

"I feel fine, but I'd feel better if you would fuck me." Rena bounced against me.

I inhaled and let the breath out slowly. The door was still open to the room, and I kicked the door shut behind us.

Rena wiggled in my arms. "That was extra. Do it again."

I dropped her gently on the massive couch. She latched her hands around my neck and pulled my mouth to hers. The kiss was fierce, but the sentiment wasn't her. My cock thoroughly enjoyed the enthusiasm, pressing painfully against my zipper. *There is no way I'm doing anything with her in such a state but damn, I'm going to have the biggest case of blueballs after this.* I removed her hands and slid in behind her on the couch. I pulled her tight against my chest.

"This is nice," she said, her voice still way too bubbly to be hers. "But it would be even nicer with your hard cock inside me."

Fuck. What did I do to deserve this torture? My cock inside her is exactly what I want and the one thing I can't have.

"Close your eyes, my love," I whispered against her ear. "When we wake up, I will eventually fuck you." Normally, angels healed fast and archangels even faster, but Uriel looked weak earlier. If he wasn't healed in the morning, I was worried Rena wouldn't be better. She didn't seem to be in any danger, but I wasn't sure I'd survive another day like this. *I might have to find a bathroom to jerk off. Angels-be-damned, I'll settle for a corner far away from her to take care of the throb on my own if she doesn't stop rubbing against me.*

She scooted back against me, but she settled in. Her head lay on my arm, and her eyes closed. I relaxed my shoulders, willing my throbbing member to do the same. Rena's breathing evened out, and the rest of the tension in my back gave way.

I brushed her hair from her face and pressed my lips to her temple. "I love you, Rena."

CHAPTER 19

RENA

I stretched my arms out in front of me. Every muscle in my body ached like I'd sparred with someone unafraid to make an example of me. My head throbbed, and I pressed my hand to my temple.

"Hey," Jax whispered. He had me tucked against him like a spoon, and I relished the closeness despite the pounding in my skull.

"Hi," I said, covering my eyes with my palms. "Why do I feel like I have a hangover?"

"You were sick," he said, his voice a soft song in the quiet room. Too gentle for someone sporting morning wood pressed against my backside. "But you seem better. You're not cold and sweaty anymore."

"What do you mean?" The memories came back in random flashes. Sweet angel's ass. Surely those were dreams and not real. I considered rolling off the couch and burying my face into the floor. "Oh, my hell. Please tell me I dreamed what is in my head."

"I can't see what's in your head, but if what you are remembering is acting like a giddy teenager who was hot for my cock, then that is true." He teased me and chuckled against my neck, pressing his lips to the same spot.

"Ugh." Embarrassment heated my cheeks. "Can I hide in..." I raised up to look around the room. The space was another one of the vast sitting rooms in the Library. "This room for eternity?"

"That's an option, but we're probably not going to be able to defeat Typhon if you remain here for the rest of your existence."

"No, I suppose that wouldn't work. So, the plan went to shit because I wasn't well. What happened to me? I remember freeing Uriel and defending Chimera and her children from the Nephilim. Everything else is fuzzy from then until now. How is my uncle? He looked awful."

"Uriel was sick too." Jax cleared his throat. "That's why you were feeling unwell. Your bond with Uriel from where your blood mixed on the feather caused this."

Shit. So little blood but that was all it took. And if I missed Uriel acting like a goofy teen, I'm going to be pissed. "Is he okay? Did he act stupid too?"

"Your mother came to check on you. She said he was doing better. I can't say if he acted like you after we parted, but he was weak. The siblings gave him transfusions." His voice was soft. "Speaking of blood. Gabriel retrieved some from Gothica. Lucifer thought you would need some help to regain your strength." Jax reached behind him on the sofa table and produced a bag.

My mouth went dry as soon as I saw the liquid. I gulped down the blood, ignoring the gag forming in my throat.

Jax held up another full bag.

I recoiled from it. "I don't think I can."

"You need to. We still have Typhon to deal with, and you need to be at your best for the fight." He kissed my temple. "And I say this with love, you are not at your best right now."

I sighed and took a bag from him because despite not wanting the claret-colored liquid, I could tell my body was stronger with each drink. "Fine. You're right. I'll drink the blood."

Jax sat up and took me with him. He reached for another of the bags on the table. I wasn't sure how many were there, but there were way more than I'd ever be able to drink no matter if I was injured or sick or healthy.

"I'll drink one more if you drink some too. You need to be at full strength yourself." I pushed the bag in his hand toward him.

He narrowed his eyes at me but took the bag. "Together."

"Always."

I ripped open the bag and tilted my head back, chugging the thick liquid. The metallic twang tasted good, but I'd never admit that out loud. The blood coated my throat and sang through my body, restoring my strength.

Jax crumpled his bag and tossed an empty plastic container on the table. "You need more than three bags, my love. Your mother said it took blood from all four of the siblings present for Uriel to be better."

Uncle Uriel was worse than I suspected. "How bad was he?"

"He was pretty weak. He collapsed when we arrived at the Library," Jax said. "I haven't seen him since we parted ways after arriving here."

"I should check on him." I didn't doubt what my mother told Jax, but I needed to see Uriel for myself.

Jax winced. "If you drink two more bags, I'll take you to see him."

I eyed the bags on the table and could feel the way my lip curled in disgust. The whole consuming blood and flesh for sustenance was the part of being a demon I sucked at. I grabbed another bag and drank it down, surprised the gagging sensation had completely disappeared. It tasted resplendent as the fluid crossed my tongue. The thick liquid warmed my insides. The fourth bag went down just as smoothly.

"I'm ready."

JAX HELD my hand as we wound through the hallway. My body was fully recovered as far as I could tell, but my embarrassment for my behavior still shrouded around me. I couldn't change what I'd done while sick, so I had to face it. I hoped the fact I was better meant the same for Uriel. We stopped at the command center where voices filtered out into the hallway, and I observed from the doorway for a moment until I found my uncle. Uriel stood among his siblings and my mother looking well. The sight of him assuaged my worry and concern. My uncle raised his head, and his eyes met mine.

"I'm glad to see you are fine," he said. "My apologies for the inconvenience."

"I am fine," I said, taken aback by the strange apology. "What about you?"

"Thanks to my brothers and sisters, I am much improved." He kept his tone formal. He hadn't been so prim with me since we met after his long sleep. If I was being honest with myself, his stiff demeanor hurt, especially since we'd grown close. I hoped this attitude was temporary.

Mother crossed the room and drew me into an embrace. "While I hate you were sick, it was good to see you lighthearted for once."

I smiled. She'd been protective of me as a child, but my happiness was always important to her. Perhaps it was because she and Father had to fight so hard to get their happily ever after. "If any part of my memory is accurate, my actions were erratic, Mother."

"You were cute," she said.

My father pulled me into a side hug and whispered,

"Jax took good care of you while you were sick. I think he's a keeper. Isn't that what you say?"

I chuckled. "Close enough, and I agree."

Michael hung close to Uriel, but Aunt B and Jophiel hugged me. Maybe Uriel wasn't as well as they were portraying him to be.

"Since you are here and feeling better," Aunt B said, "we want to know more about what Chimera shared with you. She's never spoken to anyone as far as we know."

The image of Chimera's slain child drifted through my mind, and my stomach dipped. *Would I have done the same as the Nephilim if I'd gotten there first?* I pushed the thought away. What ifs for the past wouldn't change what needed to be done for the future. The most important thing here was to get back on track with Typhon's imprisonment. The events after defeating the Nephilim were still fuzzy snapshots. My mind struggled to put the pieces together in the right order after the fight.

"Anyone have a trick to clear up hazy memories someone can't quite reach? Someone being me." I looked around the room and the others averted their eyes except for my aunts.

Aunt B glanced at Jophiel and smiled. "As a matter of fact, we do."

Aunt B stood in front of me and Jophiel behind me as I sat in a large, plush, royal blue chair. My boots and socks were removed. *Why do these ceremonies always have to be weird?*

"Is this going to hurt?" I'd do the ritual even if it did, but I wanted to prepare myself.

"No, not unless you fight the process," Jophiel said.

"She's not wrong." Aunt B crouched down by my bare feet. She grasped my big toe on each foot, applying a light amount of pressure.

"This is awkward," I said, looking down at my aunt with my feet in her hands. "I hope my feet don't stink."

Aunt B laughed. "This is definitely one of the stranger rituals, but it is effective."

"You didn't say my feet don't stink." I raised a deliberate brow at her.

She laughed harder. "Well—"

"Ssh. You both need to be quiet," Jophiel said. "Everyone else needs to leave the room now. Your energy could disrupt us."

The group filed out, except Jax lingered. He approached me, concern lining his face. "I hate leaving you alone." He kissed my forehead.

"She's not alone," Aunt B said, her tone feigning offense.

"I meant without me." He smiled at Aunt B. They were getting closer whether either wanted to admit it or not. Aunt B was easy to like, but she chose who she let in her circle. She trusted him.

"I know." Aunt B returned his smile. "Now get out of here."

"Harsh," he said. "Take care of my future wife."

I held my sigh in, but I loved hearing him call me that. My insides melted every time. I looked forward to being his wife. If the wedding ever happened. We had to defeat Typhon first and then we'd get our happily ever after like in Mother's novels I used to read to him to make him blush when we were teenagers.

He winked at me and left me with my aunts.

"Ready?" Jophiel asked.

"Ready," I said.

She positioned two fingers at each of my temples and began to hum a tune that resembled a lullaby. The music even made me sleepy. I closed my eyes. The memories played like a movie on the back of my eyelids. My memories. The knowledge Chimera had imparted to me came to the forefront. I focused on every detail spoken or inferred that she'd shared. Echidna was still the key to defeating Typhon, but the impact was in a different way than expected. We needed her on our side, but if what Chimera said was true of her mother, Echidna didn't like the chaos Typhon created either. And I remembered a promise Jax made, and my cheeks burned. *Sweet angel's ass. I hope my aunts can't see these memories, especially the ones from when Jax and I were alone.*

"I remember," I said.

"Very good," Jophiel said. "I'll close the ritual."

She hummed the tune backward. "Now, open your eyes."

I did as she said. Thank hell Jax got me to sleep, and I wasn't a giggly fool anymore.

"Barachiel, you can unground now." Aunt B released my toes.

"I need the others in here now," I said, crossing the room to look at the map of Megiddo. "Will one of you let them know?"

"Yes," Jophiel said.

Aunt B came to stand beside me. "You know Chimera chose you. She's never spoken to any angel, demon, or human that I'm aware of."

"She'd lost her child, and I helped her protect her others," I said, trying not to think about the dead youngling in her nest. "Could you and Aunt Jophiel see my memories?"

"No, the ritual does not allow for joined visions, but you mentioned pieces yesterday."

Although I was thankful my memories weren't projected, they had seen things I never would have flaunted in front of my family. My cheeks heated again. "What an awful spectacle I must have been."

"We've seen worse and some of us have done worse." Aunt B nudged my shoulder with hers.

"I know that should make me feel better, but it doesn't," I said, doing my best not to picture what similar episodes my aunts and uncles might have experienced. "I appreciate the effort though."

The others came into the room and gathered around the table. My cheeks flamed again, and I wondered how long I would keep reliving my embarrassment when I saw my family. *Months? Years? A millennium? In all that is Hell, I want to crawl under the table, but that won't make the humiliation go away.* Jax stood next to me, close enough I could feel the warmth from his body.

"Your memories are returned?" Mother asked.

I nodded. "They are, and I have the answer to how we'll defeat Typhon with Echidna's help. Assuming she will help us."

Michael was still glued to Uriel's side like the warrior archangel was a shield or pillar even though Uriel looked infinitely better. *I'll ask about that after I share the plan.*

"According to what Chimera shared with me, Typhon cannot ignore a request from Echidna much like Typhon's children cannot ignore him. Apparently, his wife would not be happy to see what he is doing. Chimera said if we can free her mother, Echidna could stop him easily." The realist side of me said nothing would be easy with Typhon, but I supposed if Echidna had some special power over him that would be a path of least resistance.

"And you trust Chimera?" Gabriel asked.

"I do. She told me this because she trusted me to do the right thing. Typhon controls his children. Despite what we thought, they do not willingly participate in his plans."

"What makes you confident this isn't a trick from Typhon to get us to open Megiddo for him?" Jax asked.

"She bowed and told me she would follow me if she wasn't under her father's control. I believe her," I said, and I had considered the same thing in the moment, so I didn't fault him for asking. Chimera could have fought me there, and she hadn't. Instead, she chose to talk about her sister...family. That wasn't the act of a monster. "Do you trust me?"

"With my life," Jax said.

"Then, this is our answer. We will enter Megiddo and convince Echidna to be our ally. Once we have her to control Typhon, we can send him to the prison where Uriel will close the door, locking Typhon away forever." And freeing his children.

"What kind of monster is Echidna?" Jax asked. "I didn't see anything on her in the texts."

"Her identity has always been hidden," Jophiel answered in a cryptic tone.

"She is a fallen angel," Aunt B said.

My eyes widened in disbelief. "What the— "

"A fallen angel fell in love with Typhon?" Jax asked.

"Her love for him was the reason she took the Fall from Grace," Michael said. "Which is why she supported Uriel marrying their daughter."

Uriel's jaw tightened, and he stared at the corner of the ceiling. Something inside me cracked open, knowing this was why he was so broken. I scooted closer to Jax until my shoulder touched his.

Jax's head turned toward Uriel like it was on a swivel. Realization swam in his eyes. "You were married to Typhon's daughter. That's what the journal was about."

Uriel winced, closing his eyes. His throat worked on a swallow. "No, but I would have married Helena had circumstances ended differently."

They hadn't made it down the altar. His emotions, albeit muffled, bled down our connection in a flood of sorrow, remorse, and self-loathing. Bile rose in my throat at how intense the sensation was even when Uriel was so obviously working to suppress his feelings from me. I touched Jax's arm. "Let it go."

"What do you mean?"

"It's a story for another day," Gabriel said, his voice heavy with sadness.

Uriel roared. The sound echoed off the walls, and I covered my ears. Fear vibrated in my spine. I gaped at my uncle as I pulled my hands away. He met my gaze, and the anguish in his eyes was heart-wrenching. The barrier evaporated. His unfiltered misery felt so overpowering. The intensity of his response passed through the bond from our blood and threatened to drag me into the dark abyss where he was drowning. My knees were weak, and I had to fight to stand.

No one moved. All eyes were on my uncle. Mother's mouth gaped open, and Father shook. Michael moved closer to his brother as did my aunts and Gabriel. Uriel's chest heaved. He'd clearly never dealt with his grief. Instead, he simply went to sleep without processing his heartbreak and loss all those years ago.

I gripped Jax's elbow and urged him backward. He looked at my hand. When he met my eyes, he took a step back. I moved toward Uriel. His eyes were wild like a golden storm raged in them.

"Morena," Michael said my name as a warning.

"Uriel?" I touched his arm, and he tensed. "Remember when you first woke up, and we were in the lab? We talked about mistakes. You helped me find forgiveness and free myself of the heavy burden I carried. You said forgiveness didn't mean anything was forgotten, but the heaviness was lifted. It's time for you to do the same."

His sorrowful stare found mine. The storm still rumbled in his eyes, but not as strong as the anguish had been. The ferocity of his misery eased until the weight was bearable.

"Can you hear me?" I asked, giving his forearm a gentle squeeze in hopes of grounding him here with us.

"Yes," he said, his voice vibrating quietly but still powerful. The swirling storm in his eyes evaporated.

"Are you ready to let it go? To finally forgive yourself?"

He broke eye contact with me. "No, but I'm in control now."

The piece in me that had cracked widened further. My uncle was cold and closed off, and I couldn't fix his grief for him. He'd carried his despair for centuries, and the pain was a festering wound without a cure.

CHAPTER 20

JAX

I wasn't sure what I'd witnessed, but the scene damn sure looked like an archangel losing his shit. He was far from my favorite, but his breakdown was horrible to watch. I wouldn't wish that on anyone I considered family. The effect on Rena had more of my concern. I was worried his bond with her would suck her into whatever pit of torture he put himself in. While I didn't want to see him suffer, I'd do whatever it took so he didn't tow Rena with him. There had to be a way to sever the bond instead of waiting for the connection to fade on its own. It wasn't that much blood that mixed.

Barachiel surveyed the group as if she was validating we were all good to continue and then moved back to the table. "Here is Eve's former chamber and the other chambers we visited. After Jophiel and I reviewed some of the texts on Megiddo, we believe Echidna's room to be somewhere in this area of the mountain. There is only one hallway leading to her stasis chamber, and we think this was deliberate."

The aunts had at least uncovered a possibility. We'd planned to hit all the chambers we hadn't explored before, and the task felt monumental. They'd given us a starting point, but not one we could portal to since I hadn't been there to visualize the area.

"It's deep in the mountain," I said, looking at the distance between this chamber and the ones we'd been to. I was in no hurry to portal into the room where both Eve and Rena died, and I was confident Rena didn't want to relive that day either. There was the empty room where Adam had trapped us. The space was vacant and not as tarnished with blood and death.

Michael crossed his arms, "And the entrance requires Jax and Morena to open it, and to do so puts them in the same vicinity Typhon and his children are patrolling now."

Rena focused in on the area of the map. "And we're sure there's not another way inside we haven't thought of?"

I ran my hand over the area of Megiddo we'd been to until I found the position of the vacant chamber. "We still have the option to portal inside, but the rooms we are familiar with are on the other side of the mountain."

Gabriel shook his head. "The journey would take half a day or longer to wind our way through to this area, and if we are wrong about where she is, then that's half a day where Typhon could have slipped into Megiddo on the wind of the portal."

"A trick he's familiar with," Lucifer said.

Rena pivoted to face her father. "How so?"

"We believe that's how he entered Hell to get Uriel."

Rena's eyebrows bunched together. "I thought he used Cerberus to do breakthrough?"

"We don't know for sure, but he seems to be able to access the remaining remnants of a portal similar to how Jax reads them," Jophiel said.

I'd never heard of someone being able to slide through a portal in such a manner, but Typhon commanded the wind among his other powers. If that was the case, any portal he got to before I could close it was an open door except to and from the Library.

"What about a portal directly from here inside the mountain? Would he be able to use the gateway if the door originated from here?" I asked Lucifer.

He looked at his siblings.

Jophiel opened her mouth and closed it. "I can't say for sure, but I believe he could. The probability and risk are high," she finally said.

I scrubbed my face with my hands and clamped down on the urge to shove everything off the table. Rena needed me to support her and be her scale. Dumping the table on the floor wasn't a picture of balance. Typhon was formidable, but there had to be a situation that gave us the upper hand in some way.

Rena let out a long breath. "Our original plan to lure him, Cerberus, and Orthus away still has to be done."

Rena and I were stronger together. Hell, we were all stronger together, but the distraction had to be done for us to succeed.

"Yes," Barachiel said.

"And still two teams," Jophiel said.

"One team to retrieve Echidna this time," Michael said.

"And one to be the bait," I added, knowing which one I would belong to.

"Nothing about this feels good." Lilith wrapped her arms around herself. "Asking a mother to plot against her family."

Lilith's compassionate side was a reflection of Eve. She hid it to not look weak in Hell, but she had much of her mother's goodness. Rena did the same, thinking of others as what they meant to the world and not a pawn to be used. While I respected the goodness in them and didn't want there to be any casualties, prioritizing others' lives outside the family made our task all the more dangerous. We were all risking our lives for this mission.

"Not her family." Barachiel looped her arm through Lilith's. "Just the father of her children who she already believes is doing the wrong thing, not to mention controlling her children. She's an angel. Even Fallen, she will want to save humanity."

I wouldn't say my opinion out loud because Rena didn't need the negativity, but I agreed with Lilith. Everything seemed heavier. Not that going into a battle would be light, but this was different. Even in the Library where the scents were meant to make you happy, the weight settled around us.

"But to ask this of her..." Lilith looked at Lucifer.

He moved closer to his wife. "Do not put yourself in her place, Lilith. They are not us. Their family is not ours."

Rena watched them carefully. Her forehead was bunched up. "Are we really so different?"

"I think we are." Jophiel pulled Rena into a side hug.

"But it is natural to want to put ourselves in the shoes of others." Barachiel hooked one arm around Michael's waist and the other around Gabriel's.

Uriel looked at me and took a step forward, lifting his arms slightly.

I held up my hand. Not hating him anymore was one thing but embracing him was going to be a no from me. "Don't even think about it."

"At least you didn't threaten me." Uriel smirked.

"What makes us different from them?" I asked, drawing all eyes. The viewpoint was uncomfortable to say out loud. "Rena and I fulfill our roles from prophecies written long before our births. This freaking Library seems to have all the answers but barely shares them." I gestured around the room to the archangels. "You only intervene when the balance is at risk. How can we say we aren't similar?"

"We, all of us, always have the power of a choice, Jax," Uriel said, clearing his throat. "The prophecies, our duties, our interventions, are always within our will to choose to or choose not to fulfill."

Lucifer shifted his feet so he could wrap his arms around Lilith. "I would have never been able to fall to be with Lilith if we didn't have the freedom to choose."

"Kind of feels like we are one step away from being monsters," I said, turning to face Rena. She looked as overwhelmed as I felt.

"How about we go for one more walk while we wait on confirmation of positions?" I held my hand out to Rena. She slipped hers in mine, and nothing reassured me more than our connection. We were always better together.

RENA

Jax and I retreated to the room with the green couch. I'd promised to tell him, so I recapped the story Chimera had told me about how in love Uriel had been with her sister.

"I don't understand how she wasn't a monster like the others." His forehead wrinkled in confusion, and his eyes squinted with skepticism.

I was offended but I shouldn't be. "Am I a monster? I'm also half of a fallen angel like their children and half vampire. If we were to have children, would you call them monsters?"

"Our children wouldn't be monsters, though." He paused.

Jax wasn't, and he was half human and demon. There wasn't anyone out there like us, but we weren't like Typhon or his children.

"Would they?"

I was so mad at him. Out of what I had said, that was what he came up with to ask. "No, but if you are thinking that is the case, then there is the door." I flung my arm out, pointing the way.

He glared at me as if he couldn't believe what I said. My anger spiked further when he didn't immediately acknowledge how ridiculous his statement was.

"I said what I said." I doubled down and stood my ground. We'd both faced a lot of judgment in our lives, and I couldn't believe he was acting like an ass.

"Obviously." He stared at me as if I'd made some kind of crazy statement. "I think Uriel's emotional state is bleeding through from your bond with him."

And maybe I was a bit harsh. My patience had worn thin from the lack of peace we'd had, and the reality had not escaped me that the rest of our lives could very well be this same crazy cycle. Plus, I'm sure the fact my blood mixed with Uriel's wasn't helping just as Jax had pointed out.

I rubbed my neck and stared back at him, not willing to apologize.

"Rena..." His voice trailed off, dripping with sadness.

"I'm not trying to be mean, Jax, but you pissed me off."

He nodded. His mouth curved down in a deep frown. "And it infuriates me you stayed behind alone to fight Chimera but here we are."

"Are we trading blows like on the sparring mat now?"

"No, that wasn't what I meant, and you know it." His eyes flashed demon red. "Hanging back was an idiot move, though, and you would have told me the same thing if the situation was reversed."

I couldn't argue with him on the latter point. It was incredibly stupid for me to stay behind to fight a monster on my own. I'd made a bad choice that ended well, and I could admit my mistake.

"You're right, Jax. Me sending everyone else back and going to face Chimera and an unexpected group of Nephilim alone was an idiot move. I'm not going to deny what I did, but I wouldn't have learned the information about Typhon and Echidna if I hadn't taken the risk. Can you explain your boneheaded comment in the same way?"

"No," he said. The tautness in his jaw eased. "I'm just on edge. I don't know why, but everything is getting under my skin. I feel so frustrated, and I want you to myself. I hate that you're bonded to Uriel. If anything had happened to you, Rena..."

We both needed closeness and reassurance and words weren't enough. Action was what we needed. Literally.

"I think I know what the problem is." I closed the distance between us. He reached for me, and our mouths collided.

There was no gentleness about the kiss. It was fierce and demanding, full of need and want. Our hands were chaotic, removing clothes in a blur.

Jax encircled my waist with one arm. He slid his hand around my nape and licked from the hollow of my neck up until our lips crashed against each other. My core tightened into a needy ache. Jax rubbed his thumb up and down over my throat. His fingers trailed down my skin toward the already hardened peak. He rolled my nipple between his fingers, eliciting a moan from me.

"Jax," I gasped out, finding his mouth. "I need you."

"You will have me, my love," he murmured, his voice lower and thicker with desire.

When he wanted me like this, the intense passion, everything else in the realms fell away. There was only him and me.

He skimmed his hand down lower over my belly, slipping a finger between my folds. A breath whistled from between his teeth. "You are so wet, Rena."

"For you. And why are you still wearing pants?"

He dipped a finger inside me. My hips bucked against his touch, and a loud and guttural approving groan escaped him.

He slid the finger in and out, adding another finger. My pleasure intensified as it wound tight in my core.

"Don't tease me." I reached for his zipper, yanking the metal pull down. I rubbed my hand against the long hardness of his shaft. "I need you inside me now."

A low rumble came from his chest. He shuffled out of his jeans. "I want your soft pussy wrapped around me."

My center slicked in anticipation. As much as I craved the pleasure, I needed the connection. "Then take me."

He lifted me, my legs sliding easily around his back. I relinquished all control to him, welcoming Jax to take the lead. I trusted him with every part of my body. He turned us until my back brushed the rough fabric of the couch. I reached between us and wrapped my hand around his rod. He pumped into my hand. My body vibrated with desire and need. I positioned him at my entrance, but his cock sprung free. He was as hard for me as I was wet for him, but he pulled back.

I ran my hand along the length of his dick.

"If you do that too many times, I'm not going to last long," he said, his voice so deep it was almost a demon utterance. His eyes closed and he sat back. "Hold on for a second."

I leaned forward and ran my tongue around the head of his hard length.

"Fuck." He grabbed my chin and tilted my face up. "What did I tell you?"

I met his heated gaze and wrapped my fingers around the base, sliding my hand up and down in a slow motion.

He growled. "You will be the death of me."

My chin was freed. In one swift motion, he had both of my hands pinned up over my head. My core throbbed, and a gasp slipped from my lips. I squirmed in his grasp.

"If we have to die one day, let it be like this." My voice sounded rough with need.

With a precise thrust, Jax buried himself deep inside of me. My head rolled back. The moan that came from my lips was a sound I didn't recognize, but I wanted more and ground my hips up against his.

A hiss from Jax's lips was my reward.

He thrust slow and deep. "Rena..."

"Don't you dare be gentle with me. That's not what I need," I gritted out.

Jax pulled back and drove into me again and again in a punishing rhythm. My core tightened and ached. I moved my hips in time with his until the pleasure blinded me to the point I couldn't keep pace.

My orgasm ripped through me in shudders. Glorious release. My body was light like I drifted in rapture.

Jax came right after me. My body still shook with waves of pleasure when he stilled. His hot release pulsed into me, and I relished the connection between us.

He dropped his forehead to mine. "Damn, Rena. You are trying to kill me."

I laughed. "Like I said. If we have to go, this is the only way I want to do it."

He chuckled and covered my mouth with his, taking his time in a gentle kiss. I loved how he could be gentle or fierce, but I loved how he did those things for me more.

"Thank you, my love." He kissed both of my cheeks. "For knowing me in a way no one else ever will."

My heart swelled in my chest. "That's love, Jax."

CHAPTER 22

JAX

I pulled Rena against my chest and held her there. Our time together in an intimate moment was limited, and I wanted to be present in the time we had. But there was a room full of archangels down the hall along with the Devil and the Mother of Night Children. "This is going to be awkward if your family comes to find us here, and we're naked on this ugly-ass, booger-green couch."

Rena laughed. The sound was one of the full laughs I was determined to get more out of her. She deserved innumerable happy moments. There had been so much upheaval the last year. Her birthday was coming up. We would have Typhon taken care of soon, and I would have my love as my wife by her birthday.

"What are you thinking?" Rena asked.

"How many times can we repeat that before anyone comes looking for us?"

Rena laughed again, and it went straight to my dick. "Let's try for at least one more."

She pushed herself up until she straddled me, rubbing her slick slit across my cock. The shaft hardened for her as if her pussy had power over my member. *Rena did.*

"I knew you were trying to kill me. Are you trying to get out of marrying me?" I smiled up and locked on her blue eyes.

Rena peered down at me with fierce intensity. My dick jerked under her.

"I told you I would marry you in a small ceremony as soon as we could." She rocked back and forth. "So maybe you can wait until after the wedding before we both die from amazing sex."

I laughed then and tilted my hips to sink inside her. Dying while fucking my beautiful love was the best death I could hope for, because inside her was my favorite place to be.

I BUTTONED MY PANTS, and Rena tossed me my shirt. She shimmied into her clothes faster than I did.

"Why are there no bathrooms in this library?" Rena asked, her voice exasperated.

"I'm guessing angels don't use them." I shrugged.

"How bad is my hair?"

"It's fine," I said, eyeing the messiness. She looked

freshly satiated, and my pecker started to harden as if we hadn't just ridden each other all over the ugly green couch. I cleared my throat. "Not as smooth as you usually wear it."

"In other words, the just-fucked look?" She smiled.

The image of her on top of me swirling her hips made my dick harder, and I adjusted my pants. "That would be a very accurate description."

She ran her fingers through her silver-blonde locks, smoothing them down. *Damn, she is beautiful. Why she is with me I do not understand.*

I tugged her toward me, cupping her cheeks in my hands. "I love you, Rena. No matter where this path leads, I just want you to know that."

"I love you, Jaxon." She smiled a wicked mischievous grin.

"Why do you always want to push my buttons?" I chuckled, grabbing a handful of her ass.

"Because I can." She bit back a smile. "And you like it."

I devoured her mouth, letting my lips linger in a soft caress before I pulled away. "I do."

"We better get back before Father sends the Hellhounds to look for us," she said, disappointment drenching her voice. She didn't want to leave either, and I took satisfaction in that.

I nodded. "We should come back to this room again. It's my favorite room in the Library."

"They might rename it the fucking room if we keep using the space for that." She shot me another one of those devious smiles that roused my desire and eliminated all my common sense. My cock responded like it hadn't had its fill already.

"I'm going to get a plaque made for outside the door to officially claim this as our fucking room."

Rena's cheeks heated. I slipped my hand into hers and drew us toward the door. "I know you aren't embarrassed about a sign after you picked the name... and the stain you left on the couch."

"I did n—" Her words were lost as she studied the darker spot on the couch. The pink in her cheeks grew brighter. "We should clean that."

"We should," I agreed, but I kind of enjoyed having the place marked. "Guess we don't need the plaque after all."

"Jax." Rena laughed. Her face sobered, the levity forgotten. "Do you feel the call?"

"Yes," I said, rubbing my chest where my leaky essence had been plugged. A pull nagged at me from the spot. "It's like when Uriel showed me his journal." I was bound to him with his essence and Rena his blood. *What is it going to take to get this archangel disentangled from our relationship? We must do something to end the connection.*

"The tug is familiar to me too," Rena said. "I know where we need to go."

"Should we tell the others first?"

She navigated us down the corridor toward the pull. Her pace quickened. "No, this is a call for us and the pull is too strong to delay. Trust me?"

"Lead the way, my love."

CHAPTER 23

RENA

As Jax and I navigated the hallways following the call, the destination became plain. The Library called me to the special room Uriel had brought me to while Jax was recovering from ending Adam. The same room I'd been called to several times before. I led Jax through the winding hallways despite his protests we should get back to the group first.

"I don't have a feather to use as a key," I said. The slot for Uriel's feather was empty in the thick metal door, making me feel foolish for coming here first. "You were right. We should have gone back to the command center. The call feels so urgent though."

"It was," a smooth voice said from behind us, startling me. I grabbed Jax's arm and turned to see Uriel plucking one of his metallic feathers. "The Library is ready to share more secrets than I might be able to articulate."

I moved aside to give Uriel access to the door, and he walked between me and Jax. The feather melted into the same spot the previous one had done before. Jax crossed the space behind Uriel to stand closer to me.

"How do you have any feathers left if you have to give one to the door every time?" I asked.

"Entrance varies by room, but I've rarely been drawn to this one until now. Until you two." Uriel glanced between me and Jax. "Something changed when you became the balance and the scale. However, my feathers do return as I heal."

Well, at least he wouldn't have a bald spot from the feathers we'd used.

The room looked the same as the last time we'd visited. Uriel walked toward a tall bookcase to the left, and I knew which shelf he'd choose because the call tugged at me too. I reached for the book, and Uriel's hand brushed mine. His skin was cold. I jerked my hand and stepped back into Jax. His hand went to my hip.

Uriel flipped the book open and handed it to me.

The text was on Megiddo, but it was the last paragraph that detailed the description of Echidna's entombment. Her resting place was deep in the mountain with only one way in and one way out. She was in stasis, according to the text, but at her wishes her room was completely sealed in a tomblike fashion to prevent Typhon from reaching her. *Extreme measures. What happened for her to lock herself away like that? Had he tried something like what he did to their human daughter?*

I stared at my uncle with more questions than when we arrived. "Has Typhon known this all along? About the lengths Echidna went to?"

"Yes," Uriel said.

I passed the book over to Jax. "This makes me second-guess waking her up to help us, especially knowing Typhon is unable to reach her. I don't want to break her out just for her to die a terrible death like your..." Uriel went rigid. Sorrow and anguish swirled in his eyes. I couldn't finish the thought.

"But did you read this paragraph?" Jax pointed to one further down on the page. "It says if the day were to arrive where he became too powerful, she would come forward again."

"The book makes it sound like she would know and free herself," I said. "Not a band of angels and demons breaking her out."

"The text is open to interpretation as are all writings," Uriel said. "Those who rest in Megiddo need a connection or a condition to wake from deep stasis."

I brought my hand over my chest where the scar marked... "Like my death woke my grandmother."

Jax shifted closer to me until his hip brushed against mine. "Those?"

"More than just Eve and Echidna have rested there?" I asked.

Uriel shifted his weight. "They have. The rooms on the map are not all empty."

I didn't like how he evaded the question. He didn't lie, but that was only half an answer. "Who?"

"We'll have to save the topic of who for another day when you are further down your journey," Uriel said.

The way he cut off the conversation hurt, but I couldn't find it in me to get mad after I'd just brought up his dead family.

"This reveal-as-you-go is bullshit, Uriel, and you know it," Jax said.

"The restriction is not intentional. Even though you are the balance and the scale, we are still limited on how much we can share without interfering," he said.

I let out a long sigh, knowing that was a very fine path all my aunts and uncles traversed. "And what exactly will happen if you give us information that crosses the line? And what is the line?"

"The divider is not so black and white, Morena. The line is various shades of grey and might move depending on where you are in the journey." He paused and let out as long a sigh as I had, but his sounded tired instead of frustrated. "For an archangel, and I mean all of us, we can help you find the answers you seek, but we can't influence the path you choose with the knowledge uncovered. We can protect you as the balance and the scale, but even has limitations."

"What happens if you do overstep on this ever-moving line?" I asked, noting he'd skipped that part. My nerves jittered with fear at what his answer might be.

"We cannot tell you about the consequences of those actions, either, as the knowledge might influence you."

"Like I said." Jax's tone was exasperated. "A bullshit answer."

"Your disagreement does not make the boundary unreasonable," Uriel countered. "We all have rules we must live by, but they are not the same set of rules."

His answer was true. Demons had a code, angels had a different canon, and humans had several sets. "I'll let that one go… for now."

"As you wish, but the answer will not change in the future whether from me or the others."

I narrowed my eyes at him but didn't question him any further.

"What I did want to show you"—he paused—"what I can show you now, as the knowledge would not influence your decisions to do what you were already going to do, is this." He retrieved a book and flipped the pages open to the middle where a piece of paper was filed in the spine. Uriel handed it to me.

I unfolded the paper. The map had an inset square drawn to look like the outside of the mountain, but the bulk of depicted the inside. "This is Megiddo." There were random lines with dots at the end of them. "These are the stasis rooms."

"They are," Uriel confirmed.

They weren't just the ones we knew but many more. So many the sight was overwhelming to try to decipher. "But they are not labeled."

"No, but you know two of them already." Uriel handed me a pen. "You should identify those."

"How do we figure out the others, and how does this help us find Echidna?" Jax asked.

I marked my grandmother's right away along with the empty room we'd found. The others were scattered around like tombs in Egypt's Valley of the Kings. "There isn't a pattern. The rooms are sporadic. Eve's room and that empty room are both on the lowest level, but the others zigzag all over the place. These three were on the other map in the command center, but we haven't visited them to confirm they are accurate."

"This is a fucking dick move, Uriel," Jax said. "You've put the answer in our hands, but no way to understand the map. This might as well be in a dead language no one speaks anymore."

I might not be as angry as Jax, but I certainly was disappointed.

"Have I now?" Uriel peered at the book where the map had been tucked away.

Jax and I both reached for it. He was faster and snatched the book up with a wink. One of the many things I loved about him. He didn't let me win at anything just because I was Lucifer and Lilith's daughter or the heir to Hell.

I crossed my arms, grinning as I waited for him to pass the text to me. I'd glimpsed the writing and knew he wouldn't have learned the ancient language in his training for the guard.

"What the fuck is this written in?" Jax's forehead bunched.

"That's Sumerian," I said, not hiding my smugness.

"You learned this?" Jax appraised me with admiration in his eyes.

"Yes, I've studied it since I was able to write my name. Aunt Jophiel was a stickler with me on this particular language and my ability to translate Sumerian." I narrowed my eyes at Uriel. "Kind of prophetic, don't you think?"

"Learning the ancient language hasn't changed your choices," Uriel said, his tone flat. He was over the questions. I wasn't, but I tucked them away for later.

Jax handed me the book. I scanned the pages the book was opened to. The words didn't make sense. I reread them and passed the book to Uriel.

"Maybe my skills are rusty." I pointed to a paragraph. "This reads like they must reveal themselves to the one seeking to find them."

"You are interpreting the passage correctly." He handed the book back to me.

The ability to hide in plain site was part of the protection, and I found comfort in how the residents of Megiddo were so safe. But that meant our cause had to be deemed honorable to locate them too.

"That doesn't help us find Echidna," Jax said.

I regarded Uriel. He worked a swallow in his throat as if he was choosing his words carefully. "Keep reading."

"Only one person has access to them all… like a skeleton key," I said, thinking on the words as I said them.

"Who is that person?" Jax asked, his voice low, almost menacing.

I let out a long breath. "If my Sumerian isn't way off, it's Eve. My grandmother."

"We're screwed then." Jax paced a few steps away.

"Not Eve," Uriel said. "Read the text again but not so literally."

I went through the same passage again in silence. The words referenced the first man and the first woman, but the first woman was the one who could open the rooms. Inside Megiddo was her temple, or maybe the mountain itself was her temple. My Sumerian wasn't perfect, so the interpretation could be either. As I reasoned through the meaning, I thought of how kind my grandmother had been. She was the Mother of Life, and her kindness was limitless even in the presence of the cruelty of Adam. "Was the mountain raised to be Eve's sanctuary and she opened Megiddo up to others?"

"Yes, and she did. But what else do you see?" Uriel urged me on.

I reviewed the text wishing I'd worked harder at learning translations. "She was the one who could open all the rooms, and I suspect seal them even though I haven't read that part yet."

"You are correct. She could." Uriel leveled me with that glacial stare only an archangel capable of his power could —as if he were willing me to get the connotation.

I'm an idiot. The answer was obvious. "She could open and seal them because she was the balance."

"Very good," Uriel said, his voice relaxed.

"But knowing Rena can open the rooms doesn't help us pinpoint the exact room where Echidna is in stasis." Jax rested his hands on the table and regarded me. Frustration filled his eyes, and I understood the sentiment well. He was right.

"Did you read the entire passage?" Uriel asked me.

I turned back to the pages and continued reading. "Guardianship will always require two to protect the secrets of the mountain." I sought out Jax's gaze, and his realization reflected my own. "It's us. Like my parents and Selene and Endymion can make the hidden door visible. The answer is both of us are required to reveal the labels on the map. Pick it up."

Jax held the map in his hands. I scrambled around the table to stand at his side, taking one side in mine. Nothing happened. I looked up from the map. "Did I misread the text, Uriel?"

"No, but like everything in our world, we must bleed for the answers."

It was a hint. A big one.

Jax growled next to me.

"It's not what you think, Jax." I touched his arm. "We just need a drop of our blood. I had to do the same thing with another book."

"I don't have fangs anymore to jab your finger," Jax said.

"That's okay." I slid my thumb along the edge of the parchment. The sting was sweet knowing I would have answers soon.

Jax did the same on the other side of the paper. I pressed my thumb to the paper and watched the red liquid seep in.

"What if the map doesn't accept my blood because I'm half-demon and half-human?" Jax asked. My heart ached. Even through all his accomplishments that was his first thought.

"It will," Uriel said. "Because you are the scale, Jax."

As Uriel spoke, our blood soaked into the thick parchment. Crimson flowed down the lines to Eve's chamber. My handwriting disappeared and was replaced.

"Eve's name in Sumerian," I said, to clarify for Jax.

The race of red stopped at the empty chamber, and I gasped. "The empty room…"

"What the fuck?" Jax said, his eyes narrowed. I followed his fixed stare to Uriel.

"Did you know all this time she wasn't even there?" I asked, not hiding my disappointment.

"No," Uriel said. "But I suspected it could be possible."

"So, she's been awake this entire time but not intervening." I couldn't keep my voice calm. My anger bled through like blood had seeped into the map. Chimera had been wrong. Echidna didn't give a shit.

"I'm not sure where she is or if she is in stasis or not," Uriel said.

"And why aren't the others filled in?" Jax asked still focused on the useless map.

"Some have been occupied periodically. They fill in over time as needed," Uriel said, averting his eyes.

"All these secrets, Uriel." I sighed. "I know you think the secrecy necessary, but I don't agree. As you would say, that's a conversation to have later. Right now, we need to figure out where Echidna actually is."

Jax nodded. "And if she even wants to be found."

CHAPTER 24

JAX

I carried the map back to the command center. Rena started to argue, but there must have been something in my expression that made her concede. My face probably said I would throat-punch Uriel if my hands were free. *He's a fucking piece of work.* While I owed him for standing by Rena when I couldn't after I killed Adam, every time we got to a place I thought I could move past our conflicts, the cold bastard did something like this.

While we were away, the group had been busy with various strategy options. It was impressive to see how Lucifer worked with his siblings. Rena laid the map on the table. Uriel said we could take the diagram anywhere in the Library but not outside of the walls. The parchment would disintegrate if we did. I pictured the paper self-destructing like in the human spy movies.

Lilith ran her hand over the paper to her Mother's

chamber. She paused there for a moment before moving to the open chamber. *Echidna's chamber.*

Lilith's eyes widened. "She's not there." was a statement, not a question.

"No." Rena shook her head. "And we don't know where she is or why she's not intervening."

"We need a different plan in case we don't find her," Lucifer said, his tone resigned.

"She is the linchpin," Barachiel said. "We must find her."

"I agree." Jophiel stepped forward. "She may need our help."

"The human world needs our help," I said, recalling the intel we reviewed daily. "Have any of you seen the storms Typhon has unleashed on Earth?"

"Of course we have, Jax," Gabriel said. "We might not know all, but those kinds of disasters reach us. We know of every single death."

"You might try acting like humans dying impacts you."

"Bear the weight of those souls for thousands of years and come back to compare," Gabriel said.

Were they so insensitive to the humans who had died at Typhon's hands? I was sick to my stomach at how little emotion they showed over the lives lost.

"We can do both," Michael reminded us. "There are nine of us. That's a lot of power."

"There's no need to take two teams to Megiddo if Echidna isn't there," Lilith said. "We should divide up and go look for her."

Lucifer drummed his fingers on the map. "Or we move forward to stop Typhon without her."

Even Echidna's children said their mother was the one defense that would make the difference for us against Typhon. I didn't like either option, but I worried about what the Overworld would face if we didn't act now. The Overworld was part of me—my human half.

"I think that's our best option. The longer we delay, the more destruction Typhon causes in the human realm." Rena flattened both hands on the table. "But we're better off if she's found. We'll make one last attempt to find her. If we're unsuccessful, then we take Typhon on without her."

I leaned forward. I had no idea if Echidna would help us even if we did find her, but Rena believed Echidna would. That was what was important to me. "I agree."

"The balance and the scale have spoken," Barachiel said. "We have work to do."

WITH OUR TEAMS and efforts focused, I relaxed some, even though Rena was working with the opposite group. Lucifer, Michael, Barachiel, Gabriel, and I were focused on a strategy without Echidna while Rena, Lilith, Uriel, and Jophiel focused on where to find her.

"It's apparent Typhon believes Echidna should be

there but doesn't know she is not. We have an advantage," I said.

"Yes," Michael said. "We can create distractions to keep him there. That will limit the damage to the human world while we locate Echidna."

Finally, an archangel shows some concern for the human realm, and the warrior of them all, nonetheless.

"Agreed, but we need a plan if we don't find her too," Lucifer added.

"She's never been one to hide. She faced off with Typhon on several occasions." Barachiel cut a glance to Uriel.

"True, and she was ready to rest after so much history," Gabriel added.

"We need a two-part plan. Keep Typhon distracted without tipping him off we are also searching other places for Echidna," I said, thinking we could launch a series of sneak attacks on Typhon. A barrage could draw his children to his defense and buy us time to look for Echidna.

"That's the same plan we had before." Michael crossed his arms over his chest.

"But we thought we knew where Echidna was then. We have no clue now."

I scanned the room, finding Rena. She sat on the giant blue couch, far larger than the one in our little side room, along with Lilith and Jophiel reading different texts. Uriel stood behind them answering questions and consulting on the passages. I wanted to choke his neck. Not just because he was close to Rena or had inadvertently bound himself to her. Still debatable to me. He was the reason we were here forced to battle a being capable of destroying entire realms. Uriel fell in love with Typhon's daughter. None of us had any control over who we fell in love with, but he had the answers we needed to defeat this powerful being and withheld them under some stupid fucking angel code.

Rena's eyes lined at the corners and locked with mine. She was the reason I kept my promise to let my grudge against her uncle go. Her lips curved up into a wicked smile. The kind that drove me wild. *Fuck, everything about her drives me mad.* My dick took notice, and I leveled the most intense look at her I could muster. Her cheeks reddened, but she licked her lips. My dick hardened, and she was all I saw. Lucifer cleared his throat next to me, and I was thankful the map table we stood at came to my waist.

"Did you hear what I said, Jax?" Lucifer asked. "Or were you too busy ogling my daughter to hear me?"

I suddenly felt like a lovesick teenager again. I'd get in trouble for not paying attention, but I was better at hiding my stares at Rena then. I didn't have to hide them any longer.

"I was admiring my fiancée and did not hear you, Lucifer," I said.

Lucifer chuckled. "Balls, Jax. You've certainly grown them this last year."

My face heated, and I figured my cheeks were as red as Rena's turned a few minutes earlier.

Lucifer continued, still chuckling. "What I was saying was I believe I can send a company of demons to keep Typhon busy at Megiddo. Then, both groups would be freed up to look for Echidna."

It was a solid plan, but he was Lucifer. "That is why you are the king of Hell. Do you think Rena is going to go for your idea?" She hadn't been on board before when we thought we were going to be in and out of Megiddo with Echidna.

Lucifer clasped one of my shoulders and Michael the other.

"That's why you are going to talk to her about it." Lucifer smiled.

I swallowed hard, and the spit choked me, making me cough. Lucifer patted me on the back. Approaching Rena with this was potentially going to be bad for me. *If she cuts me off from sex for this...*

"You are the scale to her balance," Michael said, and he smiled too. That was the first smile I recalled seeing on the archangel's face.

Gabriel and Barachiel whispered amongst themselves.

"Why do I feel like I'm going to end up in the dungeons of Hell after this?"

"I won't let it come to that." Lucifer's smile got bigger.

Surely, my future father-in-law wasn't setting me up for an ass-kicking from my future wife. I swallowed hard and peered toward where Rena had returned to her reading. *Fuck. She's going to plant a kick right in my chest when I suggest bringing an army from Hell to Earth.*

CHAPTER 25
RENA

I closed the book I'd been skimming. Neither Mother, Aunt Jophiel, nor I had found anything useful in these texts. We were going to have to act on our plan with our best guess at where to find Echidna, and we had few ideas.

Jax fidgeted as he stood in front of me. Nervousness radiated off him. "Can I talk to you for a second?"

I looked around at the others wondering what he couldn't say in front of them and why he was so nervous to talk to me. "Of course."

He held out a shaky hand to me. I took it, and he led me across the room away from the others.

"We had an idea in our group that would free up all nine of us to search for Echidna when we have some leads," Jax said, smoothing his hands over the legs of his jeans.

"Oh, that would be great." A little hope sprung up in

my chest. "When we actually have some ideas on where to look."

Jax shifted his weight to the other foot. "Lucifer could bring a company from the armies of Hell to Megiddo— "

"No," I said, making sure my tone was firm. "Not happening."

"Let me finish. Since Megiddo is currently closed due to the dust storm Typhon has stirred up, it's low risk to bring them there."

"Our armies are not known for being judicious when it comes to killing innocents," I said. "Bringing that size of an army from Hell is like releasing two hundred mercenaries to do as they please."

On more than one occasion, even small armies took out many innocents. It's why Father didn't allow any sizeable force in the human realm often, and exactly why I was against the idea.

I let out a long sigh to release the tension building from the option. The army might be our only choice. "If we can't find another option by the end of the day, then I'll consider his offer."

"That's all I'm asking for, my love." He kissed my cheek.

My skin heated where his lips touched. Damn him. "You know that's all it takes for me to cave. Don't you?"

"What? Kiss you on the cheek? If that's true, I'm going to be kissing your cheek more often."

I bit my lip at his innocence. He had no idea. "No, calling me your 'love.'"

"But you are. My love is all yours, and when I look at you, all I see is the beautiful woman I cherish above everything else. Beautiful inside and out." He tucked a piece of hair that had fallen over my cheek behind my ear. He had no idea how marred I was inside.

"And you had to say that here where there is an audience." I tilted my head so my lips brushed against his ears and lowered my voice. "Where I can't drop down on my knees to properly return such adoration."

Jax blinked and cleared his throat. He leaned in so close I could feel his warm breath against my ear. "I could scoop you up in my arms and take you to the room where your stain marks the couch. Then, you could drop down on your knees and take my cock in your mouth until the head hits the back of your throat."

My core tightened. I choked on a swallow and coughed. He shattered the thought of innocence I'd had earlier. I delighted in him this way when he was almost feral for me. "We can't have this exchange here."

"I know." He groaned.

"Later," I said, giving the promise we both needed.

His heated stare leveled me, but he broke the connection and turned back toward his group. I needed a bucket of ice water dumped on me. Since freezing liquid was not an option, I walked back to my cohort.

"We found something that might be useful." Jophiel turned a book toward me.

I read through the text she pointed to. "You think she's hiding there?"

"It would make sense." Mother shrugged.

"Does it?" I asked, unsure what she meant. "Why would the Mother of Monsters be in Santa Fe, New Mexico?"

"She is a fallen angel, Morena," Uriel said. "And the area's beauty is reminiscent of our home."

"The Loretto Chapel is often visited by angels," Jophiel said. "As well as the mountain ranges."

My mouth fell open, and I snapped it shut. "Are all those alien sightings from you all?" I wiggled my finger between Uriel and Jophiel.

"I haven't been since you woke me," Uriel said, holding his hands up.

"I used to visit often, but it's been over a year since I made a trip," Jophiel said.

"That's not a denial." I stared them down but turned to the other group. "Jax, have you ever been to Santa Fe, New Mexico?"

"Yes." He glanced at Father and back to me. "Lucifer and I stopped in a few times a year or so ago."

Jax had a guilty look on his face, and I looked at Father. "So, you're the alien they see?"

Father chuckled. "Not intentionally."

Laughter trickled through the room.

I shook my head. "You angels are like children sometimes."

"What's in Santa Fe besides archangels posing as aliens?" Jax asked, fighting a smile.

"Echidna. Evidently, she is fond of the mountains she

landed in when she fell from Grace," I said, passing the book to him.

"The large mountain range? I can portal us close to that area."

Of course, he could because he'd been there with my father. "That's the one," I said, hesitating for a few moments as I considered our options. "And I'm going to have to take you up on your idea from earlier. We need a distraction for Typhon, so he doesn't pick up on us gathering in Santa Fe. Make it small though."

"I'll meet you there," Father said. "After I give the company their orders." Father disappeared as only he could.

If our efforts went all wrong and Typhon ended the existence of those one hundred and fifty demons, their blood would be on my hands and no one else's. I nodded to Jax.

He formed the symbols and the portal spurred to life. The blue light opened to reveal the base of the massive mountain. "Who's ready to be mistaken for an extraterrestrial being?"

"Isn't that what we are?" Gabriel asked.

Michael shoved him through the portal with a laugh. I hooked my arm through my mother's and rubbed Jax's bicep as we went through.

CHAPTER 26

JAX

The mountains were beautiful with their snow-capped peaks. I hadn't had much of a chance to appreciate them when I was here before. The last time Lucifer and I came here was to track down some Nephilim hunting demons, and the trip was at nighttime. The Nephilim had created a hideout at an abandoned ranch outside the city. I was disappointed when the half-angels didn't try to fight us more. My frustration at not being able to talk to Rena during that period had reached an all-time high. The Nephilim weren't frightened until they saw Lucifer's devil face, as if they hadn't believed he existed until they saw him. I'd killed more of them than Lucifer that night, and I carried their deaths with me. My demon side had taken over, and I'd relished in the blood lust. It wasn't the kind I'd felt in my brief time as a vampire, but it was an angry desire to destroy them before they could destroy us. Only Lucifer was with me, and the Nephilim never stood a chance. Maybe one day I would be able to tell Rena about the mission, but that night wasn't the only time I'd killed Nephilim. We had more important things to do.

"A few of us could go into town while others check the mountainside she's fond of," Rena said, moving closer to me.

"Why don't you and Jax check out Santa Fe for signs while the rest of us cover the mountain," Lilith said. "Do you have your cell phone with you?"

"Yes," Rena said.

"I have mine too," Lilith said. "You can call us if you see anything, and I'll do the same."

Rena looked at me with excitement and curiosity. I held out my hand to her. She slid her hand into mine, and I was thankful we would have a few moments to ourselves here. "Call if you see any signs of her."

"We will." Barachiel winked at us. In fact, Lucifer and the others were all smiling at us. It was like they knew Rena wanted to explore the city. It was thoughtful of them. The archangels all had their wings tucked in, even Lucifer. They could go with us, but I suspected they were giving us space to be ourselves for a while. I wasn't about to challenge a rare gift of time alone with Rena.

I took in the local artwork on display as Rena and I strolled around the plaza. Rena stopped in front of two large wood doors that were closed.

"This must be the chapel Aunt Jophiel mentioned." She peered at the large church in the town square. There were incredibly detailed carvings above the massive wood doors. A cross was nestled in the peak of the roof.

"I believe it is." I squeezed her hand. "Want to go in?"

"Yes," she said, her voice a little breathless. "This is beautiful." Rena's tone sounded soft and full of amazement. "The staircase really is something."

I read the sign and ran my hand over the banister. "They call it the miraculous staircase."

"The guy at the front said we weren't supposed to touch the stairway," Rena hissed at me.

"Do you really think he's going to stop the heir to Hell?" I scoffed.

"I know we can't, but imagine how lovely the weddings are here." Rena took in the stained-glass windows.

"Why couldn't we?" I pictured her at the front of the church dressed for a human wedding complete with a veil. I could marry Rena anywhere as long as she was happy. "We're in here now. You are half-archangel, and I'm half-human."

"We'd have to get a license." Her eyes widened with a little hope like all she needed was a small bit of encouragement to go for what she wanted.

"Why don't we see if they have the availability and go from there." I lifted her hand and kissed the tops of her fingers. Warmth gathered in my chest and spread out around my heart to see her looking forward to an event rather than dreading an outcome.

We walked back to the gentleman who took our donation to enter. He'd been friendly enough earlier.

"Did you enjoy the chapel?" The man at the desk asked.

"We did." I smiled and looked at Rena. "Very much so."

Rena's palm was sweaty against mine. "Would it be possible for us to get married here today?"

"Not today, but we could fit you in tomorrow evening." The man smiled almost as if he'd heard. "You'll need a license and someone to perform the ceremony though. Let me give you directions on where to get one and the names of a few JPs." The man retrieved a map of the city from the stack on the counter and scribbled down directions to the clerk's office. He handed the paper to me, and my hand shook as I took it, suddenly overcome with nervous adrenaline. *Can we pull this off?*

We cleared the large carved wood doors, and Rena tugged me away from the crowd gathered to view the chapel. "We don't have to do this if you aren't ready."

"I've been ready," I said. "I'm just worried what your parents are going to say about us getting married in a church."

"It's a non-denominational chapel. I don't think they will have any issues with a ceremony there. Father is an archangel. You don't really think he'll have a problem with it, do you?" Her voice was wistful as if she dared to dream something different than what she knew she was obligated to do with the binding ceremony.

"No, I don't. Are you ready, my love?" My pulse raced as I lifted her hand and brushed my lips over the inside of her wrist. "There is no rush other than my impatience to make you mine."

"I'm already yours, Jax," she said. "But I want to be bound to you and you to me in every way we can."

My heart pounded so hard from joy and love, that I was sure the hole in my essence Uriel plugged with his own would burst open. During my childhood, I might not have thought I was worthy of love, but she always did. First as friends and then as we became more so did the bond grow between us. My devotion to Rena was infinite. There would be no end to my commitment or what I would do for her.

"Then that is what matters." I held up the map and pointed in the direction that matched the instructions. "Looks like the office is just around the corner."

We walked up the steps to the two-story adobe brick building. There was a terrace above the entrance. A gentleman inside the double metal doors directed us down a hallway. We followed his guidance until we came to a wood door with six framed-glass panels on top and turned to wood about halfway down. I wiped my sweaty palm on my pants and opened the door for Rena. A bell on the door jingled above us.

The clerk looked us over and grinned. "I bet you're here for a license."

"We are," Rena said, meeting the gaze of the clerk. She used her demon powers of persuasion on the clerk and artfully eliminated the need for proper ID.

I chuckled against her ear and whispered, "That was impressive."

She winked at me and continued to focus on the clerk who was entering our information into the computer.

In moments, the license was printed with our names on it. Neither of us had last names, so we used lands as humans did centuries ago. Jaxon Dreamland and Morena Eden. The contract wasn't official by human standards, but we didn't live by those standards. We would be binding ourselves to each other, and the act was more irrevocable than the human marriage ceremony. Our lives would be forever linked in a way that could not be broken, even in death.

The easy smile on Rena's face and the way the sun danced over her, she looked more beautiful than even seemed possible. Warmth spread across my chest. I loved Rena with each drop of blood in my body and every ounce of my patched-up soul. She stood by me through my near-existence-ending experiences and took me back when I'd checked out after I ended Adam. I didn't deserve her, but she chose me. And I'd keep choosing her every day as long as she would let me. Rena was all I'd ever need in my life from now until the end of my existence, however long or short that time may be.

She looked up at me. "What are you thinking?"

"I love you." I leaned forward and claimed her lips.

She'd be my wife tomorrow evening.

CHAPTER 27

RENA

My heart was full as we strolled toward the mountain range to find my family. Jax and I hadn't found any signs of Echidna's presence in Santa Fe, and my hope my family had found the Mother of Monsters dwindled. My excitement swelled at the thought of Jax becoming my husband tomorrow, though, and the feeling grew with each step we took. He loved me in spite of my role, my future, and my parentage. He loved me for the me very few got to see, and I loved him for the way he was never intimidated by me. For the way he revered my body when I needed it and ravaged me when I wanted it that way. For the way he understood and listened to me, even when I had the craziest ideas.

"Do you think they will be surprised when I show them our license?" I waved the envelope containing the paper in front of him.

Jax sucked in a breath. "I'm just hoping Lilith doesn't kill me over it."

"Not my father but my mother?"

"Your father might be the Devil, but he's still a dude. After the planning your mother put into your coronation, I can't imagine what she has planned for your wedding. The fear I have for her wrath has no end."

I laughed. "You are right to be scared of her."

He tugged me around in front of him and cupped my cheeks in his hands. "You are worth any wrath Lilith might deliver."

His lips devoured mine, and I sank into him. He walked me back against a tree. My body was pressed between the hardness of the tree and Jax's firm chest. The position was like my own personal bliss. Jax leaned back. "If we don't stop, your family will be hearing you scream my name."

"I don't care," I whispered in his ear.

He put a little more distance between us. "I know you mean it now, and the blush that crosses your face when you think someone knows of our intimacy drives me wild. The thought of that look makes me want to fuck you right now to see it, but I don't want you to ever be embarrassed by me."

My heart slowed as he gave me space. There wasn't a scenario where I'd ever be embarrassed by him or because of him. I, myself, was another story. There had been plenty of embarrassment over the things I said when I was sick. I held out my hand to him, and we continued on our way in silence for a bit.

There were no familiar scents nearby, just the smell of oak, cottonwood, juniper, and other woodland things. We were safe, but I understood what he meant. "I would never be embarrassed by you, and I hope you know that. My own actions... I might be by those but never you."

Jax's fingers tightened on mine. He stopped, tugging me with him off the trail.

"What's wrong?"

His eyes widened and dust pelted us. I threw my wings out as a shield. Pebbles stung and bit at my feathers. Jax drew me behind a tree with him. I pulled my wings in. My back was to his front as he wedged me between him and the tree, but the stance wasn't the same safe feeling from before. I felt exposed here. The tree was far too narrow to hide us from the danger... whatever it was. Looking out in front of us, I saw through the dust to the source. My wings were pinned, but they wouldn't do us much good against this enemy. *Typhon.*

His gross snake legs swirled in a grey haze, and I swallowed down the bile rising in my throat.

"How did he find us?" I whispered under my breath.

"I don't know," Jax said under his.

"Apparently, the company Father sent failed."

"Any ideas?" Jax asked against my ear. "Now would be a good time for them."

"The only weapons I have are the dagger at my waist

and my devil face." Neither option seemed like an effective weapon. There was no way to get close enough to him with my dagger. The remaining tool in my armament was one very few knew about, and one I wasn't entirely sure I knew how to use anymore. This opportunity came to us for a reason. *If I can reach inside where I buried that special gift, we might be able to take him here.* "I could use my demon powers. It looks like he's alone, so this could be our chance."

The pressure holding me against the tree disappeared. Wind whipped against my back that hadn't moments ago. "Jax?" I swung my head around, twisting my body.

Fear entwined with panic burned through my belly until I was almost sick. Orthus held Jax in his jaws. Saliva dripped from the giant dog's mouth. Blood trickled down Jax's arm and onto the grass below. His face was only partially visible to me, but the eye I could see was closed.

I reached for my dagger and slid the blade from the sheath, stretching for the power locked too far away to obey.

"If you will agree to my terms, I'll let him go unharmed." A large voice boomed around me.

Orthus clamped down on Jax, and my future husband grunted as if in pain.

"What are your terms?" I shouted over the roar from the dust storm Typhon had created.

"Return with me," he said.

"Return where?" I peered up where Jax was unconscious in the giant dog's mandibles and seeing him in peril cleaved my heart in two. He needed help, and I had to decide.

"Eden," he said like I should know. His first prison was there until they created the one that held him for centuries.

"Let Jax go, and I will go with you," I said, playing back what I knew about Eden. There was a chance I could imprison him there. A slim chance but I'd take the opportunity. There wasn't another choice in my mind if Jax was in danger, and I had any power to stop it.

Typhon nodded, and Orthus set Jax down in a gentle, smooth motion. It should be a relief to see him out of those massive jaws, but he wasn't moving. Everything in me wanted to go to him, but Orthus stood between us. I still had my dagger, but I wasn't fast enough to take on both Typhon and Orthus with a single weapon. I tried to reach out to my bond with Uriel to send a message, but I didn't know if he could feel me the way the archangels did. Orthus looked remorseful for her part, and her reaction was unexpected. Typhon spun a portal in grey hues. *Well, that answers that question.*

He ushered me through the portal first, and it was as if all color disappeared from the world until my foot met the ground of the garden. I'd been through many portals. Most of the demons' were red and cast a crimson tint for a brief moment. Jax's was blue like his essence, and everything felt like spring going through his portals. I guess it made sense Typhon's would be colorless since he didn't seem to have any humanity in him.

Eden looked the same, but the garden was eerily quiet. The flowers still bloomed, and the trees were green. But the silence was unnerving. Not to mention we still had prisoners here on the mirror side, and there was a feeling I couldn't shake. Something familiar and uneasy. *Adam's remains.* Bile rose up, and I swallowed the bitterness back down. I wasn't sure how I would get out of it if he wanted me to free the prisoners on the mirror side.

"What do you want with me?"

"Do you know the story of Uriel and my daughter?"

"Yes," I said, observing the way his face softened at the very mention of his human daughter.

He continued as if I hadn't answered or had said something different. "He took from me something so special. The world did not deserve her. Helena was the only one who hadn't been born a monster. I do love all my children, but she was special."

"I can understand that." *Born? The texts we read said she had been created in human form. Echidna is a fallen angel. She could have given birth to any of her children, but I assume he means born of his making.*

"Can you now?" he asked. "You have Lucifer and Lilith as your parents. What do you know of loss?"

I knew the guilt and hardness grief could create in one's heart because it was what I felt every time I spoke of Eve. I, also, recognized the actions of someone like Typhon. He might be more powerful than Adam, but he wasn't any better. "My grandmother is now in a place I can no longer reach her, and she can no longer return to

Earth because she helped me. She had to hide her identity because of an obsessed psychopath, and I had little time with her after I found out who she really was to me."

"Your grandmother?" he echoed. "You mean the one who was the balance before you?"

"My grandmother," I reiterated. "Eve." First and foremost, she was family, even if I hadn't known the relationship until this past year. She was not a thing or a role like the balance any more than I was.

He studied me as if he was used to people acquiescing to him versus standing by their opinions.

I didn't budge under his assessment. The only reason I didn't fight earlier was because I was certain he would have killed Jax and anyone else I loved to get me here. I returned his observing stare and swallowed down my disgust to keep my face neutral. Nothing about him was welcoming. What had Echidna seen in him?

"You are unusual, balance," Typhon said, his tone carrying a hint of amusement.

"My name is Morena," I said, forcing myself not to grit my teeth. "What do you want from me? Is your plan to kill me to get back at Uriel for your perceived wrong? Because he grieved your daughter for centuries. He still grieves. He felt her loss."

"No, I'm not looking for revenge. I want you to bring my daughter back."

My heart broke. With Echidna as her mother, she was the daughter of a fallen angel. She should be in the same place my grandmother was, but Helena was made too. The power in me didn't have a way to even reach them or visit them like I could if they were in Hell.

"Angelic beings like your daughter and my grandmother go to places you and I cannot travel to. There is no way to even communicate with them." I softened my voice, understanding how deep his pain was. He'd have to pay for his crimes against the humans and my family, but he was, also, a grieving father. I understood grief all too well.

He eyed me with a hint of suspicion as if he thought I was trying to mislead him. "You can. You are the balance and can bring anyone here to our present that you choose."

I wasn't sure where he got his information, but I assumed he meant Eve's special abilities. "My grandmother was unique. She had a gift that allowed her to do things no one else could do, and she used her artistry until it took away her ability to exist in realms I can visit."

"The balance can do restore life."

"No, I can't. She could, probably because she was so pure of heart. She was goodness. I am not."

"Yes, you saved my daughter, Chimera, and her children." There was something akin to kindness in the expression on his face, but he was too brutal for that.

"A single good act doesn't make me a good being or even mean I have a good heart. I did what was right at the moment. Your daughter and her children didn't deserve what the Nephilim would do to them," I said.

He cocked his head as if scrutinizing me. "Do you not understand your power, Morena of Hell?"

"Just Morena, and I understand the responsibility of my choices."

"I don't think you do," he said. "Let me show you." Typhon swirled a finger in a circle like he was stirring a drink. A tiny funnel spun to life. "Look into it."

I leaned over to peer down the cone of the tiny tornado. Images appeared of my grandmother as she did the deeds only she could. A wave of grief hit my insides like the swirling of the miniature whirlwind and threatened to bring me to a cold, dark place. There was, also, pride. Eve had been magnificent in how she wove her goodness into the world. Typhon thought I had all her power, but that wasn't the case. I was … just me. The heir to Hell and those inherent abilities. No special power like hers other than a gut check that hit me when my decisions were impactful to keep the balance. I smiled at the image of my grandmother healing children and adults through the centuries. She was special. The gift was always her.

"It's not that I don't understand what she did. I love who she was, but that's not who I am. She was Eve. The first of her kind, and the only one I know of who could do what she did for a sparse few."

"Stop putting limitations on yourself, Morena of Hell."

I rolled my eyes. He'd been imprisoned for a long time, but he didn't deserve my respect. My biggest concern was how to get out of here, and angering him didn't seem productive to my cause.

"You will remain here until you find the power to bring my daughter back to me."

Fuck. He wasn't getting it. *And what is he going to do when he realizes I'm telling the truth?*

"Rest for now," he said. "Our work will begin when you are restored."

"I'm not tired."

He reached his hand in the air as if he was grabbing something, but there wasn't anything there... at least from what I could see. Typhon blew a small, for him, breath across his palm. I couldn't keep my eyes open. My lids were heavy, and I stopped fighting them too close. Everything was dark around me.

JAX

I woke up alone on the ground with dirt matted to my skin. Panic shook my entirety. Typhon had taken her. He'd taken Rena. I counted the ways I would dismantle him and make him pay in a similar way as I did Adam, even if doing so took my soul. She would come home but telling Lucifer and Lilith... saying where Rena was out loud. I had to do it. An envelope caught my eye from the ground. Our marriage license. I let out a growl that turned into a roar. Birds, squirrels, and other wildlife nearby scattered through the trees and underbrush... maybe for miles.

Lucifer and Lilith reached me first, and the others arrived behind them.

"Are you okay, Jax?" Lilith asked, looking over my bloody shoulder. "Where's Morena?"

"I'm fine." I closed my eyes against the pain and anger mixture twisting in my stomach. "Typhon took Rena."

"Where?" Lucifer demanded.

"I don't know. I was a little unconscious."

Jophiel came to my side and examined my arm wound from Orthus. "We can fix this, Jax."

I wasn't sure I wanted to be healed. The reminder of how I'd failed to protect was what I wanted more. I deserved the pain. Relished the ache. It kept me grounded in what was at stake.

"We need to get you to a secure place with a lab," Barachiel said.

"I want to find Rena first." I glanced at Lucifer. His eyes were full of the fires of Hell, rage barely contained. He wore the same look Rena had at her angriest. There was a safe house in the area kept so restricted I wasn't sure Lilith even knew about the location, but it wasn't mine to disclose. I'd simmer in the pain before giving away a sworn secret. "I can portal us to the Library."

"No," Jophiel said.

"There is a place," Lucifer said. "I had it set up for one of the generals to do experiments."

"Will he and his experiments be there?" Lilith asked.

"No." Lucifer leveled a wicked smile at her. "Turns out he was a traitor."

I knew exactly which general Lucifer spoke of, and that demon deserved the end he received. His experiments were done at human and vampire expense, and he didn't care what age they were. He'd done a good job hiding his deeds, but Lucifer had his suspicions. I wasn't part of the squad for that mission, but I heard the details. The bastard tried to run and took two of my classmates out along the way.

Lilith nodded. "And the location is close?"

"Just a few wing beats away," he said.

I took a step forward, but my knees went weak. I reached for a tree with my injured arm, and the spike of pain plummeted me into darkness.

I woke up on a cold metal table. The slick surface reminded me of what we'd seen during a training mission at a human morgue to collect a demon who turned out not to be dead. I sat up and looked around. Jophiel and Barachiel were at work with lab equipment and scientific instruments. There was a serious stench of death in the air. My stomach roiled at the pungent scent. *Fuck. It's bad to turn my stomach.*

"Oh, you're awake," Jophiel said. "The smelling salts worked."

"A little too well." I fought the urge to cover my face with my shirt.

Jophiel extended my arm out to my side. I winced at the stabbing pang, but I didn't move or cry from it. "Barachiel, I need your help."

Barachiel moved behind me. "Oh." There was surprise in her voice.

"What?" I gritted out.

"Nothing we can't fix." Barachiel patted my uninjured shoulder. Pain radiated out.

"I'm poisoned," I said. It wasn't a question. We trained with poisons in the guard and how to power through the effects. I recognized the way the toxin spread setting my veins on fire in a different way than Rena's touch.

"I'll not lie to you, Jax. What you are sensing is Orthus's poison. Had she not pierced the skin you would have been fine. Her venom entered the puncture wound from her saliva."

"There was a lot of that in my hair and on my clothes," I said, forcing a chuckle. My attempt to lighten the mood fell flat with the archangels to keep myself from going full-on rage. If I didn't think of something other than the fact Rena was with Typhon, I might tear this entire place down to go after them, even as weak as my body kept reminding me it was. "Where are Michael and Gabriel?"

"Tracking for Morena," Jophiel said. "We're hoping they can sense them given..."

"Since he just took her." I closed my eyes to rein in the fury inside me.

"Eyes open, Jax," Barachiel said. "We don't need you fainting on us."

"I have no intention of passing out, but I do need you to patch me up so I can go after my love." I kept my voice steady and strong to hide how exhausted I was. Never mind I didn't know where to look, but I would return to the place in the forest I last saw her.

"And we will," Jophiel said. Her quick clipped response grabbed my attention.

"Why am I sensing a but in that statement?"

"Orthus's poison isn't like an herb-based poison." Barachiel came to stand in front of me. "We need some of her saliva to make the antidote, but getting it will be challenging."

"I'm covered in her slobber," I said. "Can't you use what's on me?"

Jophiel shook her head. "No, that is contaminated with things like the fibers from your clothes and your skin oils. We need it straight from her."

"And what neither of you are saying is I'm going to be too weak to go after her myself before too long." I pushed down the frustration building in me. My existence...my life with Rena couldn't end like this. I'd free my love even if it cost me everything to do so.

"Yes," Barachiel said. "That is true, but Uriel is hunting Orthus."

Jophiel took my hand, and a sense of calm came over me. "Uriel had a bond at one time with his partner's siblings. Not a strong one, but the connection does make him unique in being able to locate them."

Uriel's grief tangled him up in a bad way, but he loved his family. He'd do what needed to be done to bring Rena home, and that was a piece of hope for me. "What do I do in the meantime?"

"Keep your heart rate low. No unnecessary movements," Jophiel said.

"In other words, stay where you are and stay calm." Barachiel squeezed my hand. "Being the scale doesn't save you from a human death in the human realm with this kind of poison."

"Be a frozen statue. Got it." I ignored the spikes of pain shooting down my back. "And no naps?"

"No naps," Jophiel said. "I know this will be tough for you, Jax, but trust us."

"Trusting you is not tough. Being still when the love of my life is in the hands of a monster is impossible," I said, fighting the deep, bone-aching tiredness from the poison.

Lilith entered the room. I hadn't even noticed she and Lucifer had left me until then. The lack of observation was a sign the poison had already dulled my senses.

"How are you feeling?" Concern creased Lilith's forehead.

"I'm fine," I said, hearing the strain in my voice.

"I could give you blood," she said. "That might postpone some of the effects."

Vomit came up my throat at the idea of what life was like during the brief period I was vampire, but the hurt in Lilith's eyes erased my disgust. She'd saved me from a death that would have separated me and Rena for centuries if not millennia. My chest tightened around my heart.

"It won't," Barachiel said. "Orthus's poison will not respond."

"Is Lucifer with Gabriel and Michael?" I asked.

"No, he's here," Lilith said. "He's sending the army

back to Hell. He figured Morena wouldn't forgive him if he let them stay."

I smiled. "He's right, but I'm surprised."

"He..." She paused. "We don't believe he will hurt her. He wants her help."

"Her help?"

"Yes, Lucifer believes, as do I, Typhon wants Morena to resurrect their daughter as Eve did with Morena."

"Does Morena have that kind of power? And his daughter has been dead for centuries. Is it even possible to bring someone back after that long?" Rena wouldn't agree to pull someone back after that kind of time. She'd been so concerned with not disturbing Eve that I couldn't fathom she would even entertain Typhon's ask.

"No, the ability was something unique to Mother," Lilith said. "I don't know about the other."

"I do, and the answer is no," Barachiel said. "Eve could only resurrect while the soul was still in the same realm. Once the soul passes to its final resting place, the essence of the being cannot be resurrected."

"Nor should we disturb them." Uriel's voice came from the doorway. He stepped through holding a covered jar. I flinched at the harshness in his tone, but relief hit harder knowing he had the poison to make the antidote. "I have it. Orthus willingly gave her venom to me. She was still in the forest as if she was wandering. Her remorse was apparent. She didn't agree with Typhon's choice either."

"That goes along with what Rena said Chimera told her. Typhon controls them, and they can't resist him." I grabbed my head to stop the room from spinning. The urge to lie down was overpowering and difficult to ignore. The aunts said to keep my eyes open, so I managed to stay upright.

"It would seem so," Barachiel said, taking the jar from Uriel's hand. "And by looks of this donation, Orthus was generous."

"She wanted to come with me," Uriel said, a touch of sadness in his tone. "But I told her knowing our location was too dangerous for us. She agreed."

"It was the right thing to do," Jophiel said.

Uriel examined my wound. "I feel your pain."

I might have thought about hurting Uriel more times than I cared to count, but monster poison had never been on the list. There was no satisfaction for me. "Because of the sliver of your essence in me?"

"Yes," he said. "Our connection will dissipate over time, but with the relation fresh, I feel the burning ache as much as you do."

"Sorry." The lack of satisfaction I felt, along with knowing the torture Uriel had endured to protect his family, made me feel bad he was experiencing this with me.

"Don't be," he said. "It's good to feel something. I'm sorry it is at your expense though."

"Not your fault," I said.

"But we both know the blame is mine. Everything Typhon is doing today is because of me." Uriel kept his voice low. I pitied Uriel. I knew all too well what it was like to blame yourself for an evil being's actions, and that was something we had in common.

Barachiel shook her head, and she looked like she had as many as Cerberus. *Definitely the poison spit.*

Barachiel laid a hand on her brother's shoulder. "No, Uriel. All of this turmoil is Typhon's fault alone. He sent Nephilim after his daughter, whose mother was a fallen angel. Her death is on his hands."

"If I hadn't loved her..." Silence filled the air as his voice trailed off.

"I'm no expert, but I do know loving someone is never wrong. Doing ignorant things like sending Nephilim after someone you love is."

Uriel blinked a few times and stood. He clasped my good shoulder. "Do us both a favor and don't die, Jax."

I scoffed, holding back the grunt of pain from where his hand was. "If I did die, Rena would find me and kill me again."

Uriel chuckled. He walked over to where Jophiel and Barachiel worked, and I let out a slow breath. The throbbing in my arm lessened with my exhale, but the discomfort got worse by the minute.

Jophiel walked my way. My eyes bugged out of my head at the long needle attached to the syringe in her hand. I started backing away. "Where are you putting that?"

Barachiel stood on one side of me and Uriel on the other. They each took an arm. "What are you doing?"

"I'm not going to lie to you, Jax." Jophiel maneuvered to the side the wound was on. "This will hurt."

"Don't I get something to bite down on?"

"You can squeeze my hand," Uriel said, a twinge of humor in his voice.

"Fuck you," I said. "You miserable— "

A sharp searing pain impacted my shoulder. "Fuck me," I rasped out.

Jophiel pulled the needle out.

Sweat beaded along my upper lip. "Aggh."

"We're not done," Jophiel said. "But the others will not be as deep."

"Just do it," I gritted out. "Get fucking torment over with."

She repeated her movements and true to her word the puncture wasn't as deep. The pain was real though. Dampness accumulated along my brow and ran down the side of my face.

"All done," Jophiel said, sounding happy.

I let out a breath attempting to find my center, but I knew that wouldn't happen until Rena was safe.

"Your body should take over the healing now. You should be feeling better already."

The agony morphed into a dull ache I could handle, unlike the torment in my heart. I tested my arm by rolling my shoulder. There was a slight pinch from the movement but nothing more. "I'm good. Let's go get my girl."

CHAPTER 29

RENA

Typhon had his back to me facing the massive tree in the garden, and I reached for the dagger at my waist. I unsheathed my weapon in a slow, smooth motion. The blade glimmered as I slid it across my palm. Blood beaded along the cut. I waited for the pull to my father, but nothing happened. *What in Hell's fire? Did I not cut deep enough? The depth shouldn't matter. Only that I drew blood. Blood to blood.*

"Sheath your blade." Typhon turned and faced me. "All angelic and demonic power has been blocked here. Eden can only be entered through the original passage."

"What passage?"

"Through Megiddo. It was the original passage that became what you know as the intersection today." He sat on a bench, but I kept my distance, afraid his fucking snakes would make an appearance. "Please put your blade away."

Typhon used 'please' with me. The nicety caught me off guard, and I did what he said. I sheathed my dagger.

"Why leave that passage open but shut everything else off?"

"I will know if anyone comes for you before we are done," he said as if I should have known that answer.

"I told you I do not have the power of Eve. She was... different." There weren't words in any language to describe the magnificent being my grandmother was. Her existence had been a treasure to the realms, particularly the humans who she lived among for so long, creating life. Maybe there was another one of her children out there who eventually could be what she was, but me, her grand-child, wasn't the one. I'd taken life...a lot of it. Different beings. I couldn't believe giving life was a gift for me.

"Why do you assume you can't?" he asked.

"Why do you ask questions you already know the answer to?" I asked the obvious question he'd set up so nicely, but I bit to see his reactions—where he wanted to take the conversation.

"My daughter who Uriel stole from me. Her return is why we are here."

Uriel hadn't stolen her from him. He loved Typhon's daughter and wanted to build a life with her. Typhon had only himself to blame for her death, but it didn't seem prudent to call him out on his culpability at the moment. Even if I controlled power like my grandmother had, I would not disturb someone who had been at rest as long as his daughter. There were repercussions. *Always.* Even if the price was life-force like my grandmother had sacri-ficed for me.

"Are your other children here?" I asked, wondering if Chimera would help me escape. A plan would've been good, but I didn't have a solid idea of how to get out of here without my powers. If I could end him, then I could maybe muster up a portal...maybe if my power cooperated on that request for once.

"No, there was no need to bring them here."

"You should be very afraid of the wrath my father will bring down on you," I said, testing his reaction to see how sure he was of the block he had in place.

He laughed. The son of a bitch laughed like a fucking jolly Santa Claus. I clenched my fists and pressed them to my side to keep from punching the asshole.

"I cannot be touched by your father or your father's siblings."

What does he mean he can't touch him? No one was more powerful than Father.

"What are we waiting for, then, if not my family?" I attempted to tease some answers out of him.

"I've answered this question, and I'm bored with repeating myself. We're here in the birthplace of human-ity, and my daughter was human."

Realization found its way through my scattered thoughts. I understood exactly why he'd chosen Eden. "You don't want me to resurrect her. You want her to be reborn."

He appraised me. "You are as smart as Chimera said."

His words patronized me whether that was his intention or not, and bringing a soul into this world reborn wasn't possible. "You know not even my grandmother could do that, right?"

"But you and she are not the same as you have pointed out to me unnecessarily multiple times."

He is patronizing me. My anger spiked, but I held the annoyance in. I couldn't chance letting my composure slip since he had my demonic powers turned off here. I was practically defenseless. *Fuck. I can't even get a message to the rest of them to tell them not to come.* There had to be some way. I had to figure out how to end this fast before my family was endangered. *Think Morena. Think. Why can I not put a fucking thought together?*

"Why don't you sit so we can chat?" He gestured to the perfectly placed stone bench and took a seat himself.

There was absolutely no fucking way I was seating myself next to him. If his legs turned to snakes again, I would totally lose my shit as if I wasn't already. *Zero chance of that.*

"What makes you think I have this power you seem to believe I have?"

"I do believe," he said. "You are the one prophesied many lifetimes before yours."

"I'm the balance. I'm half-demon and half-vampire. That is my origin...what I am."

"How have they not prepared you for this?" He sighed. "Maybe they did not know, but I would have expected the archangels to have known of the prophecy."

"What prophecy are you talking about?" Typhon was delusional. If there was some prophecy of someone so powerful to pull a soul from eternal rest, surely that kind of text would have been known and repeated many times. I was certain my parents or my aunts and uncles would have told me the story, especially if they believed the person to be me. My destiny was to be the balance and Jax was my scale. We were next in what was probably an infinite line for the future.

"You don't know your own history? How you were conceived?"

The last thing I wanted to think about was my parents being intimate, but that wasn't what he was referring to. It didn't take special abilities to know he meant how my mother cut open her womb. I learned what Mother had to go through to carry me, and the very dagger at my waist was an important part of my conception. *Is that what he means?* "Yes, I've heard the story of how my mother came to carry me in her womb."

"But do you know all of the details of how it came to be and why it worked?"

"I'm more curious how you know of the circumstances given you were locked away for centuries before I was even born." I narrowed my eyes at him looking for a crack in his façade I could break through.

"I know all that my children know. While they were not able to take form, their ability to move as apparitions afforded them opportunities to gather knowledge."

"You used your children as spies," I said. He treated his

children as weapons and tools. That wasn't love, but his confession made me realize two things. For one, the admission made me more determined to free the children from his control. Two, I appreciated the loving relationship I had with my parents despite their imperfections and mine.

"They are my progeny," he said, as if that were all to say on the subject.

"Which doesn't mean you own them. They are living, breathing..." I didn't know what to call them.

"Monsters," he said, softly. "I know what you and your family see them as, but they are my children."

"Chimera showed me kindness when she was not under your control. She hardly seems like a monster to me." Perhaps I shouldn't have said the truth out loud, but he likely knew what was in his children's minds since he used them as spies.

"And she was appreciative of your selflessness in saving my grandchildren," he said.

"Are they okay?"

He met my gaze with a hint of sadness. "They are. Except for the one the Nephilim took, of course."

"I'll never understand how warped the half-angels are." I hadn't meant to expose the private thought, especially to him, but the words tumbled out. The poor little thing had barely started life when the Nephilim ripped the youngling's existence away.

"Their hatred is the product of an old grievance. Do not judge them too harshly."

Was Typhon suggesting I have sympathy for the beings responsible for his daughter's death and his grandchild's death? He'd sent them after his daughter, and yet he was suggesting I shouldn't judge them. "They killed your daughter."

He winced. "That is up for debate."

"I don't think it is. I've heard multiple accounts of the situation."

"Multiple accounts from those who all have a shared origin," he said.

I trusted my aunts and uncles and their accounts. Typhon was never going to see the truth no matter how much we debated about the reality of what happened with Helena. I needed to focus on getting out of here. He mentioned one way in and one way out with our powers disabled here. If I could find the exit to Megiddo, the crossroads, I could use my dagger to summon myself back to my father. That was my current task, and I needed to figure out how to implement my plan without tipping him off.

CHAPTER 30
JAX

I landed on my ass back in the lab for the third time. Orthus had told Uriel where Typhon had taken Rena, and I was desperate to get there, even if I hated the thought of going back. The others had stopped trying to go through with me after the first two failed attempts to portal to Eden. I hadn't tried a portal to the silent room in between the two halves. The unyielding heaviness of the space between Eden and the mirror side conjured up blood-tinged memories of how bad a state I was in after I ended Adam with Michael and Uriel's help. Maybe a portal would work in that room. For Rena, I would try, because she was the reason I came back from that dark place. She was home for me.

"Stop, Jax," Michael said. "Typhon has some barrier up keeping us out of Eden."

"I could try a portal to the mirror side of Eden or the silent passageway between."

"He's locked us out for a reason," Uriel said. "And it can't be good."

I stared at Uriel in disbelief. I wasn't sure if he was in shock, or if he thought we all were idiots. "You think?"

Uriel opened his mouth, but Barachiel stepped in front of him. She couldn't block him completely, but she made a barrier between us as if she knew I was about to punch Uriel. "There is one place he wouldn't be able to block."

"The intersection," Michael said, nodding. "It's our only move until we can break whatever lesser magic he is using to lock us out."

"You're underestimating him, Brother," Jophiel said. "He has never used lesser magic, and it would take an act much stronger to lock us out of Eden."

"She's right." Lucifer entered the room with his hand laced with Lilith's. Lucifer's face was solemn but stern. Lilith looked shell-shocked, and stunned was not a normal look for the Mother of Night Children. She was a fighter, so to see her distraught increased my concern to the next level.

"I'm going to need you to elaborate on that," I said.

Uriel shook his head. "You believe I would be so foolish to think he wouldn't expect us?"

Lucifer ignored Uriel and leveled a glare at me. I knew I'd crossed the line. If we were in Hell, he probably wouldn't have let the demand slide, but he'd allowed me to get away with a lot and the reason was Rena.

"He thinks she is the one, written about in an ancient text, who can choose souls to be reborn," he said. "Give them a second chance. We were told of this prophecy after Eve walked the human realm, and we assumed the individual mentioned in the writings was her."

Lilith cleared her throat, but her eyes were unfocused. "There is no basis to support Rena is the one we've read about in that vague prophecy."

"I know of this text," Jophiel said. "The being was angelic and has moved on from the realms we dwell in just as Typhon's daughter has and as Eve has."

"Your understanding matches what we have read as well."

Michael, Uriel, Gabriel, and Barachiel all swung their heads to face Jophiel. I assumed they shared something in the archangel group text of their subconscious.

"I knew the being who did this," Jophiel said, anguish saturating her tone. "I can assure you she is no longer able to facilitate such actions."

Her sorrow was the sour kind one feels at the loss of love. She loved the person who wielded this gift. Yet, she wasn't jaded. She was kind and helpful not just to Rena but to me as well. Jophiel could have let me die when my soul splintered, but instead, she clued me in to what I needed to do to be whole for Rena again. I wanted to hug her, and I'd never wanted to hug an archangel more. *Fuck it.* I crossed the short distance and wrapped my arms around her.

She hugged me back. "Those events were a long time ago, Jax. I'm fine."

I held onto her for a few more moments until she let

go. When I moved away, I stayed close to her in case the memories came back. I didn't know what it felt like to lose that kind of love, but I did know the sheer torture I endured when I pushed Rena away for the brief time I was vampire. As painful as that was, I suspected the grief Jophiel felt over her lost love was more than I'd borne.

My shoulder was healed, and I knew how to get to Rena. I was not sitting here and waiting until it was too late. "I'm going in through the intersection in Megiddo. You can all choose for yourself whether or not you are going with me, but you must decide fast. I'm spinning up a portal in about thirty seconds."

I turned my back on the beings in the room and formed the symbols to portal inside Eve's room. She wouldn't be there, of course, but her stasis chamber was a place I'd been to. I'd weave my way through the maze inside the mountain to find the intersection to Eden. The trek might take time to navigate on my own, but I would find my love. I walked through the portal.

To my surprise, they all followed me. I don't know why I was shocked they would come. I guess I thought they would want to reason through their own path.

"I'm glad you all trusted me enough to come," I said.

"Not so much trusted your decision as we didn't have a better idea." Uriel clapped my shoulder and headed out the doorway. The opening was no longer bound by blue energy as it had been when Eve was in stasis. I swallowed back the dread that had taken up residence in my throat and followed Uriel.

"Do you know the way from here?" I asked him.

"I do," he said. "Or I did at one time."

The others joined us in the hallway, and Uriel and I took the lead together. He'd saved my existence more than once and fought for Rena. He had my respect and my gratitude.

"It's this way," Uriel said. Torches lining the walls flamed to life as he passed them.

"Any idea how we will beat him?" I asked. "Typhon?"

"Barring our powers inhibits the majority of his own as well," Uriel said. "Making him easier to kill."

"Thank fuck," I muttered under my breath. Visions of unsheathing the swords at my back and burying them into the head of Typhon consumed my thoughts.

"It's a death sentence to his children though," Uriel added. "The outcome for them would be better if we could send him to my prison, as Morena calls my choice of sabbatical."

Uriel might have been trying to break the tension with that awkward turn of phrase, but I wasn't in the mood to joke. If we could end Typhon, that would be my preference. We didn't know for sure any prison we made would hold. The answer I kept coming back to was ending his existence. "She'll never forgive us if we take out his children by killing him." *She'll never forgive me.*

"No, she wouldn't," Uriel said.

A vibration ran through my body. "Did you feel that?"

"Yes," he said.

"Was it an earthquake?" I asked.

"No, the burst wasn't seismic. That was a pulse of power." He watched me as if he expected to say more. "Are you feeling anything else?"

"I'm drawn to a turn up ahead... to the right." I couldn't explain the call. The pull was magnetic like I had to go investigate the source. The summons yanked at my center similar to when we were rescuing humans from the tornado outbreak Typhon unleashed on them.

"Just as the balance can sense tasks, so can the scale," he said.

We paused for the others to catch up.

"Jax has a call as the scale up ahead. Be ready as we do not know what is waiting for us."

Our group split to each side of the path and eased our way forward in a single file on either side. I reached the edge on my side and Uriel on his. The pull was so intense I fought the urge to sprint ahead. Uriel nodded to me. I peeked around the corner, seeing a room sealed with blue light like how Eve's had been when she slept and traded her life for Rena's. A day that haunted me because Rena died in my arms. I loosed a breath at the memory.

I hadn't expected to see that kind of barrier, but Eve had prepared me for this. If there would ever be an opportunity to thank her, this would be one of the moments I would recount. I held my hand up to the blue sheen, and the shimmer parted like expected me.

Uriel stood at my side. "After you."

I stepped through the arched entrance. The room was smaller than Eve's. For a moment the cell appeared to be empty until I saw a woman with blue eyes seated in a wingback chair to match their shade. Long, dark, wavy hair cascaded around her shoulders. Although she was the kind of beauty men waged wars over, there was a hardness to her. Rena was more beautiful, especially with the softness she exuded along with her strength. This woman wielded her beauty like a shield and a sword, and I supposed that was what the Mother of Monsters had to do.

"Echidna."

She smiled. "I heard I missed you in Santa Fe. Pity. I could have shown you and Morena around. Where is she?" Echidna peered over my shoulder.

I winced. "Your husband took her."

She blinked a few times and her mask slipped, the hardness of her features giving way to desperate concern. "He what?"

My disquiet multiplied at seeing how quickly she transformed.

Uriel stepped through and stood next to me. "He took the heir to the throne of Hell to Eden."

"Hello, cousin," Echidna said, eyeing Uriel with apprehension. She peered around him. "Cousins."

Lilith stepped forward, back to her strong self, taking Echidna's hands and kissing each cheek. "It's good to see you awake."

Echidna's mouth curved in what had to be a genuine smile. "Lilith. I'm so glad you came with the others."

Understanding hit me like a slap across the face. *Holy*

Hell's fire. Lilith was our secret weapon. She and Echidna were old friends if their warm greeting was evidence.

"What has he done now? Do you need my help?" Echidna asked, directing her question specifically to Lilith.

"Typhon believes Morena is the resurrector, but we are all aware that she lived long ago and rests now. Your husband wants Morena to claim your daughter's soul for rebirth."

Echidna gasped. *Did she not know or was this fake surprise?* She'd known we were in Santa Fe but not that Typhon had taken Rena from there. My suspicions rumbled under the surface even if she appeared genuine.

"He was obsessed with her death. He never accepted she was gone or his role in it." Her mask fell away completely, and weariness lined her face. "What do you need me to do?"

"The thing only you can," Lilith said. "Talk some sense into him."

THE INTERSECTION with Eden was narrow. I had to turn to the side to get through the opening, and the tightness of space did not help the constriction in my chest. "At the risk of sounding like an ass, are we there yet?"

"Close," Echidna said from her place between me and Lilith.

Lucifer had the lead in front of me. "Save the sarcasm for when we are home."

"So, you're saying I did sound like an ass?" My nerves were wired, and I needed some kind of outlet. There wasn't enough room to grab the required air to laugh or for the adrenaline-driven tremors to vibrate my body. The confined space was like being trapped, and I needed out of there.

"I see light," Lucifer said.

"He might have the entrance guarded," Echidna said. "We should move slowly."

Fuck slow. I wanted to shout, but my leathers rubbed against the wall and reminded me there wasn't room.

The same blue sheen from the rooms in Megiddo shined from the entrance. Relief washed over me as the space opened. It was a lock, but none of us knew if it was there as part of Megiddo's defenses or Eden's or both. A vibration ran through me, but the sensation was different from the other times. The call of the scale mixed with the pull of Rena—the draw ushered me to a missing piece of myself. *Rena. It's guiding me to her.* Our love led me, and nothing would change my mind about it.

"This is for me," I said. "The scale is the key."

"Are you sure, Jax?" Lilith asked.

"I'm certain," I said, stepping within arm's reach of the shielded space. I held my hand out in front of the blue light and gently pressed my hand into the essence-like protection. The energy shimmered and disappeared just as it had when Rena had been locked in Eve's chamber. A second vibration ran through me—stronger than the first like a homing beacon. "Typhon likely felt the jolt, so we should get moving."

"I felt the shift of power, so he most certainly did," Echidna said.

The intersection planted us right in the middle of the maze. Not the start or the end, but the damn middle. If we chose the wrong way, we'd have to backtrack to the center and then out the other way. "We should split up."

"I don't think that's wise," Echidna said. "We will stand better together. A unified presence increases our chances of survival."

"Anyone object to that?" I asked, not caring what anyone else was doing because I was going for Rena. No one replied. Their concentration was on the path ahead of us. "Silence is acceptance. Looks like we're taking your advice."

"I am trustworthy, Jax. I know you think because I'm married to Typhon I cannot be, but I have never gone back on my word in my entire existence."

"Lilith trusts you. That's enough for me." And there wasn't another option, but some things didn't need voicing.

"I want my word to mean as much as hers. It's hard loving someone who doesn't consult you on their decisions." She studied me, but I didn't squirm. "I suspect you might know something a bit about that. Maybe a little experience with the person you love making a decision and cluing you in after the fact."

Typhon was nothing like Rena. She would never do the harm he had. A piece of me resented Echidna trying to use that as common ground, but I understood her angle too.

"I do. Our story isn't a secret. My duty is to support her, and that's what I plan to do." I'd known what Rena's role was at a very early age, and I knew I'd be there by her side in some form or fashion. Being with her in any way was a gift I could never repay. Being with Rena as her husband would be nirvana.

"But it's never easy being left out of decision-making," she said.

"It's not always like that, and if I'm being honest, I'm just as guilty as she is in that department." I had disappeared after I ended Adam and scattered him across the human realm. My actions haunted me to this day both in the vicious way I avenged his acts against Rena and the way I handled myself afterward. I was lost in the evil terror I'd had to take on in order to inflict the savage death. My fuck up was epic in justifying my actions to myself as Rena deserved better than to see me that way after what she'd been through. I wasn't sure I'd be able to come back from the dark place I descended to either. She was the reason I kept trying and found myself enough to return.

"I will make my husband understand the error of his ways." Her determination was admirable, if she was being sincere, but achieving her goal was much harder than saying those words.

"How are you so sure?"

"Because I am his weakness," she said softly.

It was the reason we'd come for her, but she ended up finding us.

"We're here," she said, her voice confident. "I'll go first. He will not harm me. You stand behind me until he lets Morena go."

We found Echidna, so she could stop him. *This better fucking work.* I nodded, agreeing with the plan, and turned to the others. The tension bracketing each of their faces was a mirror of what built inside me. The anticipation of seeing my love was dampened by the tightness in my chest. Her scent found me with the softness of those sweet peonies and the strength of the fire that burned in her soul.

Echidna held out her hand, and I waited at the corner. She stepped forward. "Typhon."

"Echidna." Typhon's voice was full of warmth for his wife.

"Why do you have the heir of Hell here?"

"You know why," he said, unwavering in a loving tone. "And why have you brought your former family here?"

So much for surprise. Not that we expected to pass through undetected, but it would have been nice.

Echidna motioned for us to come forward. I stepped from the corner and stayed behind Echidna as she'd instructed, my gaze landing immediately on Rena. She was unharmed, and the relief came over me in a wave almost as strong as the pull. My knees weakened, and I forced myself not to give into it.

"The heir of Hell is the balance and betrothed to the scale. This is not our business to interfere. To do so invokes a terrible karma on us." Echidna made the briefest eye contact with me, but the gesture was enough to convey I needed to be ready.

CHAPTER 31

RENA

Echidna's voice was melodic and sincere as if she was singing a song to her husband only matched by her beauty. She spoke to her husband as a mother still grieving. "We've paid the penance for our crimes over and over, and we are at a place where that can all end. Don't create a situation where we must continue to pay."

My chest tightened, my heart aching, because I knew what it was to lose someone important to you. No matter how long or short the time they are in your life, the loss was still painful... sometimes heart-crushingly so.

I found Jax's gaze, still not believing he was here...with Echidna. His presence lightened me and brought relief. Relief Jax survived the attack Typhon forced Orthus to commit. Relief he seemed fine. Relief he was here.

My family and Echidna came through the intersection in Megiddo. Jax had done that. I instinctively knew he was the reason they found me because somehow, he always found me. But my fear wiped away the elation I'd had at the sight of the group. We had no power here. Not while Typhon blocked it out. *Do they know that?*

Echidna had Typhon's full attention. If there was a time to kill him it was now... but that would end his children. I couldn't do that or allow their deaths to happen. We were all at the mercy of Echidna's ability to persuade him to stand down. Only if she were to fail would I consider ending Typhon where he stood.

"Walk with me, husband." Echidna moved forward, touching Typhon's arm. His attention solely focused on her as she looked up under her lashes at him. "Let us speak in private."

"I know what you are doing, wife," Typhon said, but there was no malice in his voice. He observed Echidna with an expression of love. His eyes twinkled with amusement. "It is why I haven't sought you out, but I'm glad you are here."

She leaned in and caressed his face. "Then stop this madness and leave with me."

"Our daughter—"

"Deserves the place of peace she's in now."

Typhon began to cry, and the tears were massive. The liquid filled the space at our feet like a flash flood. Echidna wrapped her arms around him, and he sobbed into her neck.

"Go," Echidna mouthed to me.

I ran over to Jax and grasped his hand. Tears burned

my eyes at the contact, but tears would have to wait. "We need to go now." I motioned for the others to follow us. Echidna did her part distracting Typhon, but that only gave us a small window. Our escape had to be fast.

We'd made it a few yards into the tunnel when Typhon's yell reverberated around us. "Nooo."

The terrorizing sound leached inside and rattled me all the way to the bones. I covered my ears, sure my eardrums were about to rupture from the decibels the sound achieved. The walls shook and crumbled around us.

"Move," Jax said. His mouth moved like he was shouting but his voice barely reached me. I tried to run, but the passage was so narrow we couldn't move fast. No longer able to cover my ears and run, the sounds of the passageway's demolition by Typhon's one word were equally deafening. The remnants battered my back as I barely stayed ahead of the debris flying around us. Fragments rained down. I tripped on a hunk of rock and fell into whoever was in front of me. *Michael?* The wall crumbled under the hand I used to steady myself. If we didn't cover the distance to Megiddo fast, the tunnel would be our tomb.

The light ahead was different than the passage, and we were closing in on the glow. *Megiddo.* A breadcrumb of hope planted in me. *We are going to make it.* I didn't slow down despite the encroaching screams of my extremities from the beating they took from the rocks. My body begged me to stop, but I pushed through.

I reached the other side just behind Jax and watched

as our group made it through. Mother, Jophiel, Uriel, Barachiel, Gabriel, Michael, and Father. Echidna wasn't with us, and I hoped that didn't mean Typhon would punish her. My family had all cleared the intersection, and I relaxed. The blood and bruises were already healing on all of us, but our torn clothing would be a reminder. A small chip no bigger than a quarter fell directly in my line of vision, and I followed the piece's path where it bounced at the feet of our group. *Fuck.* The momentary relief I felt died as another larger shard landed near the first.

"Run," I screamed and pushed the shoulders in front of me toward the torch-lit Megiddo hallway.

"Can you portal us out of here?" I asked Jax as I ran beside him.

"Yes, but where? Where are we safe?"

"Anywhere but fucking here," I gasped out. "Library, Hell, Gothica. Literally anywhere."

Jax began to form the symbols to get us the fuck out of the mountain before the mound came down on our heads.

"Get ready," I shouted above the rumbling noise. "And get close together. We're portaling out."

Jax flung his hands forward, and the blue light of his portal appeared a yard in front of Mother. "Now!"

I'd never considered throwing a portal to be a particularly useful skill. *Until today. Until Jax.* One by one we each made it through the portal. I collapsed onto the gravelly sand. *Sand?* I ran my fingers through fine dust and looked up. Jax had portaled us to the stone paved path quite a few yards from the entrance to Megiddo. Before I could even ask why, Megiddo imploded on itself like a shriveled pumpkin.

My awe gave way to sorrow. Sorrow for Echidna and the others who rested in the mountain by the good doings of my grandmother. "Weren't there others in stasis in there?"

"A few," Uriel said. He dropped to his knees as did his siblings, including my father. Mother knelt beside Father.

Jax and I exchanged looks, and his was as full of sadness and weariness as mine. This was my fault. All of it. I was the one Typhon was after, and I was the reason innocents had died.

Mother took my hand and urged me to kneel with her. I did, but the numbness crept in on me. Jax took the position next to me and grasped my hand in his. *This was so fucked up.*

"What have we done?" My voice came out rough and broken like the stone that had fallen on us.

Jax tugged on my hand and pulled me into his lap. "Look at me, Rena."

I turned my head to him.

"We did not do this."

"No," I choked on the words as if the dust was still in my throat. "We didn't do this. I did."

JAX

I wrapped my arm around Rena's waist and stood, taking her with me. She was surprisingly steady on her feet considering what she had been through. Her face was cold against my hands as I cupped it. "Listen to me. You did not do this. This is not your fault. There is only one person responsible for this, and that is Typhon."

I searched her face for understanding, but those beautiful blue eyes were almost vacant. She gaped at the mountain, but my hands were still on her face. As gently as I could, I turned her back to look at me.

"What happened today is not on you. You don't have to say the words out loud but repeat them over and over again in your head like a mantra until you know it's true."

The others stood and gathered around us. Lucifer curved his arm around Rena from one side and Lilith from the other as if they were grounding her here with us. I could see her slipping away, and she would continue to do so if we stayed here.

The ground beneath us rumbled as if the earth were going to swallow us whole. "Lilith, is Gothica safe for us?"

A geyser of rock spewed into the air from the middle of where Megiddo once stood. Typhon rose into the air with Echidna in his arms. I retrieved one of my swords from its scabbard. Typhon advanced toward us.

"Please," he said. "Save her."

It was only then I noticed how still and limp Echidna's body was. The crushing weight of her sacrifice settled over us.

Gabriel's' wings rustled next to me. "She lives but barely. Without assistance, she will move on."

"She was worried that the balance would be crushed and went in the tunnel after her." The scent of death coated the air. A tear dripped from Typhon's face and made a puddle in the sand and dirt.

Rena jerked free of our hold. Her purplish-black wings extended to their full width. I reached for her, but she rocketed into the air. "Do something." I looked at Lucifer and his siblings. They all had wings but kept them tucked away. Gabriel's retracted too.

"We cannot interfere, Jax," Uriel said. "This is part of her destiny."

Chimera appeared in the area below where Typhon hovered. She wailed. Orthus and Cerberus joined her.

Rena floated in front of Typhon. She placed her hands on the head and chest of Echidna. A purple vapor covered her hands. The tinted haze moved over Echidna's body until a shroud of mist enveloped her completely. I was in awe of what I was seeing. Was that Rena's essence? Not blue like mine or Adam's or Eve's but purple?

"She is like Mother," Lilith whispered, her voice cracking on the last word.

Echidna's chest rose and fell, first in a slow motion and then faster. *Echidna is moving.* The scent of death dissipated. Echidna sat up as if she hadn't been dead or near death. *Holy fuck.* Chimera watched them and moved closer. The wailing from the monster siblings ceased. I pressed the heels of my palms to my eyes and rubbed, not caring I ground more sand around them. When I opened my eyes, Echidna reached for Rena's cheek, and she wiped something away. *Is Rena crying? Echidna too?* I couldn't tell from this distance. Rena turned her head to Chimera and stared as if they shared a message without ever using words. Rena lifted Echidna from Typhon's arms and dropped her. She landed on Chimera's back.

Typhon roared, and Rena looked back at us. "Uriel, now."

Uriel leaped into the air with such force dust stirred up. I blinked away the debris. Uriel bypassed Rena and collided with Typhon. They slid across the sky and disappeared from view with a flash of bright white light.

Rena floated back down to the ground in front of Chimera. Echidna slid from Chimera's back to stand in front of Rena.

Echidna wore a confused expression. "You could have killed him and ended the threat permanently."

"I could have, but your children would die too. That didn't seem like a fair price to me."

Surprise glided across her face before she settled back to neutral. "They came willingly, ready to make any sacrifice necessary."

Rena patted Chimera's neck. "I know they did, but it's not fair to ask something like that of them."

Echidna clasped Rena's shoulder. "Your compassion is great, and I do not wish to see my children's existence wiped from the world. I hope you do not come to regret that decision."

THE NAUSEATING scent of the laboratory infiltrated my nostrils like an assault of bad memories. Coming to this torture center was a better option for Echidna since the archangels weren't sure how her Fallen status would mesh with the Library's defense system. She wasn't an archangel and might not be afforded the access Lucifer and Lilith were for their status. I didn't question the archangels on the decision. They were the experts. But the fact I could enter and Rena could enter made me question if Echidna had a soul or if that had been the price for the daughter Uriel had loved.

"We need to find Uriel," Rena said. "He should be back by now."

"Maybe he ran into Typhon's henchmen or something," I said, joining the group discussion.

"Doubtful," she frowned. "He should have done the angel thing right back."

"He had to lock the door. Maybe that takes a bit longer." I tried to ease her worry, but my own worry claimed my thoughts. She was right. He should have been back right away.

"One of us should go check on him," Barachiel said. "I can go."

"No, it should be me," Michael said.

"You would know if..." Rena paused. "Can you sense him?"

Jophiel took Rena's hand. "We can't communicate with him, but we would know if he was ..." She swallowed like she was holding back or searching for words. "If he was somewhere else."

The revelation was a relief. I turned to Barachiel and Michael. "I would go with you, but I'm guessing that's not an option."

"No, it's not, but we wouldn't risk you if it was." She gave me a small smile and turned to Michael. "Ready?"

"Ready," he said, and they disappeared in a flash of warm white light.

"What if something happened?" Rena looked at me. The distress on her beautiful face worried me. Her anxiety was high, and we hadn't talked about what she did for

Echidna yet. That topic would be one to tackle after she was better, and Typhon was securely locked away.

"A lot of something has happened, and we're all still here. Michael and Barachiel will bring him back." I hated placating her when I wasn't sure he would return.

"I can't sense Typhon, either, if it makes you feel better," Echidna said, grabbing one of the small towels on the counter. There was no bitterness in her tone. Her face twisted in confusion as she dampened the cloth under the faucet and began to wipe away the dried blood on her arms. "And I can always sense him."

Rena examined her. "How are you feeling?"

"I have no memory of the time I was injured. The gap is strange because I can remember centuries but not that brief period. My mind tries to fill in the missing parts."

"Maybe that's the way it's supposed to be," I said. I didn't know what came after for us but shouldn't Echidna? She was a fallen after all.

"I don't know," she said. "I don't know what our next existence looks like."

"But you're a fallen," I said.

"A fallen angel, Jax. I was never an archangel or privy to the knowledge only they possess."

"Even at the Library?" Rena asked.

She nodded. "Even there. I wasn't granted passage to some of the special reserved areas the archangels were. There is a hierarchy to everything, even angels."

The order of angels made me uncomfortable. It was

too close to some of the mistreatment I'd faced from full-blooded demons my age.

I walked over to where Jophiel stood alone. "Are you okay?"

"I worry about my siblings as anyone else would." She patted my hand. "We are a tough crew though."

"Very tough," I said.

"I saw the paper," she said.

"What paper?"

Jophiel smiled. "A marriage license."

Oh. I hadn't realized anyone had seen the license. I didn't even know where it was after the attack. "Yes, we had planned to surprise everyone with a wedding in Santa Fe. I guess that's not going to happen now. I doubt Rena wants to go back to the town."

"Sometimes you return to the place where a memory went wrong so you can replace the moment with a good one," Jophiel said.

The church was a good memory for us. I'd be willing to go back if Rena would. It was the after part that was hard to think about, and the part I expected Rena might not want to relive. "That's a great idea, but if we revisited all of the bad memories, we'd probably all need therapy for the rest of our existence."

"Not all of them. Just the ones that deserve a mulligan," she said.

A do-over. Maybe that was exactly what Rena and I needed. A chance to right the events of that trip, and she loved the square in Santa Fe. When the dust settled, I would broach the subject with her.

A surprise wedding might be just what our family needed. *Our family.* Rena had referred to all of us as a family before, but I'd been the outsider. Now I thought of us as our family. *When did that happen?*

I searched the room for Rena. She was in the corner talking to her parents. My future in-laws. Lucifer and Lilith. I didn't hesitate when I walked over and wrapped my arm around her waist. She sank into my side.

"They will be back, and they will be fine." I pressed a kiss to the top of her head.

"Jax, Lucifer and I think you should take Rena back to Hell," Lilith said, her tone firm as if it had been decided.

Rena stiffened in my arms. I squeezed her waist. "But you don't want to go, my love?"

"Not until I know they are safe."

"And that is what your gut says is the right thing?"

"It is." She nodded, inching closer to me.

"Then we will wait." I wouldn't force her to do something she didn't believe she should do.

"Thank you," she said. "And thank you for coming for me in Eden and for saving us all by portaling us out of Megiddo." She raised her head, and I met her blue eyes, dull from the weight of the circumstances. Her face was full of unspoken words and tears, and she broke me in that moment. I never wanted her to hurt, and the one thing I could do, fuck her until she forgot it all, wasn't an option. Instead, I held her close, so she would know she was safe.

CHAPTER 33

RENA

I needed Jax nearer to warm the cold settling in my body, but we couldn't get physically closer here. As soon as the rest of my family was safe, I'd show Jax my gratitude. I'd cherish him in a way equal to if not greater than how he worshiped me with his respect and support. He pulled me tighter to him, and I clung to him.

"Do you want to sit down?" He brushed the hair away from my face with his free hand.

My parents ventured over to where Gabriel, Echidna, and Jophiel were talking.

"No, I'm too nervous to sit." I'd fidget and squirm, and that wouldn't help the time pass any quicker.

"I could put you in my lap and hold you still," Jax said.

A small laugh escaped my lips. "Don't tempt me."

"So, you like sitting on my lap." He wagged his eyebrows.

"Oh, I do. Your lap is my favorite place to sit." I wagged my eyebrows back at him.

Light flashed. The warm white light of the angels filled the room and then dissipated just as fast. Uriel, Barachiel, and Michael stood in front of us soaking wet.

"We couldn't hold him in Uriel's personal prison," Barachiel panted out.

"We can't let him back out into the world," Echidna said. "He will not stop."

"Where is he now?" I asked.

"He disappeared, so we don't know. We'll have to wait for him to make a move," Michael said. "But we should be ready. He will not be as easy to capture next time."

"You thought that was easy? We took an entire mountain out," I said. "What will we have to do this time?"

"End him," Barachiel said.

"It's our only option," Uriel added.

Echidna audibly inhaled and let the breath out. "He is my husband. I do love him and our children more than my own existence, but Typhon cannot be allowed to destroy you and the realms."

"But your children?" I studied her.

"They know they have a duty greater than what lies in this realm. They have been prepared for that since they were young. Just as you have your purpose, they have theirs." Her face was firm, and I wasn't sure if she covered her emotions with a mask or if she was as strong in her convictions as she acted.

She was so agreeable to the death of her children, and it was immoral. Our kind, angels, demons, and vampires, often operated in morally grey areas, but ultimately, our actions were done for the greater good. Her children had done some horrible things but done while under her husband's control. Whether they were innocents would be debatable, but everything in me said there had to be another way. A way to end Typhon's terror without killing his children.

"Found him," Gabriel called from the other side of the room. "And he is trying to get your attention."

"How do you know?"

"He's sent at least a dozen tornadoes bouncing around Dallas," Gabriel answered.

Fuck. Stassi. "What's the number?"

"Twelve," he said.

Uriel placed a hand on Gabriel's shoulder. "I think she's asking about casualties, Brother."

"None so far, but these are early reports and some tornadoes are still on the ground."

Innocent human lives would pay the price for something Typhon wanted from me that I couldn't give. If I had to cross the moral line to save them, could I do it? Would I do it? I might not be able to save everyone in this situation. Chimera's two remaining children were at the forefront of my thoughts. If I end Typhon, they would be lost as well. *Is this even my decision to make?*

"Echidna, the last thing I want to do is end your children, but he is forcing me to act. Are you sure you can live with this? Because I'm not sure I can." My heart ached like one of Cerberus's heads was clamped down on it.

"They don't belong in the human realm, Morena. They never did. They know this."

"I have an idea," Jax said, his tone full of hope. "What if we sent them to the jinn realm?"

Jax's jinn powers gave him a direct line to the dream realm, so it could be a viable option.

"To the dream realm?" Jophiel wondered.

"I don't know if death would find them there or not," Barachiel said to Jophiel.

Uriel rubbed his chin. "It could work. They would be able to haunt the nightmares of humans there."

Jax cut his gaze toward Uriel. "They already haunt their nightmares while here."

"But they are corporeal now, not shadows and smoke. Has anything like that been done before?" I asked.

"No," Jophiel said. "But that doesn't mean the plan wouldn't work."

"We need to be in the Library," Barachiel said.

"You four go." Michael looked at Jophiel, Gabriel, Barachiel, and Uriel. "I'll stay here with the others."

"I'd like to go," Echidna said. "It is to save my children."

"What are we going to do while they are gone?" I asked Michael.

"We're going to help those Typhon so willingly injured. They are humans. Innocent lives in this battle."

And hurt because of me. "You're right. They need our help, and I need to check on Stassi. She and her future husband were going to her mother's in Oklahoma, so she should be safe."

"You're still in touch with her?" Jax whispered.

"We're still friends, Jax," I said. "They were taking their new partner, Christina, to meet Stassi's mother. The three of them are seriously committed, and you have nothing to worry about because you are the love of my life."

After everything Jax and I had been through, he still had some jealousy or insecurity around us. *How can he not know he is the center of my world?* I leaned over and brought our lips together in a soft kiss. "Only you, Jax. You are the very beat of my pulse."

He slid his hand into my hair at the base of my neck. "And you for me."

"Jax, can you come look at this map?" Michael asked.

Jax's hand fell from my hair but found my hand. We walked over to the screen where Michael had the map pulled up. "This looks like the worst hit area. Are you familiar with any of the places near this location to portal us there? I can't carry this many people."

"Yes, I'm familiar with this neighborhood." Jax pointed to an area on the map. "It's risky not knowing how the damage has changed the view, but I can step through to make sure the landing spot is safe."

Michael nodded. "Watch for downed electrical lines and broken gas lines."

"Let's go." The thought that people could be dying every minute we stayed here hurt me.

Jax formed the symbols to take us there.

JAX

The view was some of the worst destruction I'd seen. *Worse than watching Megiddo implode.*

"The subdivision looks like a war zone," Rena said, standing beside me on a mound of rubble. "Like an actual bomb went off."

"The desolation reminds me of the safe house blowing up but it just keeps going on and on," I said.

Michael stopped in front of us. "Morena, I have confirmation that Stassi is safe at her mother's house."

"Thank you." She touched his arm. Her intense stare focused on the disaster in front of us, scanning the destruction. "Let's save some humans."

"You'll have to enlighten me on how this doesn't count as interference later," I said to Michael.

"That answer is easy. These innocents were not meant for this fate." Michael jumped from the pile of debris to a patch of ground free of any remnants of homes. Rena and I followed. I looked up at the debris pile we'd been standing on. Lilith and Lucifer were still on top of the heap, and I realized it was a partially collapsed home.

"Anyone here? Can you hear me?" No response came, and I didn't sense any life in there. I peered up at Lilith. "Are you picking up anything?"

"Not here, but there." Lilith pointed to a two-story home still standing but missing half of the upstairs and all the windows. She and Lucifer joined us below, and we made our way over to the remains of the house.

"Something in my chest is pulling me there too," Rena said. "I think the balance is calling me to this person."

"This structure is close to coming down," Lucifer said. "We need to be fast or it's going to fall in on us."

"I'm the fastest," Lilith said. "It should be me who goes in."

"Hell has not frozen over yet, Lilith," Lucifer said. "I will enter."

"No offense, Father," Rena said. "But you're kind of large to go in."

I stepped forward. "We're wasting time. I'll—"

Rena flung her hand in front of me, halting me not only mid-sentence but mid-stride.

"This is a call for the balance. It must be me," she said, effectively silencing all of us.

"Be wise," I said.

She disappeared into the weakened building with catlike movements. Rena would be fine. She was skilled and trained to handle situations. *And she is the balance. Yes, she will be fine.*

"Should we go in after her?" Lilith asked.

"She will lock us up in the dungeon if we do," Lucifer said, a hint of humor in his tone.

I turned my head and stifled a laugh. Lucifer and I both tended to be sarcastic when we worried, and I realized we had that in common. Besides, he wasn't wrong. Rena would be pissed if her parents trekked in after her.

"Jax could go," Lilith offered.

My laugh disappeared.

"He does not want to end up in the dungeon either," Lucifer said, glancing at me with a smirk.

Lilith faced Michael. "You go. She can't do anything to you."

"That remains to be seen, and I can't interfere with the balance's mission," he said.

Smart archangel.

The structure shook. A portion collapsed and dust pelted me. I sprinted toward the home. "Rena?"

Michael and Lucifer were on either side of me. Lilith swiftly made her way around the perimeter in a methodical fashion.

"Rena?" I called again. She didn't respond. Panic slid down my spine in the form of a cold chill. I placed a tentative foot on the board in front of me. The wood groaned in protest. I tried another one, and the plank protested less. I inched my way forward. "Rena?"

"I'm here." Her voice audible but distant. Even with my expert hearing, the words were hard to make out.

I positioned myself closer to where I thought her voice had come from. "Talk to me, my love."

"I have the child," she said.

Child? A child was trapped in this mess. "I'm coming to you."

Michael joined me on an adjacent board. We cleared the debris as quickly as we could. Michael was faster. He heaved two pieces away to my one, but we created an opening. I shimmied into the makeshift entrance and looked around. There wasn't much left of the house. A massive hole went straight down to the crawl space of what was once a split-level home. Damp earth and blood scented the air. My heart pounded an alarm in time with dripping water. "Rena?"

"This way." I let my relief out in a breath. She balanced in what had been a bathroom. In her arms was a young human child. The little girl couldn't be more than five, but she was too still for one that young. Her eyes were too wide.

I glanced from the child's face back to Rena. "Is she hurt?"

"No, but her parents are. I need to get her out. Can you help her mother and father? They are in the bathtub."

"Michael and I will get them. Come toward me with gentle steps." She inched forward as close to the edge of a gap about six feet across. Below her was a nest of electrical lines and water from broken pipes. She and I had both jumped further in our pasts, and she'd easily clear the break if she could use her wings. The space was too tight to jump high or use her wings. The layout was a disadvantage, and she wouldn't be able to use her arms because she held the child. "I'll catch you. You can do it."

She peered down below, and I noticed sparks from a broken line.

"Ignore it. You can do this, Rena."

She backed up and ran with as much speed as she could get in the short space. Rena flung her body forward with precision, and she landed on the balls of her feet at the very edge. I wrapped my arms around her and pulled her and the child backward. We fell against Michael. He caught us with the kind of strength expected from the warrior archangel.

"Get them out of here," I said.

Michael left through the hole we had made and disappeared. Rena was safe. The little girl was safe. I had to find the parents. I turned and ran toward the gap Rena had just jumped and cleared the distance easily. A cracking noise rang out, and the board beneath my feet gave way. I leaped forward and landed on a more structurally sound section.

The bathroom was visible from here, and I observed two unmoving figures in the bathtub. *Please don't let them be gone. That little girl deserves parents.*

I knelt next to them. I looked up and saw pieces of what had been a bathroom directly above this one. It wasn't unusual to see that kind of architecture in modern human homes, but the state of the upper level looked like the floor had given way. *Were they upstairs and fell through to the tub below?*

The mother stirred, but the father was out cold. Both had heartbeats. Hers was erratic. His was too slow. The mother's arm appeared broken, but she could have internal injuries. *How had the child been kept so safe?* "Michael, I need your help."

"I'm here, but you know I'm limited," he said. I glimpsed the grim set of his jaw.

"Carry one," I said. "The wife appears to be the least injured, so take her if you are concerned about interference."

Michael lifted her out of the tub and went back the way he came.

The man's breathing became shallow. We had to get him to human doctors soon. The gap was larger now, and I had the same issues Rena faced. Can't jump too high and not much room to gain speed. Plus, the gap was wider. Can't portal because humans might see. *Fuck it.* I backed into the bathroom and ran full-out at the rim. I launched across the opening and landed well past the edge on the opposite side. The man groaned in my arms. *Good. He's alive.*

"Michael?"

"Here." He peered over the edge. I handed the man to him and climbed my way out of the opening.

Lilith cradled the child in her arms. Rena knelt beside the woman talking to her. Michael still held the man.

"Any sign of help?"

"None so far," Lucifer said.

I grabbed a throw pillow that somehow in the chaos had remained with the random couch among the piles of debris. I lifted the woman's head gently to place the pillow under her.

"It might take time for them to come," Lucifer said.

I stood up and followed him a few feet away so the humans wouldn't hear us. "We need to get them care," I said. "Especially him. He is badly injured."

"I can heal him," Rena said, joining us.

"Someone could see you," Lucifer said. "That's too risky. You should not interfere just as Michael cannot."

"Then why do I have this healing power now? The balance called me here for a reason."

"Your power was not meant for humans," Lucifer cautioned. There wasn't judgment in his voice. His tone was more concerned.

Rena looked at me, but the pull that told me the human needed to be saved was strong. I disagreed with Lucifer. "I feel a similar draw to make sure they survive. My vote is to do it."

CHAPTER 35

RENA

*I*f not to save innocents hurt because of me, then with whom and when was I to use this power?

The balance urged me to save the father of the little girl. I peered at Jax, and he had that look on his face that he wanted to say something but wouldn't because Father was there.

"You are both being unreasonable. Think of the consequences for using your powers in the open here among humans."

"I am thinking of the repercussions, and I'm weighing the decision. What do you think, Jax?" I faced him so everyone else was blocked out, and it was just the two of us. *Did he feel it too? The call to help them?* I needed an ally, and I trusted Jax to be that person, not only as my future husband but as the scale to my balance.

"I stand by my agreement. I think you should do what

you think is right." He glanced over my shoulder and shifted his weight between his feet.

I rested my hand against the side of his face. "I'm not looking for anyone else's opinion but yours. You are the one I trust above all others. You are the scale. Should I help him?"

He rubbed over his chest in the same spot the warmth of the call manifested for me. "Both times you asked me, the first word that popped into my head was yes."

I nodded. "Thank you."

Michael wrapped the woman's arm in a sling. She'd passed out from the pain, but her injuries weren't as severe as the man's were. The balance was telling me to focus on him. I knelt to where Mother and Father had made a makeshift stretcher to carry the little girl's father out of there. His breaths were shallow, and his heartbeat had slowed to almost nothing. He was near his end, and I didn't need the power of the balance to tell me that. My demon senses knew what death felt like. A twinge skittered through me at the memory of my own death. There was no more time to delay.

I placed my hands on him as I had done with Echidna and closed my eyes. *Heal.* His heartbeat steadied but was still weak. *Your daughter needs you. Heal.* Warmth flowed into my hands, and I opened my eyes. The purple light engulfed him as well as my hands and arms. It was similar to how I mended Echidna. The man's heartbeat grew stronger, and his life force was palpable in our connection, like honey in Earl Grey tea.

The warmth in me subsided. The purple light retreated from his body to my hands and up my arms to the warm spot in my chest. The space around me was strangely cool afterward. *Have I done it? Will he live for his daughter?*

The man's eyes opened. He stared up at me but didn't say anything. His face was a mix of confusion and pain.

I patted his shoulder. "You'll be fine. Rest now."

The man's eyes closed as if healing had taken as much out of him as it had me to restore him. The way weakness settled in my bones and made me tired was real. I stood, but my head was light. My legs wobbled, and I was unsure if I could remain in the position. Jax was there. His hand slid around my waist and a soft blue haze covered us. Some of my strength returned.

"What was that?" I asked.

"I thought it was you," he said.

I looked at my parents and Michael and found confusion. Michael moved closer.

"The balance saves but the scale restores," he whispered, his tone carrying some awe.

"What?" Jax asked.

"The musings of a very old prophecy," Father said.

I closed my eyes understanding what prediction he meant. "The one Typhon said mentioned me, but none of you thought it was me."

"Yes," Mother said. "We thought it was already fulfilled and couldn't be you."

"But it is," I said. "I need to read this prophecy. After

we save the people here." I turned to Jax. "If my partner is up to the task?"

"I'm always here to support you." He smiled.

Jax, Father, and Michael took the people with minor injuries to the staging area. The first responders arrived less than a half hour into our search efforts. They'd set up as deep in the area as they could get with their ambulances, tents, and tables. Mother and I continued to look for more survivors. The dedication of the first responders was evident in the speed, care, and efficiency with which they triaged the patients. There weren't any others injured as badly as the man I'd saved, so my power stayed safely tucked away. I listened for a tug and the warmth in my chest was a sign of relief there was no call. Typhon hadn't inflicted any other damage we were aware of past this disaster, but that didn't mean he wouldn't. I'd done what I was meant to do here. The time was right to get back on mission.

"It looks like we've done all we can here," Father said as we gathered together on the outskirts of the human's triage area, out of sight but where we could still monitor.

"Yes," Michael said. "We should join the others at the Library."

"I'd like to know what I am," I said, confused for the first time in my life about what it meant to be me.

Mother stood in front of me and took my hands in hers. She had pride in her eyes, and I wasn't sure I'd earned the accolades. "You are and will always be my and Lucifer's daughter."

I wrapped my arms around her. She'd believed I was special and destined for things bigger than Hell my entire life, but I don't think this was what she had in mind. *Would I be able to resurrect or call souls forward for rebirth like Typhon thought?*

Eve's unwavering goodness made her the right choice for that kind of power. I didn't deserve nor want the responsibility. If I did have the ability, the temptation would be too great to use it for personal reasons. I still had to wonder, though, if I did have the potential given I was the balance. There was only one place I would get those answers, and that was in another damn prophecy. Prophecies were my new normal.

"Your portal awaits," Jax said once we were in a secluded area where the humans would not notice a swirling blue mass.

I pulled away from my mother and slipped my hand into Jax's. The doors to the Library appeared in front of us along with the sweet apple scent of this realm.

CHAPTER 36

JAX

The scent of the Library reminded me we were safe from Typhon here. He couldn't enter. My portal had brought us to the front door. I'd thought of the entrance and our souls instead of the room we'd been using for meetings. I rolled my shoulders, releasing the tension, and reached for the door handle with my free hand.

"Do you know where the others are?" I asked Michael, my hand still firmly in Rena's.

"Yes, in the room we've been using," Michael said.

Our group walked in silence. Our steps barely made noise. We'd witnessed horrific damage today, and the destruction was a fraction of what Typhon was capable of. If that hadn't renewed everyone's commitment to extracting Typhon from this realm, we deserved to lose. But we wouldn't. We couldn't.

The quiet emptiness of the halls was unnerving

after listening to sirens the last few hours. I studied Rena. She peered down the long hall as if she was in another world, but that's how I imagined her mind to be...a long string of intelligent inner monologues. I turned back to the direction we were headed. If we had time, I'd sneak off to the room with the couch that was still marked by us. I would clean the spot eventually. When I found some cleaner in this place. My dick twitched at the memories of how Rena looked on that couch. *Not now.* I inhaled and let my breath out.

"You okay?" Rena asked.

"Yes, just thinking about a green couch." I peeked at Rena and was rewarded with a pretty pink blush across her cheeks.

"Don't even think about it," she whispered under her breath.

"Oh, I'm thinking about it," I said. "But I know we don't have the time. Until then, I'll just keep thinking about it."

"As long as you're not thinking about it when we go into battle with Typhon."

"Of course, I will. That's my motivation."

Michael cleared his throat. When I peered over my shoulder at him, he gave one shake of his head. I looked at Lucifer who had a stern set of his face. Lilith hooked her arm through his and just like that, the tension released from his body. *Would they have been the balance and the scale under different circumstances?*

"WHAT DOES THIS PASSAGE MEAN?" I pointed to the paragraph I was referencing for Jophiel.

She scanned the text and back to me. Then she looked across the table at Rena. "Let me read it out loud." She cleared her throat. "Only a righteous decision will be honored by the scale."

Rena blinked a few times. "I can only save those who the balance power tells me to save. If I use the gift on someone whom I'm not meant to save, you will not be able to restore me, Jax."

"And if that happens?" I ask. "If Rena uses her powers to save someone the power doesn't think is worthy? What happens to her?"

"The outcome would depend on how much of her power she uses." Barachiel sat next to Rena. Her voice lowered. "She could go into stasis and heal. She could end up like her grandmother."

My gaze froze on Rena. "That is not going to happen."

She nodded but averted her eyes. *So stubborn. My love is ready to sacrifice herself, but I will not let that come to pass.*

"Typhon is sending tsunamis into several countries," Gabriel said, coming to stand at the table. He ran a finger along the populated coastlines of a dozen countries. My stomach roiled. Lucifer, Lilith, Michael, and Echidna joined us. Each wore a solemn expression.

My vision tinted red. *The fucker has no regard for a*

human's fragile life. As a half-human, his attack on them felt personal.

"Innocents?" Rena asked, staring at the map, and not meeting anyone's eyes.

"Too many to count yet," Michael said.

"It has to be done." Echidna's jaw tightened and throat bobbed while she focused her gaze on Rena. "I'll go say goodbye to my children. Then, we end the terror."

Rena pursed her lips and nodded. She was deep in her head, and who with a conscience wouldn't be. *Typhon. That's who.*

Light flashed and Michael took Echidna to say her goodbyes to her children.

I covered Rena's hand with mine. Her body jerked. She was on edge.

"Let's go for a stroll, my love." *Do we have time for a break?* Probably not, but Rena needed to get out of her head and into the right frame of mind for the upcoming fight. And what waited for us was going to be a battle.

"I can't. I need to—"

"Obsess," I finished for her, my voice soft. "Walk with me."

She let out a long sigh as if walking with me was a chore. It was that singular focus she had when she committed herself to finding an impossible answer. And she usually found an alternative, but there wasn't going to be one in this situation. I'd dealt with the same struggle when I ended Adam. He was going to keep hurting her until he couldn't anymore, so I ensured he couldn't.

"I know you'd rather be seeing what you could find in the books, but sometimes you need to let me take care of you," I pulled her close and guided us toward the small garden. "And this is me taking care of you."

She smiled, but the gesture didn't reach her eyes. "I do appreciate what you do for me, Jax. Everything you do. I just feel alone in trying to save Echidna's children. Even she's given up."

"Echidna has just known longer this would be the outcome. She's had centuries to come to terms with the reality. You are just learning the answer. It's a different perspective." I pulled our entwined hands to my lips and kissed my knuckles. "One of the things I love about you is that you believe everyone can be saved."

"Well, not everyone," she said.

I pressed my lips to the tip of her nose. "Most everyone."

"They don't deserve this," she said. "Echidna's children. They didn't have a choice."

"No, they don't, but they don't belong in the human realm either." The decision was hers, but she had my full support. Even if the end justified the means in this case, it didn't make the outcome easier. I took her hands and wrapped them around my waist. "They deserve to be somewhere they are not viewed as monsters." I encircled her with my arms.

She let out a sigh, the short, huffy one she did when she knew I was right but might not be ready to agree with me.

"I'm not going to push you. I brought you here to give you space to clear your head." I brushed my lips against hers. "I'm at your service however you need me."

"Just hold me," she said.

I tightened my grasp around her, and she relaxed in my arms. Her head rested against my shoulder. "I'm afraid, Jax. I'm afraid that doing what needs to be done will make me like him."

Her fear gutted me because I knew what she meant. It's why I had to take some time after I ended Adam's existence. "You are not like him, and I'm not sure there is anything you could do that would ever be as malformed as what he has done."

"I'm not so sure," she said. "I think of his death often to end the slaughter he inflicts on innocents."

"Sometimes we do things others might consider bad or ruthless to make a path for those who are innocent to thrive. That does not make us bad people." I focused on her eyes. The confusion in them was her reality, and I empathized with her. Taking a life wasn't a task held lightly despite what some of demonkind thought. For those of us with a soul, the deed stayed as part of us, and I didn't want that for Rena. "I know you, Rena. You are dissecting your decisions, but there is only one option left on the table here."

"You're right," she said. "I know it has to be done, but saying what I must do out loud is a failure to me. I couldn't figure out a way to save Echidna's children."

That was my love. If she couldn't save everyone, she

viewed her actions a failure. "Did you try looking at the situation from their perspective? Perhaps they want to be somewhere they are not constantly called monsters."

"It's possible," she said. "I wonder what they will experience when we end Typhon. Will their forms here turn to dust when their souls leave their bodies? Will their bodies burn?"

I hadn't thought of how their demise would happen. I suppressed a shiver remembering what it was like watching Lilith's second-in-command turn to ash in front of us. Nor could I forget the piles of ash from vampires that lined the floor of Gothica after the attack not more than a year ago. "Your aunts and uncles would have more knowledge in that area. We can go ask them if you want."

She leaned back and peered up at me. "No, let's stay out here a little longer. The answer isn't going to change the outcome."

"That is one request I can comply with without question," I said.

"I'd like to see a sunset in the human realm again," she said. "The way the light slides down the sky in a dance of oranges, pinks, and blues."

"Or a sunrise?" I inquired.

A blush crossed her face again, and I knew she was remembering the sunrise in Picher we shared.

"Another request I can fulfill for you after we defeat Typhon. I'll be by your side for all the sunrises and sunsets you want to see in the human realm."

She kissed my cheek. "How did I find the one person who could ever be perfect for me?"

"I ask myself every day how was I so lucky you chose me."

I leaned in and claimed her mouth. When I pulled away the world seemed empty without her touch.

CHAPTER 37

RENA

Echidna had returned by the time Jax and I made our way to the room with the rest of the group. Her red-rimmed eyes met mine, and her pain radiated into me. Her goodbyes with her children were not easy, not that I expected them to be. I fought back tears for the children who would be lost. They were adults. They were monsters in this realm. But they were Echidna's children. And Chimera's infants...

Why do I care so much about them? Because they are innocent. What I didn't understand and wasn't sure I ever would was how Echidna could offer them up so quickly as well as her husband, whom she professed to love. She was a fallen, though, and angels' perspectives were warped in some ways. The angels, especially the fallen, had a different moral compass than the humans or those of us from the Underworld. I studied her, and I saw the anguish on her face. She grieved the impending loss, but she believed it was the right thing to do.

My head reconciled why Typhon must be ended. He had killed countless innocents to try to have his daughter reborn. But he didn't seem concerned that his other children would perish to stop him, and that's the part my heart couldn't come to terms with.

"Ready?" Jax whispered close to me.

"No, but I'm resigned to what needs to be done."

Jax's eyes softened. "I will strike the blow. Their deaths will not be on you."

"But this is my decision as the balance. That's the same as dealing the death blow." No matter if I was the distraction and didn't actually strike down Typhon or his children, their deaths would be mine.

"You are the balance for the greater good. Not just one person or one family," he said. His argument made sense, but it didn't make the outcome any easier to digest. My soul ached for the loss to come, and I stared at my hands as if the blood would already be there.

"Jax, time for our portal," Father said, his voice solemn.

I nodded to Jax. He formed the symbols and the familiar crystal blue light spurred to life. The opening was big enough for us all to go through together, a sign of how much stronger Jax's ability had become with all the use these past months. Bone weariness settled over me as we gathered on the other side. Here I was going into a fight, putting my family at risk, and while I believed in the goal today, there would be no satisfaction in the kills. I let out a long breath.

Jax's hand rested on my lower back, and a warmth radiated out from his touch. I let the heat eat away at the coldness inside me, waking my body from the exhaustion. He was like a demon heating pad set to my personal temperature, and he was exactly who I needed beside me. I looked at Mother and Father. They were assessing the area like Michael, Jophiel, Barachiel, and Echidna. They were going willingly to give the same sacrifice I was in the impending battle, but I planned to do everything I could to make sure my life was the only one of my family's truly ever at risk.

A roar rumbled around us, and I shifted into warrior mode, tucking back the conflicted part of me. I unsheathed my blade and readied to defend the group. Cerberus rounded the corner barreling straight for us. He stopped quite a few yards away.

"Cerberus." I used my demon voice to carry but inclined my head toward him so he knew I meant no harm.

He tucked a leg under and dropped down. *Was that a bow?* He lowered his heads, all three of them. *Sweet angel's ass. It is a bow.* He rose and met my gaze with the center head. "Morena of Hell, my sisters and I support you, even when we are forced by our father to do things we do not believe in. We recognize your authority and swear our allegiance to you such as it is."

He might as well have speared me with one of his long

claw-like nails. They would rather move on than be a tool at their father's command. I placed a fist over my heart and inclined my head toward him. "Thank you, Cerberus. I accept your allegiance and will make sure all who will listen will know our success today will be because of you and your sisters."

Chimera landed next to him. "Morena, my friend, thank you for the sacrifice you make today. I knew when you came to my children's defense you were the one we waited for centuries to arrive."

I flattened my hand over my heart. "I am proud to call you my friend, Chimera, and I hope I live up to your image of me today."

Orthus and Hydra joined their brother and sister. Hydra was fucking terrifying with eight of her nine heads looking like snakes. The single human head was beautiful, but I couldn't look at her very long. She couldn't help how she was born, but my fear of snakes was in overdrive being near her. She must have sensed my apprehension because she took a step away. I was about to take her life in my hands. She owed me nothing, especially not space.

Echidna walked out among her children. Her skin shimmered as she touched each of them. "My touch will only block him from them for a short time, but it will give a window."

"He will call for us once he knows you are here," Chimera said. "He may have already felt your arrival."

"I wish our friendship had more time to grow," I said, blinking back tears.

"We will meet again," she said, her voice holding much more confidence than mine.

"We should go before he knows we made contact with Mother," Cerberus said to his sisters.

"Thank you," I said. "Thank you all." The sentiment wasn't enough, but those were the only words I could get out. I watched them go with the hope I would do their sacrifice justice.

Once they were out of sight, I unsheathed my dagger and rolled my shoulders, letting my wings extend to their full length. I'd spent years holding them in but not today. My parents were originals and so was I. *Time to own it and send Typhon to where he belongs.*

"Morena," Mother said with a gasp.

"I'm not going into this fight without all the tools in my arsenal," I said.

Jax unsheathed his double-fighting swords. "I agree."

Father let his wings unfurl in their snow-white glory.

"Lucifer. Really?" Mother said, her tone annoyed.

The other archangels followed suit. I stifled a giggle. We were a sight of seven winged beings, a vampire, a demon, and a fallen angel. I surveyed Echidna.

"No wings?" I asked.

"No, Typhon clipped them not long after we lost Helena. He was afraid I would return despite me telling him that was impossible." Sadness filled her eyes along with a flash of anger. "He wasn't always so horrible. There was a part of him that was good once, but that piece of him has long been dead. Gone when his focus shifted to reuniting his entire family on Earth."

Her desire to end his reign of terror suddenly made more sense. He'd inflicted pain on her and their children. Not just pain. What he did had a name. Abuse.

It was wrong to do a battle cry as we headed in the direction Echidna's children had. Instead, I offered something more relevant. "Today, we bring peace to your children."

Typhon's back was to us, but I doubted he was as oblivious to our presence as he appeared. Goosebumps raised along my arms. *He definitely knows we're here.*

He turned slowly to face me. "Are you ready to do what I asked of you?"

"I cannot perform the task you have asked, and even if I could, I wouldn't do that to your daughter while she is at peace."

"Then I will remove you for the impediment you are just as I did the one before you. And I'll keep doing so until I find the one who will."

Jax growled beside me, sounding more vampire than demon. The scream down our line drew my attention. Jophiel's mouth was open in a painfully high-pitched shriek. I covered my ears. Her sword flamed to life. The flames licked up her arms and out over her wings. I glanced down the line at the other archangels. Gabriel's wings dripped fire from Heaven, and his sword flamed in the same glow. Michael's sword looked like a giant torch.

All of them invoked the fire they could touch, including Father, rimmed in Hell's fire.

Hell's fire. An easy whisper tickled my mind as the fire responded instantly. The molten liquid dripped from my wings—the white-hot light of the archangels but the deep lava like Father's.

"You have one last chance to go willingly to live in solitude so that your remaining children can live. No more chances will be given." I had to make one last attempt, even if it hadn't been part of the plan.

"I reject your offer," Typhon said. "Children." It was all he had to say. The command initiated the control he had over them. Chimera, Orthus, Cerberus, and Hydra lunged forward.

"Hell's fire," I said in my demon voice. Dust flew out away from me with the vibrations. The flames roared up from Hell around us in a protective circle. The monsters' self-preservation kicked in, and they backed away from the heat. Or maybe Echidna's touch allowed them to resist their father.

Typhon reared back and blew out a gust of wind. The flaming wall flickered but did not fade. Did he really think Hell's fire would be extinguished so easily? I summoned the flames, and they would not retreat until I dismissed them.

I rocketed myself into the air until I was level with him. My other winged companions joined me in the sky. Typhon had us in size, but we had him in number.

A funnel cloud formed over our heads. "How the fuck do we fight that?" I ground out.

"Can you raise the fire higher like a dome?" Father asked.

"Yes, but he could get away if I do."

"Better he gets away than we all perish."

I nodded, but I had an idea. "Get everyone lower and closer together."

Father maneuvered his siblings closer to our family on the ground.

Our original plan was already disrupted, but there was an opportunity to protect those I loved and take on Typhon myself. I hovered over my family and locked eyes with Jax.

His face scrunched up like he knew I was about to go rogue. I wanted to apologize to him for making this decision on my own, but there was no time to pacify my guilt.

"Hell's fire protect them." I raised my hands and shot to the other side as the dome closed over my family. They would be protected. That was all that mattered. A white glow to my side caught my eye. Uriel was outside the dome.

"What are you doing?" He'd barely survived Typhon last time.

"You're not doing this alone," he said, his tone full of conviction.

Wind whipped violently around me and Uriel. A tornado dropped from the sky. The twister landed hard against the dome but bounced off. A twinge of relief washed over me, but I turned my attention to Typhon. He focused on how to break my protection of the group on the ground. The moment I'd been waiting for had arrived, but I hadn't thought of this scenario.

Uriel flew next to me. "What's the plan now?"

"I hadn't thought past trapping them all in the dome."

A small smile crossed his face. "You are such a risk taker. How long before the others break free?"

"They won't be able to break through the barrier. Jax might be able to portal to the other side eventually. Lesser demons can't, but Jax is stronger." I shrugged.

"Then, we better end this before we test that theory," Uriel said.

"You go from the right, and I'll take the left?"

"It's a plan."

CHAPTER 38

JAX

ot wind gusted around and made it difficult to stand. Another tornado reverberated around us but couldn't break through Rena's power. The barricade was like a massive shield.

The heat in the dome was intense, but nothing no one in here couldn't stand. Lucifer tried and failed to cross the threshold. The flames only answered to her. I'd tried to portal us to the other side, but my gut understood the failure before my brain registered it when I was bounced back inside the flame walls.

"What were you thinking when you formed the portal?" Lucifer asked.

"I was thinking we need to get to the opposite side of the inferno wall and on the ground directly in front of it."

Lucifer nodded. "Try again but set your intention on Morena. Fighting with her out there."

Michael moved closer. "That could work. Most demons wouldn't be able to focus a portal like that."

"Only me, but Morena blocked me intentionally. Jax needs to set his intentions as strongly as she has." Lucifer motioned toward the flaming wall. "Move closer to the structure. As close as you think you can get to Morena's position."

I stood in front of the wall in a spot where I could see Rena on one side of Typhon and Uriel on the other. *I should be there fighting at her side.* The knot in my chest grew, wondering if I would make it to her in time. I swallowed against the thickness in my throat and formed the symbols.

Blue light sputtered and hissed in front of me, but the portal opened. "We'll be exposed when we go through. Be ready."

"We're ready," Lucifer said. "All of us."

"Some more than others," Jophiel ground out.

I'd always considered her one of the softer archangels, but she evoked her warrior persona for this battle.

As soon as I stepped one foot on the other side, something large shadowed the space above me and seemed to be closing the distance. I surveyed the object flying overhead. *Fucking no way.* It was Uriel. Or rather his limp body fell like a boulder directly at me. I stuck my arms out and moved to catch him. He thudded against my forearms. Stings erupted across my skin as his feathers sliced into my flesh.

Uriel was weak. Too weak to continue fighting, which

was highly unusual for an angel much less an archangel. His eyes were closed, and I passed him over to Gabriel.

"I cannot take him from the battle. To do so would bring dishonor to both me and him."

"Keep him safe until we are done then." I tracked Rena's movement near Typhon. I didn't have wings. *How in all that is Hell am I going to fight with her from here?*

We were so far off the original plan that there was no getting back on track. I surveyed the archangels and held my hand out for them to hold position while I assessed for next steps. Lucifer let out a low growl but stayed put.

Cerberus, Hydra, Orthus, and Chimera stood on the sidelines. Echidna's power to block Typhon's hold on them appeared to be working. Her power wouldn't last forever. Echidna had told us that much.

Rena looked down at me for a split second and at the dome of fire. I gave one subtle shake to not touch it. He would realize the rest of us were free at some point, but the move bought us time while Typhon didn't realize we'd escaped. He was focused on loosing a barrage of lightning down on Rena, which she expertly deflected and dodged. There wasn't enough of a break for her to react. I had to get in the air, and there were only a few ways that could happen.

The wind intensified to gusts like a hurricane. *How is Rena staying up there in that? I can barely hold my position without being thrown backward.*

"What's the plan, Jax?" Lucifer asked, stepping to my side. Michael came to the other.

I was the one who always had a plan, but I didn't here. It was like the wind drained all my senses. I didn't have wings and couldn't fly to the fight, but the archangels could. They were able to assist Rena in an aerial battle, and Typhon had certainly brought one. I studied the building behind us. *A fertilizer plant.*

"I have an idea on how those of us who can't fly can create a distraction while the rest of you take to fight," I said.

ECHIDNA, Lilith, and I each found a fertilizer room to set about a dozen bags of the smelly stuff on fire using makeshift torches lit by the fires of the dome. I emerged from my room. Echidna and Lilith were running at top speed in my direction.

"Move it, Jax," Lilith said.

I fell in step with them and hauled ass down the hall. My heart pounded. This idea was a gamble. The three of us could survive most injuries if we didn't clear in time, but I didn't want to find out how long it would take to heal. I looked over my shoulder to see if our progress was visible. The result was satisfying. White smoke billowed out.

I cleared the entrance on the heels of Echidna and Lilith. A boom shook the area around us and was likely felt by Rena and Typhon if they were paying attention. I wobbled but regained my footing and kept going until we were a good distance away.

Michael floated near us, his wings stirring up a small breeze that wafted some of the smell away. "That's a small one." He inclined his head toward the factory. "Prepare for a bigger one."

The ground shuddered. Dust and debris exploded in the air, spattering against my skin. I ignored the pricks where the particles pierced my flesh. The earth rumbled, and I was certain the next discharge would be even bigger. I led the group to what I thought would be a safe distance and managed to cover my ears seconds before the building erupted in an inferno of fertilizer.

Fiery, shit-scented globs pelted the ground around us, but they also propelled like rockets toward Typhon. *And Rena.* My chest tightened with fear. I pushed the panic down deep. This might not have been my best idea, but it accomplished the goal. Typhon turned his attention away from Rena and the archangels in the air with her to our group on the ground.

Although he couldn't control Hell's fire without Rena or Lucifer connected to it, Typhon commanded the wind to direct the inferno from the dome to the remains of the warehouse. The flames married with the blaze there. He fashioned the flames into a fire tornado. The funnel grew until the whirlwind hovered over us like a swirling embodiment of Hell. Pieces of the warehouse broke away and spun around the burning cone. The fiery storm burned a path toward us. I positioned my body in front of

Echidna and Lilith and braced for the burning pain that would accompany death by fire.

Echidna grabbed my wrist, yanking me backward. She held her free hand up, and something pulled tight inside me. The deep blue essence of light radiated out around us. Echidna formed a shield of essence around the three of us. The act was eerily similar to what Adam had done, but I didn't feel drained or controlled. No, the power was more like what Eve had done, gentle but protective. I shook myself from thoughts of a darker day capable of dragging me into distractions that were difficult to come back from. Sweat dampened my brow. I dabbed at the perspiration and pulled back a shaky hand. My breath was ragged, but it wasn't from Echidna. *In one...two...three. Out one ...two... three.*

I scanned through the blue sheen to find Rena. She and Uriel were the two closest to Typhon. Uriel wasn't completely healed, but he was on his feet. I couldn't hear what they said over the roar of the flaming tornado bearing down against Echidna's shield. I glimpsed Echidna. Lilith held her up. Sweat beaded along Echidna's hairline and brow. Her grip was firm on my wrist. All of her strength remained focused on keeping the shield in place. She was siphoning from me to power the barrier keeping us safe.

Typhon's children must be back under his control. Chimera, Orthus, Cerberus, and Hydra entered the fight against the archangels. Lucifer, Michael, Barachiel, and Gabriel were all focused on the monsters. Rena was in

Typhon's radius along with Uriel, who must have recovered enough to re-engage. Typhon had Rena in his direct line of sight. There was no one else to assist. I wouldn't hide behind the shield. Rena was the balance, and I was her scale. It was not my duty but my choice to fight alongside her. Echidna didn't look like she could hold on much longer, but I tried to pry her fingers from my wrist.

The firenado grew but moved away from us enough that the air cooled. I turned to Echidna and ground out, "Let go."

She dropped to her knees, and Lilith went down with her. The blue light shimmered and dissipated. I was on the move and under Rena's position. *How the fuck can I get up there in the fight with no wings?*

Typhon was big enough I could land on his back if I portaled there, but I could fall to my death if I misjudged it. Or worse, be eaten by one of the snakes on his lower half. I wasn't as fragile as a human, but we were in the human realm, which made me weaker.

Chimera stalked toward me. *Well, fuck.* Of all the monsters, it had to be the one Rena befriended who came after me. I would pull punches for her, but I wouldn't choose her life over Rena's. I unsheathed my sword and prepared for her attack.

"On my back," Chimera said, stopping in front of me.

"What?"

"Get on my back before he has control again," she said.

She could toss me off once we were in the air, but she could be taking me to fight beside my love. *Would Typhon command her to dump me once we had his attention?* Or worse, use me as a tool against Rena. Either way, I couldn't fly, and she was my best option to get to Rena. *My only option.*

Echidna and Lilith made their way to my side.

"My daughter wishes to help, and I will help her do so," Echidna said, sounding weak but firm.

"His army, Mother," Chimera said. "They are inbound."

"I feared as much." Echidna's tone turned solemn.

"Do I even want to know what his army consists of?" I asked.

"Serpents," Lilith responded.

"Snakes," I said. "Rena is going to lose her mind."

Lilith looked up to the sky. "And she isn't close enough to him to end him with her dagger."

Echidna touched Chimera, and blue essence light flowed between them. Chimera's eyes turned bright blue. *Not between them. Echidna gifted life force to Chimera.*

"Give me your hand," Echidna said.

I glimpsed Lilith as she nodded her encouragement. Apprehension slid up my spine, but I dropped my hand in hers. She positioned my palm between Chimera's eyes and added hers on top of mine. Her voice came out smooth and even, speaking a language I wasn't familiar with.

"She is bonded to you. Your commands will override Typhon's if you and Chimera are near."

I considered her words, unsure if this was the right

choice, but if climbing on a monster kept Rena safe, it's what I'd do.

"Chimera is not permanently bound to you because you can choose to end the bond at any time." Echidna swayed, and Lilith caught her weight.

"Echidna, we need to get you somewhere out of the fight so you can recover," Lilith said.

"I'm not going anywhere."

Lilith exchanged a look with me, and I recognized the withered look on Echidna's face so like what Eve's had been. Echidna had expended all or most of her life force. There would be no coming back from this. No second chances. Just like Eve had, Echidna would leave the human realm. The fallen would typically go to Hell and serve Lucifer, but she'd never sworn herself to him from what I understood. I wasn't sure where she would go, but I hoped it was the same place as Eve.

"Thank you," I said, gripping her shoulder for a moment before making my way to Chimera's side. There was more that should be said for thanks and gratitude but no time to say it. "Do I just take a running start?"

Chimera shifted on her feet. "I couldn't say. I've never let a human on me before today."

"Running start it is then." I stepped back and ran full speed toward her, leaping into the air. I calculated the distance and twisted my body to land between her shoulder blades. "What do I hold onto?"

Her body rippled in what could have been a shrug. "Again. No human has ever sat atop me."

"How about your mane? Does that work?" Panic made my limbs shake as I scooted up. *I can do this for Rena.*

"Hold on and stay hidden." She said, her voice filled with annoyance but didn't confirm my request.

I wound my hand into her mane, the hair coarse like a lion's, and at the same time, she launched into the air. My stomach plummeted below me as we rose. I peered through the fluff around Chimera's neck as we neared Rena and Uriel. Typhon would have to look to see me on her back, so I hoped he assumed she was acting on his behalf.

"He's trying to control me," Chimera said, and I realized she didn't speak the words. She was in my mind.

"I can hear you in my thoughts," I said.

"Yes, you do not need to use your voice. Just think the message to me," she said, sounding pissed she had to explain telepathy to me. "I am annoyed."

"Noted." I thought back.

"He wants me to take Rena from here and wait for him while he kills you and the others."

"We're not going to let that happen."

"His command and assumption of my compliance will give us an advantage to get close to Rena." She used my nickname for my love a second time. "Is Rena not your preferred name for her?"

"It is, and I agree with your idea." Chimera and I flew toward Rena at an angle to keep me hidden from Typhon's view.

Rena scanned over us, surprise on her face.

"Trust us," I mouthed to her.

CHAPTER 39

RENA

Jax was on Chimera's back. *How in the fires of Hell did that happen? And what is his plan?*

"Your army approaches, Father," Chimera said to Typhon, distracting him from me.

His army?

"The serpents are hungry," he said, his eyes glittering.

Serpents? Fucking snakes? Like his legs? I dropped in altitude from the sheer panic radiating through me. Very little struck more terror in me than snakes. I inhaled and let out a controlled breath as I climbed back up even with Chimera and Jax. *One... Two... Three...*

I can handle the snakes. I can do this. If I end him now, maybe the snakes will die like... I glanced over at Chimera. The crushing weight of what would be her death hit me as it did every time I thought of her fate. My chest felt weak as if the breath had been knocked out of my lungs. *Focus, Rena.*

The dagger was poised in my hand, and I readied myself for the strike I had to deliver much like the serpents Typhon coveted. My next maneuver was a risky move, but a risk I'd rather be taken by me than the others. Typhon wanted me alive, but he had no need of the others. I nodded to Uriel. He would protect me from the monsters should Typhon call them to him. Chimera must have been touched again by Echidna to allow Jax nearby. Uriel only had Orthus, Cerberus, and Hydra to worry about. *Only.*

I called on my demon speed and shot high above Typhon, flipping over to come behind him. I surveyed the distance between my dagger and Typhon's neck. *No time to second guess.* I lunged forward and thrust my dagger up through the base of his neck into his skull. The scrape of metal against bone, then the lack of resistance, told me I hit my mark. He plummeted toward the ground below. His arms flailed back trying to reach where I impaled him. His black, inky blood spewed out from the wound, and his movements slowed. I wanted to watch his impact to make sure he was dead. *Jax is on Chimera.* My head snapped to where they had been, and I saw them falling. Chimera's body turned to ash and disintegrated, leaving Jax in a free fall. *No. He will not die here.*

My heart raced as I dove straight down for him. I reached my hand out to him, and our fingertips were close. "Grab my hand." I lurched forward and extended my hand, slick with Typhon's blood, sliding over his to grasp his wrist. He wound his fingers around my arm, and I lifted him up.

"Rena!" Jax shouted, his eyes wide. I turned to look over my shoulder. Typhon was rising next to us, his snake legs reaching out to bite at me. To bite us. Uriel shot up between us, thrusting his flaming sword into the underside of Typhon's jaw. The serpents on Typhon's enormous legs latched onto Uriel, one after another. Jaws snapped onto Uriel, but he was silent as he held his sword in place. Uriel, Typhon, and the snakes were a tangled mess. The snakes divided and divided again, inflicting bite after bite on my uncle. The writhing mass fell toward the ground, and I wouldn't be able to stop them while holding onto Jax. I couldn't cover the distance with Jax and get back to Uriel before they slammed into the ground. The only thing I could do was watch. I closed my eyes just before the impact, and the blow was thunderous. I opened my eyes to see Typhon shattering into a million pieces. *Where is Uriel?*

I located him on the ground and blew out a breath, grateful he was alive. *Uriel.* He was hardly moving. My uncle managed to get up on his knees but no further. His movements were slow and lethargic. The agony from so many serpent bites must be excruciating. His shadowed stare rested on me, and my gut said the celebration for our victory over Typhon was short-lived. My uncle was gravely injured.

I landed near Uriel and let go of Jax. Exhaustion radiated through my body. My knees gave way, but Jax propped me up against his side and helped me to Uriel. I dropped to the ground next to my uncle. "We need to get you healed. You are a mess of bites. No telling what your insides look like."

My voice sounded harsher than I meant. His emotions were clear, but the confusion behind his vacant look meant he was uncertain if the battle had been successful.

"We beat him. He shattered." I rested my hand on Uriel's shoulder and blinked back my tears. He needed my strength, not my sadness.

"Gabriel, take him somewhere safe," Michael said, his voice solemn. He turned to me. "Archangels were once very skilled at taking a hit for the team, even taking on snakes when we have to." His tone was forced with lightness.

"We have no time left," Uriel said. "We must act now and before he forces you to do something that should never be done."

"We did it, Uriel." I squeezed his shoulder. "We beat him." And his children were gone. The sight of Chimera turning to ash and disintegrating in front of me crashed down like Megiddo on me. So much loss today. I wondered if Echidna would really be okay with her children gone.

Uriel shook his head. His wounds weren't healing on their own. He needed help to heal. "No, you must burn him. This is only temporary. He will reform, bringing the monsters with him."

My knees nearly buckled. The fight wasn't over. I dug deep for every ounce of strength I had left because I would not leave here until Typhon was gone forever.

"Fuck," Jax said under his breath. Then he pointed to the giant fire burning in front of us. "We have the fire."

The fertilizer plant would have to do. I turned to Gabriel. "Get Uriel the help he needs."

Gabriel didn't say anything but lifted Uriel and disappeared in a flash of light. The solemn expression on the archangels' faces gathering around me said what I was afraid to ask. Uriel was in a bad way, worse than the torture Typhon had inflicted.

Jax, Michael, Aunt B, Aunt Jophiel, and I picked up the disgusting slimy lumps of Typhon scattered around the space. Mother walked up with Echidna leaning hard against her. Father came up behind them. We had all survived this far. We were going to survive it all intact. I wanted to let out a breath of relief, but I held back. The gruesome task of burning Typhon still had to be completed.

"I can help here," Echidna said. "Lower me to the ground, Lilith."

Mother eased Echidna down. Echidna spread her hands out on the ground. A low hum from the touch vibrated through us. Even the tiniest pieces of Typhon lifted from the ground and debris. She raised her hands and directed the pieces to the fire.

"Fitting in that he should burn with the shit," Jax said, hatred dripping from his voice.

"I'm not going to argue with that," I said. Death is normally a time for respect, but he didn't deserve esteem or admiration.

Aunt B and Jophiel sat on either side of Echidna. All the pieces accounted for, her body went slack into my aunt's arms. She could rest now. A deep sadness settled over me but was swept away with a breeze of peace. My aunts began to sing in a low melodic tone. When I came to the front, I understood the sorrowful tune. Echidna had passed. They mourned the loss of an angel. I dropped down in front of them and took Echidna's hands in mine. We were not free of loss. Today's battle was won with Echidna and her children's sacrifice. "Thank you and your children. Your story of bravery will be retold and not forgotten."

Her hands turned to light in mine and soon her entire body was glowing as well. The sight was beautiful but haunting. A body with wings made only of the soft warm light of angels formed and disappeared.

"She is with her children now," Jophiel said.

"All of them," Aunt B said.

My relief that they no longer had to deal with Typhon and were finally all together again was tainted with a mix of sorrow. I looked around at us and amazingly, my family was still here. My gaze went to Jax first. *My love. My scale. My everything.* Then around the group. Gabriel had taken Uriel to be healed. "Where did Gabriel take Uriel? To the Library?"

A roar erupted behind me. I turned. Typhon formed in the fire. He looked like a fire demon. Something broke inside me. Anxiety that we might not be able to end this tyrant. Fury at all the threats we faced. Horror this might be how the rest of our lives would go. My chest burned, and a prickle spread out over my torso and into my limbs. I held my arms out, palms facing Typhon.

"Hell's fire," I shouted. Hell's fire poured out of my arms and wings at Typhon. My head pounded with panic that the blaze would energize him in this form, but all the anger for what he had done and who he'd hurt poured out of me with dark vengeance from the very bowels of Hell. He turned to ash much like I'd watched Chimera do.

My vision became unfocused and closed in around me. I grabbed my temple, but my arms were weak and sticky with Typhon's blood. My stomach roiled and bile rose in my throat. I tried to take a cleansing breath but couldn't get air.

"Rena?" Jax's voice was distant. He sounded so far away like when we had been in the dream realm. Everything went silent and dark.

CHAPTER 40

JAX

Rena collapsed in front of me, and I lunged to catch her before she hit the ground. The world went silent as I zeroed in on getting to her. Something jerked me back. I fought against it with all my strength, but I couldn't get free. Time seemed to slow. I was helpless as my love hit the ground aflame. A cloud of dust enveloped her. My arms were freed, and I scrambled to the ground and cradled Rena in my arms. She wasn't moving, and my vision blurred. I struggled to make out her face.

"Rena? Don't you dare leave me, my love."

Her eyes blinked open briefly but closed.

"Help…" I didn't look up, but sound returned in a haze of shuffles.

"You need to form a portal, Jax," Lilith said, her voice was gentle.

"I can't let go of her," I said. "Not this time."

"I can carry them both," Lucifer said. He knelt next to me. I tightened my grip around Rena. "I'm going to lift you as one, Jax. You can hold Rena, right?"

"Make her better," I said. "Wake her up."

He placed a hand against Rena's cheek. "We will, Jax, but we need to go to the Library."

I nodded and stood in one swift motion. Rena didn't stir. Holding her was almost like touching the fires of Hell but without being burned. I kissed her forehead and handed her unmoving body to Lucifer, so I could call a portal. She was mine to protect, and I'd get us to the Library. My mind was numb, and it took a few moments to focus on the symbols needed. I formed the correct ones and took us back to the Library.

LUCIFER AND LILITH told me Rena's extreme emotions set off her full demon power. The transformation was evident in how she glowed with Hell's fire. Lucifer had held me back while she was still glowing because that kind of power can cremate a lesser demon. I was the scale and protected in many ways, but I was still half human and we'd been in the human realm. I understood, but I don't think the image of my love falling to the ground, after incinerating whatever the fuck Typhon was at that point, would be erased from my mind. Ever. Lucifer said it takes most demons centuries to develop, much less wield the kind of power Rena did, but she wasn't like most demons. Her body wasn't used to that kind of drain, and the expenditure of energy took time to work up to using. She'd recover, but they said recuperation could take days, weeks, and maybe months given what she did on the battlefield. Her body had shut down before it got to the point of no return like Eve and Echidna. A shudder ran through my body at the thought of how the outcome could have been different. Rena's youth and likely being the balance had been the factors on her side.

A dull ache had been hanging in my chest all morning. I rubbed my hand over the area, pressing the heel of my palm into the exact. I hoped the pain was a symptom of stress and not an omen of another terrible being to face, especially so soon after Adam and Typhon. I was tired. Rena was in a coma. Uriel wasn't healing like he should. We'd lost so many along the way, and our family needed time to recover if the universe saw fit to grant us such time.

Day three of me sitting in this same godsdam chair. I'd moved her from the couch to the bed Michael and Barachiel had found somewhere and brought into the room. *Our room at the Library.* I claimed the chamber as soon as we arrived with her here, refusing to let them put her anywhere else. But she still hadn't moved or twitched, not even her eyeballs behind her lids like when she dreamed. My hope for her recovery was strong, but the longer Rena went without waking up, the more patience I lost. I'd been cross with Lucifer and Lilith when they came to sit with her and told me to go take a shower. Rena would be surprised to find that a bathroom had finally materialized in the Library, and I was convinced she manifested the lavatory. I'd chuckled when I told her that story, and for a moment, I thought she had moved a finger.

Jophiel told me to talk to her, and I'd whispered in her ear how much I loved her and needed her and that we were all still together waiting for her to come back. Nothing I said seemed to reach her though. Gabriel suggested I read to her, but the books I discovered were all depressing, and I decided against those. Gloom and doom didn't seem like what Rena needed to entice her to wake up.

An agonizingly sharp stab hit me, and I clutched my chest. If demons could have heart attacks, I'd think that was the source. I was half human though. The pain diminished and faded away. Since I was still there, I assumed my heart was not stopping. Maybe it was Rena reaching out for me from whatever state she was in. Something moved. At least I thought it did. Her finger.

"I can't wait to marry you, Rena," I said, leaning in close and placing her limp hand in mine. Hope swelled in me that I didn't imagine the change. "I know the woman usually does most of the planning, but I'd like for us to go back to the chapel in Santa Fe to commit to each other. The thought of professing our love in front of all our family and friends there does something to me."

She didn't move, and I leaned back into the chair. *Why did I think just talking about a wedding would bring her around when nothing else had?* The piece of hope wedged in my chest fractured a little, and I fought to hold the fragments together. Fifteen minutes...or it could have been longer went by. My sense of time had warped so I wasn't sure, and I stared at the finger I was certain had shifted.

A knock came from the door, and I shifted to face in that direction. Barachiel poked her head in. "Can I come in?"

"Of course," I said. I guessed I'd growled so much the first couple of days, the others were afraid to enter. "Sorry if I've been possessive."

"You could go rest. I can sit with her," she said.

"No, I got some rest on the couch," I said.

She nodded, pulling up another chair. "She will come back to us, Jax. Have you been talking to her like Jophiel said?"

"Yes, but I feel stupid recounting random stories. Like she's going to wake up and ask me what all the nonsense was I said while she was sleeping."

"She's healing and assimilating with her full power. Not sleeping. There is a difference," Barachiel said.

"I know. It's easier for me to think of her as sleeping," I said, looking at Barachiel. Her eyes were red-rimmed and blotchy. "Are you okay?"

"I will be," she said, her voice wavering. "Uriel passed on a short time ago."

I inhaled a deep breath. That explained the sharp twist in my chest where his essence was placed. He and I were more frenemies than anything, but I didn't wish this on him. Rena would take the news hard since they had become so close, and my heart broke for her that she didn't get to say goodbye. "I'm sorry for your loss. He and I were never going to be best friends, but I did respect him. Will he be with Eve?"

"And Echidna," she said, her tone mournful. "He respected you, too, and he thought you were the perfect match for Rena. He admired how you weren't afraid to speak your mind to her or Lucifer." Barachiel smiled then.

"Rena will be broken when she hears he passed, and she didn't get to see him." She would beat herself up over not being able to save him, even though he'd made his choice just as she had.

"She will, but she will have you to get her through it." Barachiel patted my knee. "I'm just sorry she will not be able to see and feel how happy he is."

"Is he?" I asked. He'd been so solemn here, and I guess broken in ways I better understood after the last couple of years. "Can you tell he's happy to be in his next realm?"

"Oh, yes." She smiled. "We can still communicate. The reception is a little different than when we're all walking the same realms, but we can still do it. He's very happy and content for the first time in centuries because he is finally reunited with his love."

"That's good," I said, truly grateful he'd found a place where he could be happy. "It will help Rena to know that."

"What about this wedding you two were planning? When can we expect that?" Barachiel asked, clearly trying to make me less pensive.

"I was just talking to her about our nuptials. I'm hoping she still wants to go with the chapel in Santa Fe for our wedding. The sanctuary felt... right for us. I don't know how to explain it."

"You don't have to. Santa Fe is a beautiful place. Spiritual and magical," she said.

"Do you think she'll remember what happened when she wakes up?" The task would belong to me to explain everything to her if she didn't, and the undertaking was one I'd bear as her scale. She didn't deserve to relive the horrific events. Our win had a cost that would stay with her from Echidna's death, and now Uriel had joined in the sacrifices made for our triumph. His death would be hardest on her, and I'd hoped he would last long enough for her to awaken and have a goodbye with him.

"She was like an overheated battery, so her mind might be a little fuzzy when she wakes up. The memories should return"—Barachiel tilted her head to the side—"if she wants them to."

I'd been holding all my anxiety and fear in to be strong for three days, and I wanted to rip my skin off to let the turmoil out. My trust in Barachiel opened the wound. "I miss her. Even though she's here, I miss her."

Barachiel reached over and took her hand. "We all do but keep talking to her. She will be mad about missing anything."

I chuckled. "She will suffer from fear of missing out for sure."

She stood and patted my shoulders before squeezing them. "I'll be back later to see if you need a break."

I wouldn't need one, but it made me feel like family that she would offer.

MY NECK ACHED, and I realized I'd dozed off. I leaned forward and took Rena's hand in mine. Her skin was hot. She'd been warmer than normal since the manifestation of power with Typhon, and Jophiel told me she probably wouldn't come out of the deep sleep until her body temperature returned to the typical range. There wasn't anything to be done about the timing. We could only wait for however long the cool-down period took.

I kissed Rena's knuckles. "Remember when we danced in that club on your birthday trip to the human realm? I nearly lost my mind with jealousy when Stassi showed up and kissed you, but the Nephilim attacked and all I could think about was getting you to safety. I had no right to be jealous. We weren't together, and that was my fault for not telling you everything upfront, including how I felt about you. I thought I was doing the right thing, but it was my biggest fuck up and regret that I didn't tell you exactly what my goal was. It was you, Rena. Always you."

The door opened without a knock, and I didn't bother to look for who entered the room. Lucifer was the only one who came in without bothering to announce his intent.

"How's our girl?" Lucifer asked, straddling the seat next to me.

"She'd hate you calling her a girl and not a woman, but she's the same," I said.

"You're right, Jax," he said. "Sometimes I feel like she is moving further and further away from me and Lilith, and there's nothing I can do to stop the progression."

"She has become her own person with her own beliefs, but she is still your daughter. Rena loves you and Lilith unconditionally." I turned to look at him. His face was twisted in worry. *How did I get in a position to console the Devil?*

"She is and always will be our daughter, but you are her future. You are her anchor. Her home. The place where she seeks stability now. Not Lilith and me." Sadness tinged his words.

"Do you think she sees me that way?" I asked, my voice cracking on the memory of what I'd dealt with after I ended Adam. "Will she see me that way when she wakes up?"

"Whether she sees you that way or not is irrelevant because it is so," he said in the final way only Lucifer could.

I ran my free hand over Rena's. "I hope that is true because she is my heart, my soul, and my home."

Peonies and fire drifted on the air in the room, and I scanned to see where the scent could be coming from. Nothing. There was only one person I knew who smelled like that. Rena's finger twitched in my hand,

and I sat up straight in my chair. "Did you see that, Lucifer?"

"What?"

"Her finger moved," I said, unable to keep the anticipation out of my voice. Unlike before, the single movement was strong like she tried to wrap her finger around mine.

"Are you sure?" he asked.

"Yes, I'm positive," I said. Her finger moved up once and down once on mine.

"I'll go get, Jophiel." He tore out of the room at demon speed.

"Rena?" I said next to her ear. "Can you hear me, my love? I'm ready for you to wake up if you are ready to come back to me." Her entire hand gripped mine, and it was firm as if she hadn't been out at all. I squeezed back. "I love you."

CHAPTER 41

RENA

Bright light slipped through the slits in my eyes. I blinked against the intensity. My lids were so heavy. *Why won't they just open?* My body was hot, and I ached all over like I'd sparred for days without any recovery time. I wanted these covers off of me. My mouth was dry, and I couldn't get enough spit to form a swallow. The scent around me was a familiar woodsy smell. *Jax.*

"She's awake." Jax's voice was … relieved.

"Where am I?" I forced my lids open. The light in the room was too bright, and I squinted against the glare while my eyes adjusted.

"The Library." Jax's knuckles brushed against my cheek.

"Water?" I asked.

Jax pressed something cold against my lips, and I swallowed it in a gulp. The liquid went down the wrong way, and I coughed several times.

"Easy," he said, pulling the glass away. "You've been out a little while."

"Did we do it?" My voice came out like I'd swallowed gravel.

"You saved the world, my love," he said, soft and gentle.

Mother and Father came into view. Neither looked like they had slept since the battle. *When had it been? I couldn't figure the timing out.* Mother took my hand in hers and patted it. Father squeezed my knee.

"Are you thirsty?" Mother asked. "For something substantial?"

My stomach growled in response.

"Sounds like she's hungry," Father said.

"Please do not bring me any flesh," I said, my stomach roiling at the thought.

"I'll go get you some blood," Mother said, passing my hand to Father.

Barachiel and Jophiel came to my bedside followed by Gabriel and Michael. But no Uriel. They smiled, but their faces were solemn. Maybe my uncle was healing. He wasn't fully recuperated when we went into battle. Jax scooted onto the bed with me, and Aunt B took his chair.

"Where is Uriel? Is he still recovering too?" I asked.

Silence filled the room like lead. I closed my eyes. The memory of me pouring fire into Typhon after Uriel sacrificed himself on the battlefield filled my mind. He'd been bitten by those nasty fucking snakes. I recoiled at the memory. Tears welled in my eyes. I didn't want to ask the question burning my tongue, but I opened my eyes to Aunt B moving toward the bed. "Did he survive?"

Aunt B leaned in closer, resting her hand on my shoulder. She squeezed, and I met her mournful gaze. Tears filled her eyes too. "He succumbed to the wounds he sustained in battle. He has moved on, but he is reunited with his love and their child. They are reunited."

I understood. He'd only wanted to be with his family again and now he was. The knowledge should fill me with joy for him, but grief and guilt blocked any happiness from taking up space.

"That's why the power of the balance didn't want me to save him. He was ready to reconcile with her. They finally have their time together." I grieved the loss of his friendship. The loss of my uncle. But he got what he wanted too. They were together once more. I inhaled a breath and let the air out in slow bursts. I didn't want to break down, especially knowing he was reunited with his soulmate.

Aunt B's lips pinched together, and she nodded. "He is happy. It is only we who grieve."

Centuries or a millennium could pass before any of us see him again. "But you can still communicate with him through the angel-conscious thing?"

"We can," Gabriel said. "Although his voice is not as strong in our minds as it once was."

It was enough. It had to be. He was safe. He was with the love of his long life and their child. "I'm glad they are together."

"You didn't know him before," Jophiel said. "But we saw him the most like his old self when he came back to help you. Now, that he is with her again, he is himself. We have you to thank for that, and he wanted us to tell you thank you."

Tears rolled down my cheeks, and I didn't hold them in this time. By not saving him here, maybe I had saved him after all.

I pushed myself up. My back was stiff and protested the movement. Jax adjusted the pillows behind me. I thought of Uriel and hoped he really was happy. An image hit me like a hallucination. Uriel, a beautiful woman who resembled Echidna, and a raven-haired little girl. They were all sitting on a blanket in the most beautiful rolling field that overlooked a pond. Sun shined down on them, and they were smiling. Uriel's wings were tucked in or missing altogether. The little girl hopped up, stretching out her arms as if she were flying circles around them. Uriel leaned over and kissed the cheek of the woman. He turned, and it was like he was looking directly at me and smiled. The image was so vivid it seemed real.

"I think I'm not quite awake or something. I am awake, right?" I looked around the room for confirmation. I was still in the awful bed.

Jax squeezed my hand. "Yes, my love. You are awake."

"Do you see Uriel and his family?" Jophiel asked. "His message for you?"

"Yes," I whispered, tears welling in my eyes that he was finally with his family. *He found them.*

She smiled. "This is a gift with your power expanding. You will eventually be able to communicate back to him. We can teach you."

My grief eased some to know there would be glimpses of him and his family. To know he was with his family was a gift, but I wasn't sure if I was ready to have all the archangels in my head, especially my father. "Where is he? Where are they?"

"Normally, the name is not spoken as the quest to find it is never-ending, but because you are the balance..." She looked at Jax. "And you are the scale..." She looked back at me. "There is precedent for you to know."

Father cleared his throat. "They are in the Elysian Fields. When Uriel passed, his wife and daughter were able to join him there. Eve and Echidna are there as well. You may be able to share images or thoughts with them in time as well."

"But I don't hear you," I said, meeting Father's curious look and scanning the other archangels in the room. "Any of you."

"That might change as the days pass, but you might only be able to communicate with those that are in the last realm," Aunt B said.

"Only time will tell how the sense develops," Gabriel said. "You are an original, Morena, and the normal rules don't apply to you."

"I, for one, would appreciate being able to communicate with you in a freer manner," Michael said. "I'd be glad to help teach you should that be something you wish."

"Thank you," I said. "Thank you isn't enough for what you all have done but thank you for standing by me in not only this battle but the journey. We've lost some irreplaceable warriors, leaders, and good beings with Uriel, Eve, Echidna, and Alessia." I reached for Mother's hand, and she squeezed mine in return. Alessia, mother's number one, had saved vampires during an attack on Gothica when Uriel's ascendant was making everyone act as if they were insane, but she had been mortally wounded in the process. The memory of how she'd evaporated into ash hung in my mind. "Their sacrifices will not be forgotten. I would like to do something on the Library grounds in their memory, but we can talk about that on another day." I swallowed against the lump forming in my throat. "Thank you, family, for staying with me while I recover. How long has it been?"

"Four days," Jax answered. "Four very long days."

"My body feels like it's been much longer," I said, rolling my shoulders. Some of the tension released, but my muscles ached.

"I'll go get you some blood," Mother said, leaning over to kiss my cheek. "Then maybe the others will go so we can chat."

CHAPTER 42

JAX

’d excused myself with the others and took a quick shower when Lilith brought Rena blood. By the time I returned, Lilith was leaving.

"She was getting a little fidgety without you here," Lilith said, meeting me at the door. I closed it behind her.

"What did your mother want to talk to you about?" I asked, sitting on the bed next to her. Her color had returned, and she looked like my love. I'd almost lost her again, and Eve wouldn't have been able to bring her back like she had before. No one could. That thought made my stomach weak and crushed down on my chest. The weight of that knowledge lifted as she smiled. She was going to be okay.

Rena snuggled up to me. "You smell so good. Just some motherly advice. Plus, she said she wouldn't push for the big wedding anymore, but I told her the timing wasn't right to talk about that."

"You don't want to get married now?" My heart broke even asking the question, and I dreaded the answer.

She sat up and leaned over, pressing a hand to my cheek. "I still want to marry you, but I have a very specific location in mind. I didn't think you would be in any hurry to go back to Santa Fe despite a dream I had where you did."

I closed my eyes and let the relief wash through me. When I opened them, she regarded me with concern. Concern I needed to ease. "That wasn't a dream. I told you I wanted to marry you in the chapel in Santa Fe when you woke up."

"You did?" Tears sprang to her eyes, and one leaked out of the corner. I ran my thumb over her cheek, swiping the dampness away.

"I did. Will you marry me in Santa Fe, Rena?"

"Of course, I will." She grabbed my face and pulled it to hers, pressing our lips together. Her lips were like the sweet smell of the Library, so welcoming and I wanted more. She was recovering from a near-death experience, and her ability to heal was more important than my own needs.

I tugged her hands away. "Easy. My restraint is barely holding on right now, and I know you. You'll want a full shower and whatever else you do before I get you dirty again."

"The way you said that does something to me, Jax." She slid her hand down my chest toward my dick.

I grabbed her hand. "I want you, Rena. To feel you

against me and know you are real. If you touch me there, I'm going to bury my cock into you until I feel you tighten around me. I've been waiting days for this."

She licked her lips, and I took a deep breath to keep from pouncing on her. *Where the fuck are the interruptions now when I need one?*

"You could come shower with me." She wagged her eyebrows at me. "Then, you wouldn't need another one after we're done.

"And you're not worried about others hearing us?" I asked. "Because I will fuck you until you scream my name so loud your voice echoes through the halls of the Library."

"If you can find a shower, I promise you the last thing I will be worried about is who will hear us." She stared at my mouth. When Rena looked up through her lashes, her eyes filled with heat and hunger.

My desire tightened in my hardening cock. "Are you sure?"

"Mother brought me blood, and I drank several bags. I'm good to go. I promise," she said. Her mouth went to my ear, and she clamped down with her teeth.

My dick twitched so hard I was sure it would burst through my zipper. I scooped her up in my arms.

She laughed. "I can walk."

"Not taking any chances," I said. "You'll need your strength for what I'm about to do to you." I rounded the corner and kicked open the hidden door Barachiel showed me when I asked why there weren't any bathrooms in the

Library. Turned out there were bathrooms either hidden in certain rooms or manifested by someone, and the room Rena and I claimed happened to be where one chose to appear.

"Don't tell me this was here all along?" Rena groaned.

"No, it showed up sometime after we … claimed the room," I said, setting her down in front of the counter. "But there are others hidden in the Library that were here." Her back to my front, I caged her in with my arms. Toiletries like toothpaste and other items were brought in for us. "Is everything you need here?"

Rena peered at me in the mirror. Our eyes locked and she leveled me with her heated demon-red eyes. "The only thing I need is here." She slid her hand back to my hip and pulled me forward.

My cock pressed against her lower back and the top of her perfect ass. I closed my eyes and let out a breath, regaining my restraint. "I'll be in the shower waiting for when you're ready."

She leaned back against the counter and watched as I peeled off my clothes. Rena studied my chest, trailing her hand over it until her palm rested on the faded scars of Orthus's bite. She ran her fingers over the marks. I shivered under her touch. "Do they hurt?"

"No, and Jophiel says the scars will eventually disappear."

She nodded, placing a kiss on one of the puncture wounds. The touch made me want to lift her to the counter and rip the thin gown off.

I spun her around gently. "Hurry up and do what you need to do."

She looked in the mirror as if she saw herself for the first time. "Who dressed me in this?"

I barked out a laugh as I ducked my head under the water. "Your mother brought it to me."

"I would never wear this." She picked up the toothbrush and slathered toothpaste on the bristles. Her eyes flicked to me. I leaned back under the hot water, letting it flow over me as I crossed my arms to watch her. Her gaze fell to my dick, and my member was pointed right at her as if it was a divining rod for her pussy. She squirmed at the counter and rinsed her mouth out. Her eyes were still fixed on my hardness.

She turned and faced me, pulling the material over the top of her head. I reached down and stroked my cock in slow motions as I took in the curve of her neck. My stare roamed down to the turgid peaks of her breasts, and lower to where the small tuft of hair failed to hide her apex. I wanted to bury my cock in her, but we would do this at her pace. She wasn't fragile, but she needed control today. Something she hadn't felt like she'd had. I'd let her have power over me for as long as she needed it.

She pulled open the clear glass shower door that was fogging up from the steam. "I like seeing you touch yourself."

"You do?"

She ran her hand up my chest over the scar nearest my heart. "I do." She slid her other hand down and placed her fingers on top of mine. *Fuck.* She would be my death. "Which do you like better? Yours or mine?"

"Definitely yours." I growled.

She batted my hand away and stroked me. My head fell back against the wall. Pleasure rippled through me. "Rena."

"I like how you react to my touch," she said, her voice like velvet. "How hard you get. How your dick throbs for me."

"Fuck," I muttered. I loved hearing her talk like that, but I could not form the words. Her touch was still extra warm, and the heat intensified with each sweep she made. I moaned from how close she brought me to the edge with just a few strokes.

She let go of my cock, and the disappointment was like being impaled by a sword. "Wash my hair?" she asked.

Ahh. She's teasing me, and I'll take every bit of it.

I grabbed the shampoo bottle and squeezed out some in my palm, rubbing my hands together. I buried my fingers in her damp hair and massaged. She moaned from deep in her throat. The guttural sound almost undid me. My dick slipped against her wet stomach.

"Lean your head back." My voice was so rough I barely recognized it.

She leaned back, and I worked the soap from her hair, watching the suds run over her breasts and down further.

"Jax," she said, breathless.

"Yes, my love?"

"Take me. Fuck me hard."

My mouth was on her, devouring her. I licked my tongue across hers and tasted the minty toothpaste she'd used. I trailed my hand down to her core and over the bundle of nerves. She bucked against me. I slid a finger into her hot slickness. "You are so wet."

"You just figuring that out?" she said, in the breathy voice that made me harder when I didn't think I could be.

"Fuck, Rena."

"Yes, please," she said.

I slid my finger out and lifted her by the back of the thighs. She wrapped her legs around my waist, and I positioned her against the wall of the shower. My dick lined up with pure perfection for her slick pussy. The head of my cock dipped in.

Rena gasped. "Please, Jax."

"You never have to beg for me. You have me. All of me," I said, thrusting deep. I gritted my teeth against the instant rise of pleasure and planted one hand against the wall to steady myself. My vision clouded with my aching need as I settled all the way in her. I held still as she adjusted to me and licked from the side of her neck up to her jawline.

She whimpered and her head tilted back, pushing her hips against me. I cursed under my breath.

"Look at me, my love. I want to see your desire for me when I'm inside you."

"Jax," she said, my name a breathy moan on her lips. I devoured her mouth and nipped her lip, needing to release some of the tension so I could last for her to ride the pleasure.

"Yes." I stroked up in a slow penetrating rhythm. "Let me hear how you want my cock."

"Faster." Her breath came in little puffs.

I moved faster, burying myself up to the base.

"Don't be gentle," she panted out. "I won't break."

I wasn't being gentle, but she could have me any way she wanted. I pulled all the way out and slammed into her.

"Yes, like that."

I repeated the rhythm over and over, relishing her gasps and moans. The softness of her slick center threatened my control. Her core tightened around me, and I knew she was close. My tempo became wild as I pounded into her sweet pussy. I reached down between us and stroked her clit.

She clenched, and her pussy contracted around me in a flutter. "Jax." I rotated my hips so I pressed against that special spot, dragging her orgasm out. Her nails dug into my back. I groaned into her neck, biting at the soft skin. The burning tingle on my back from her scratches sent me into my release. I shuddered as my seed spilled into her. My cock throbbed in her as my orgasm kept going.

My forehead rested against hers. "Damn, Rena. You will kill me in the most exquisite way."

She laughed. "That was... exactly what I needed."

I lowered her legs and held her against the shower wall while she gained her steadiness back. I kissed her forehead. "I love you." I brushed my lips across hers. "In every way it is possible to love someone."

CHAPTER 43

RENA

My heart pounded in my chest. Jax was everything I needed and more. He grabbed a towel and dried me off.

"I'm not putting that gown back on," I said, eyeing the modest sleepwear I'd been put in. "I don't care if I have to walk the halls of the Library naked."

Jax froze in the middle of drying himself. "That's an intriguing thought, but what I have in mind doesn't require clothes."

I peered up at his face, and damn if that unique way he looked at me wasn't in his eyes. He took me in like I was all the food he needed to survive. Like he'd eat me alive. Dampness slicked my center once again.

He moved fast, hooking his hands under my thighs and lifting me until my legs were wrapped around his middle. I devoured his mouth. Despite the shower, his rich demon scent like burning Fall leaves drenched me. He paused at the doorway to the room. I broke the kiss long enough to glimpse over my shoulder. "Not that bed. We need to burn that. The couch."

His lips blazed a trail down my throat. He nipped at the spot at the base of my neck that made me squirm. A ripple of pleasure pulsed through me, and I moaned. Jax lowered me to the couch on my back. He circled my nipple with his tongue as his fingers worked the other one. I arched my back into his touch. He traced a line with his tongue from between my breasts and lower to my belly. I wound my fingers through his hair. His tongue ran along the delicate flesh of my center, and I bucked against him.

"You said I didn't have to beg, so put your mouth on me," I gasped out.

His mouth covered my clit and he sucked. My back arched as pleasure pulled again. "That feels good."

"Just good," he said in a hum against my sensitive skin.

"Great," I blurted out. "Spectacular." I'd spout every adjective he needed to hear to describe how damn good his mouth on me felt and sweet angel's ass the caress felt unlike anything else.

He lapped, savoring me, until I was on the edge. I murmured sounds that weren't words. He inserted a finger and then another one and stroked in time with the sucking. A whimper slipped from my lips as I rode his fingers, chasing an orgasm, sure I'd explode once I reached the peak.

He ran his tongue in circles over my clit, and I came

hard, shattering on his fingers as his mouth siphoned the pleasure from me. His name came out as a scream.

My body shook and trembled in aftershocks that just kept going. The pleasure was unlike anything I could recall. I might have died a little. Jax kept his mouth on me. I pushed him back and pulled him toward my face, tasting myself as our lips came together.

"Damn," he muttered as we broke apart. "When you came, it vibrated inside me. I almost did too."

"You almost found release from mine?" I looked into his heated eyes.

A wicked smile spread across his face. "Almost."

I pitched forward pushing his shoulders back until he was reclined on the cushion, and I was kneeling between his legs. His nakedness was on full display, and I drank in every bit of his hard muscular lines. He was like an unquenchable thirst, but I'd drink every drop I could. I trailed my finger from his collarbone to one of his nipples. I flicked my tongue across the responsive flesh and blew a breath of air over the skin until it hardened.

He gasped and writhed under me, and I pressed my thighs together, ignoring my own desire because I wanted to revere him. He was an altar worthy of everything I could give. I rose and dragged my nails down his chest and over his abdomen in featherlike movements. His muscles flexed and contracted under my touch. Jax's reaction to me was all the power I needed.

"Rena." He said my name like it was a prayer. Jax leaned forward and slid his hands from my hips up my back until my breasts pressed against his chest. My nipples hardened from the skin-to-skin contact. His mouth met mine in a hungry dance. I relished the connection and only broke away when I remembered I was on a mission to worship him.

I pushed him back down against the cushion. The yearning in his eyes made me want to sink myself onto his hard cock, but I forced myself to scoot backward until my mouth was close to his thickness. I licked him along the vein from base to tip and the drop of his seed that beaded on the end.

He wound his fingers into my hair. "Fuck, Rena." His voice was ragged with need, and I loved how he reacted to me. He ran a thumb over my cheek and down to my lower lip. I sucked his thumb into my mouth hard. His head fell back against the armrest.

I gave his words back to him from the shower. "Look at me, my love. I want to see your desire for me when I make you come."

His head shot up as my hand stroked his length. I bent forward and slid my tongue down over his shaft, closing my mouth as I sucked hard.

A groan escaped his mouth, and the sensual sound hit me right in my center. I moved my hand in time with my mouth in slow strokes up and down his hard length. Jax's hips raised up against me, but I kept my rhythm steady, increasing the pace. He moved with me, fucking into my mouth, and I wanted every bit of him, pulling him in until he hit the back of my throat.

"Fuck, I'm going to..." His cock throbbed and his warm release filled my mouth. I swallowed and kept going until he released my hair. I sat back, acutely aware of his eyes on me as I licked my lips. He sat up and pulled me down onto his chest, kissing me until I was dizzy. "I love it when your mouth tastes like me."

"I love it when you're naked, and I get a full view of you," I said, my voice embarrassingly hoarse with my desire.

"My clothes will all burn in the fires of Hell if that's the case." He chuckled against my forehead.

"That might get awkward in council meetings." I laughed. "But it would definitely make them more interesting."

"Worth the stares if I get to have you like I have today. All of you," he said, his voice a bit wistful.

I understood what he meant. Our lives were going to be full of meetings and tasks for the balance and the scale. I traced circles on his chest. "You can have me like this every morning, every evening, and any time in between you name."

"Even in a meeting?" His eyes danced with amusement.

"I'll gladly leave a meeting to fuck you," I said.

"And my dick is hard all over again." He caressed my face. "I love you, Rena. I love your bravery and your intelligence, but most of all, I love your heart."

For some reason, those words hit me deeper than usual. I felt worthy of his love, and I realized I hadn't ever felt that way. I'd thought it was unfair to ask him to give up his future to stand by my side, but he wasn't just by my side. He was my partner in everything. My equal, and I was worthy of him and the love he offered.

"I love that you respect my choices and love me despite them." I smiled. "I love you. Now marry me, you fool."

Jax laughed and grabbed my hips, lifting me onto him. "I'll marry you as soon as you pick a date." He dropped me onto his cock. I moaned sliding right down on it with my slickness and was amazed at how he had recovered with demon speed into a rock-hard shaft.

"One week," I gasped out.

"One week it is." He sat up kissing me into oblivion.

CHAPTER 44
JAX

Rena and I didn't emerge from the room for hours, and the stares on us as we entered the war room at the Library, told me the others knew exactly what we had been doing. Rena's cheeks turned a bright crimson, but I refused to be embarrassed about making love and venerating the only person who could be a saint in my eyes.

"Any sightings?" The others had been monitoring the site where we defeated Typhon to make sure he stayed dead this time.

"No," Michael said. "No activity to report."

"I've heard no rumblings either," Gabriel added.

Relief washed over my entire body. We were finally free of the threat. I could relax into my role and focus on building a life with my love.

Lilith made her way across the room and hugged Rena. "You look much better."

Lucifer eyed me but hugged Rena too. "I'm glad you are strong enough to be up and around."

"There's something I want to tell all of you while we're together," Rena said. A big smile brighter than the sun spread across her face. She slipped her hand into mine. "Jax and I want to go back to Santa Fe... to get married."

The archangels all expressed their happiness for us until only Lucifer and Lilith were left. Lilith beamed, which was the direct opposite reaction from Lucifer. He scowled so hard I expected Hell to erupt from the floor of the Library and consume us.

"Then you will need this," Barachiel said, handing a thick envelope to me. I recognized it as the one that held the marriage license. "And you have my congratulations." She hugged me, then Rena.

"Let's go do... angel things," Barachiel said, ushering her siblings out of the room.

"Oh," Gabriel said. "Right."

Lucifer remained silent until the door closed.

"Before you even start, Father, you had to know this was coming. It's not like we hadn't discussed marriage. You gave your blessing months ago, and Mother has an entire room dedicated to planning a ceremony in Hell."

Lucifer dropped a long stare at Lilith before turning his attention back to Rena and me. "It's not that I didn't expect you two to come with this announcement, but you are both still so young and are coming off the defeat of Typhon. I expected the ceremony to be postponed."

He thought we'd need time like we both did after the Adam trauma, but Rena and I didn't want to wait. The bond between us was meant for eternity—at least I hoped that was fate's plan and we had earned it.

"Luce," Lilith purred from beside him. "They are bound in love and destiny. Their union is inevitable. You know what that's like."

He slid his hand around Lilith and tugged her closer. "It seems I do. You have my blessing, but the ceremony must be held in Hell. It cannot be in Santa Fe. The kingdom would erupt in chaos at the disrespect."

"But this isn't about the kingdom or your subjects. The celebration is about me and Jax and the ceremony we want to share our love with our family," she said. Her voice was calm, but I could see the frustration bubbling underneath. Rena was about to deliver a big middle finger to the Devil himself, and I didn't know whether to cheer her on or hide from the impending wrath.

I was probably risking my existence by stepping between them, but I did just that. Lilith's eyes widened a bit. "What about a compromise?" I glanced between Rena and her father. "What if we have an intimate ceremony for us in Santa Fe at our chapel, but we do a ceremony in Hell for the heir apparent's joining ceremony."

Rena blinked a few times. "I'm fine with that."

Lucifer let out a long breath. An odor of smoke scented the air. "That should be acceptable, but the joining ceremony will need to be grand."

Rena had hoped to avoid any more elaborate ceremonies, but we'd get our ceremony if she agreed to my suggestion. "I'll agree to that."

Lilith clasped her hands together. "Oh, this will be wonderful. When were you thinking? The winter will be beautiful in Santa Fe but so would spring."

"One week from today," Rena said.

"I'm sorry. I must have misunderstood. I thought you said a week from today." Lilith's mouth hung half open.

"No, you didn't. Our wedding will be next week," Rena said, her tone firm with confidence.

I wanted to sink back and melt into the wall because I feared Lilith's wrath more than Lucifer's when it came to the wedding. Lilith liked to plan events, and her only child was often the recipient over the years of the massive celebrations. Rena loved the attention from Lilith but not being paraded in front of thousands.

"You can't expect me to pull a wedding together in a week," Lilith said.

"That's the point, Mother. An intimate ceremony is small. I'll even wear a dress from a human secondhand store if I need to."

I understood the point my love was making, even shared the sentiment, but her mother was fashionable, grand, and stood on ceremony. If we had to sneak off to get the ceremony she wanted, I'd do it, but Rena wanted her family there.

"There is nothing wrong with those dresses, of course, but you will wear a gown that fits you. We'll visit the seamstress as soon as you've made your selection." Lilith caved to Rena, and I hurried to straighten my face from the shock. My future wife was skilled at handling people, and I don't think she even realized how well she did.

"I would appreciate that," Rena said. The small concession was a subtle nod, but one that incorporated her mother into the ceremony on a level Lilith needed.

"So, we're having a wedding," I said. It was a statement I hoped would end any more debate.

"It would seem so," Lucifer grumbled. "I already consider you part of the family, Jax." Lucifer hugged me, and I was worried one of us, namely me, might combust.

"Thank you," I said, awkwardly clapping his back.

"We better get busy." Lilith wrapped an arm around Rena and patted my back.

Rena shot me a pleading look over her mother's shoulder as Lilith led her out the door. She'd spent so much time with her mother before, and I'm sure Lilith missed the moments with her daughter. Rena missed those occasions too, even if she wouldn't tell Lilith that. But that left me alone with Lucifer...

I moved to the table and looked over some reports, but it was more shuffling papers with the giant presence still in the room.

"Jax," Lucifer called, and it wasn't a question. He headed toward the door, and I thought he would leave me alone in the room. "Walk with me."

Fuck me. He is going to burn me until I am ash like Typhon and no longer exist.

"Yes, Lucifer." I fell into step with him in the hall.

He was silent for a few minutes as we walked, and I wondered if he knew what he was going to say. He stopped in front of a room, and I recognized the symbol below the star at the top of the grand, golden door. It was the intricate symbol of Hell. *Here. In the Library.*

I glanced between Lucifer and the symbol, feeling like a ping-pong ball and unable to speak.

"It's my name." He ran his hands over raised characters. "Long ago, before the creation of Hell and before I fell from Grace. This was my room at the Library."

Why is he showing me this and not Rena? This was an important piece of their family heritage.

"I haven't been in here since Lilith and I chose to be together, but the books of my life would still be written, as that is what the Library does. Documents the lives of the archangels and some other angelic beings." He ran his hand over the symbol. A red glow sparked and ran the entire length of the symbol. Lucifer opened the door. "Come."

I followed him into the room. The space was vast, larger than most. Volume after volume filled the shelves. Tomes of Lucifer's doings. "I don't— "

"Understand. I wanted you to see this section." He walked to a set of shelves that stretched further than I could see. They were bound in red leather with a similar symbol entwined in another ornate one. "These are the books of my life with Lilith. Our love story started here." He pointed to the first book on one of the shelves. "The pages were being written before I even knew I was in love with her."

I looked around and realized there wasn't just this section of shelves filled with the mixed symbol. There were rows and rows of them. "Your joined emblem is on most of the books in here."

Lucifer smiled. "It is. My and Lilith's lives are completely entwined and have been since the day we fell for each other. But you have a question."

I reached for a book, but Lucifer slapped my hand away. *Guess that's a 'no touchy' their books.* "I do. Why are you showing me this and not Rena?"

"Because Rena's books were once stored in this room as well."

She'd had books in this room. *Is that how they knew she had a soul?* The question almost rolled out of my mouth. Another one burned to be asked more. "And they're not now?"

"No, and they haven't been for about five years," he said. "Even though I wasn't here. I felt the shift in history. She had started down her own path, and while she might not have understood the change then, the Library did."

"Is that normal?"

"There is only one reason." He ran his fingers over the spine of some of the books, his voice warm. "Love."

It was because of me. I remembered the day I knew I loved her. We were on the sparring mat. She'd taken me down, but I'd flipped her over. We'd been sparring for some time and were sweaty. Her hair had come loose and scattered across the mat except for the sweat-soaked pieces plastered to her face. I brushed the hair from her face, both of us breathing heavily. Her electric blue eyes locked on mine, and I saw a future with her. I saw myself waking up next to her, drawing a bath for her, holding her hand as we walked through ... the garden here at the Library. That's why the Library felt familiar to me. I'd wanted to kiss her that day, but she flipped me over and walked away, declaring the session over.

"You're remembering," Lucifer said.

"I am," I said. "So where are her books now?"

Lucifer gestured at the adjoining door. The symbol on the door wasn't the same as the entwined symbol of Lucifer and Lilith.

"The mark is Morena's name and yours entangled."

I ran my hand over the Library's representation of us, and my fingers tingled from the touch. The symbol glowed and the door opened.

"That is the first time the door has opened in five years," Lucifer said.

"So, you've known for five years Rena and I were destined to be together." Part of me was thankful he hadn't told me. Rena and I discovered what we meant to each other on our own, but the other part wondered why he hadn't at least told Rena.

"I hadn't visited the Library, but I felt the change. I felt when the books relocated and where."

I peered into the room. It was stacked floor to ceiling

with volumes, and I could swear I smelled the sweet scent of Rena mixed with the leather of the books.

"You can enter, Jax. This is as much your story as it is hers."

"Entering without her here feels wrong, at least the first time."

"I want you to see something." He urged me forward and stepped in behind me.

The books with our entwined symbols filled shelf after shelf. "How are there so many when we've not yet lived a quarter of a century?"

"You and Rena have a very long destiny ahead of you. This is just the beginning of your journey." Lucifer looked at me with tears in his eyes. Here he was just a father who wanted his daughter to be happy. My chest tightened from his love for her, and I realized he brought me here because he did consider me family. I was part of a family, belonging in a way I never had, and it was because of Rena and her love for me.

"Why show me this now?" The volume of books was impressive and what I'd hoped for me and Rena—that we were endgame for each other.

"Because there will be times when your relationship feels like your soul is being ripped away and everything is lost between you, but you must remember it is written that your lives will be an eternity of love. When she fights you because her will is strong, remember this room stands full of the adventures you will have together."

Ahh... This is the talk about how relationships are

hard. Rena and I had already been challenged in that department, but we had worked our issues out. My heart was light with the reassurance of the numerous books in my and Rena's room. I couldn't wait to show her.

"We haven't always been the greatest at communicating, but we've had conversations about it. We are doing better."

Lucifer smiled. "Communication is the biggest challenge. Lilith and I still work on that to this day. You will always need to strive for better communication."

"Will you show Rena this room?"

"No," he said. "I'll leave that up to you."

"But I can't enter through your door," I said, as we exited the room holding the life that would be mine and Rena's together. The door closed behind us and disappeared.

"Where did it go?"

"The room is now known by the owners, so it will no longer be part of this room. You will be able to find your room when you are ready. The location will sing to you as the Library does."

Disappointment curled in my chest because I wanted Rena to see our story was long and full, a direct reflection of our love for each other. She was...everything. "When the temptation to read ahead subsides."

Lucifer gave a small chuckle. "The fates will not allow you to read ahead, as you put it, unless there is a reason. You will be able to read and remember the past and present."

Rena and I had so many memories in our short time together, and I wondered if the room would be large enough to hold our future. Then again, the Library grew and changed every day. We would be able to bring our children here one day. I looked over my shoulder as the door to Lucifer and Lilith's room closed behind us.

CHAPTER 45

RENA

Mother and I were in the garden with Aunt Jophiel talking through what to do for the wedding in Santa Fe. My only request was simple. No extravagance. Mother insisted I wear a tiara with my veil, and I compromised and agreed to a small one. Aunt B had excused herself and disappeared. Michael and Gabriel had made themselves scarce as soon as we started talking wedding. A pang in my heart hit me that Uriel wouldn't be there for it, but he was happy. That's what mattered.

Father and Jax rounded the corner and joined us. I tilted my head up to Jax and smiled. "You look... happy, so I'm guessing Father didn't threaten to throw you in the dungeon or burn you for eternity."

Jax and Father both chuckled.

"No, nothing like that." Jax smiled at me, and my knees went weak even while sitting. His smile was so genuine and relaxed. I hadn't seen him smile like that in so so long. My heart swelled with the love radiating from him. He held out a hand. "Walk with me?"

I slipped my hand into his. "Of course."

"Don't be gone too long. We still have much to discuss," Mother said.

"I'll bring her back soon," Jax said, not taking his eyes off me.

"Where are we going?" I asked when we were walking down a long corridor in the opposite direction of our special room. My future husband took determined steps, though, so wherever he was taking me held importance for him.

"Where the Library leads," Jax said, swinging our entwined hands.

"You're being cryptic?" I bumped my shoulder against his.

He leaned over and kissed my temple. "Your father showed me the real magic of the library this morning, and I wanted to share it with you." He paused. "If the Library permits, of course."

"Is that what you were doing?" My heart warmed, and I matched his easy smile. "I can't wait to see what you have to show me."

"That's a loaded statement, my love. I have lots to show you that has nothing to do with the room we are going to." He squeezed my hand.

"How far is this room?" I winked at him. We might need a pit stop.

"That depends on the Library. We'll be the first to enter from the new door."

"New door? Now you really have me intrigued."

"Here." He stopped in front of a door trimmed in brocade.

The door glowed like candlelight, light and welcoming, and the most beautiful symbol I'd ever seen was embossed at eye level. A hum radiated out from it in the sweetest song—an invitation to enter. My curiosity piqued.

"What is this room?"

"Our room," Jax said, his voice soft and warm like honey.

"No, that's the other room... with the stained couch."

"Run your fingers over the symbol."

I did as he said, and the symbol sizzled. My birthmark flared in response, but the burn was gentle, not the intense fire I was used to. I rubbed the mark while glancing around, expecting to see an enemy. "Are there Nephilim here?"

"No," he said. The door groaned open in the lazy way a cat stretched. The same warm light as lit the brocade trim was visible inside. The aura welcomed me in like a warm hug. Like I belonged here.

"What is this place?" I asked spinning around and looking at the shelves full of books.

"I told you. It's the room of us," Jax said, pulling me into his arms. "The symbol is our names interlocked in some ancient angel language. The books in this room hold our past, present, and future. This is our eternal love in written form."

I gasped. "This is incredible. I thought that was only for angelic beings of the highest order like the archangels."

"Apparently, you fill such a role just as your mother and father have."

"And you," I said, aware of how breathless my voice sounded. Our love truly would be a very long love story like my parents.

"You are a part of me just as I'm a part of you. We are one."

CHAPTER 46

JAX

"We are one." Rena repeated my words, and her voice came out in no more than a whisper. Her eyes flashed demon red, and her skin flushed. She'd died and been saved by her grandmother, Eve, and almost died several other times. I'd almost met my death twice. I guess I technically had died when I became vampire. We'd triumphed and survived, despite the realms seeking out our deaths, and found our way to each other through the tragedy to the joy. I cupped her face in my hands. "We are one, my love, and never forget it."

I speared my fingers into her hair, pulling her closer. My restraint to not fuck her in our new room broke. I slid my hands down in slow motion, over her arms, and down her hips until I hooked my hands under her ass. She sighed against my lips. I lifted her onto a short bookcase. Her feet hooked behind my knees.

Books toppled from the case and scattered around us. *Was this moment already written in our books? Would someone read our story one day?* I grinned against Rena's mouth.

"What?" she asked, amusement in her tone.

"Just thinking how horny someone will be in the future reading how we fucked all over the Library."

"We've only had sex in one room," she said, laughing.

"It's about to be two, and I think we should make it a mission to fuck in as many as possible," I said, my voice growing rough with need. I leaned in so my hardness pushed against her core, too many clothes separating us.

Rena gasped, reaching for the collar of my shirt.

"Don't you—" My shirt was shredded from my torso.

She giggled, dropping the fabric in her hand. "Too late."

"If I walk out of here without a shirt, your father is going to be that much closer to turning me to dust," I said, still not sure that wasn't a real possibility.

"Maybe we should wait until after the wedding." Rena trailed her hands over my chest.

"To have sex?"

She nodded, looking around at our shelves of books. "In this room."

I let my relief out in a breath. "I thought you meant at all. I know it's only a week, but I don't think I could stay away from you that long."

"Sweet angel's ass, no. I don't want to wait a week

either. It just feels like anything here, especially sex, should be special here."

I brought my lips to hers in a gentle caress. "Being with you is always special, my love. No matter where we are, when I make love to you, you are all I see. The entirety of the realms falls away." I kissed her forehead. "There are no sounds except for your soft mewing and moaning." I placed a chaste kiss on the tip of her nose. "There is nothing except you."

Rena grasped my neck and held me still in front of her. She examined me for a moment as if she needed to read the truth in my soul, and finally, love softened her features. Her lips collided with mine, and she devoured me.

CHAPTER 47
RENA

"Why is it so hot in here?" I asked for at least the fifth time.

"The air conditioner is turned down as far as it can go without freezing the unit," Stassi said.

My temperature was stable as long as I was in any realm except the human realm. It fluctuated if I visited for any amount of time, which was apparently a random side effect of my demon powers coming in so early. The elevated temp was something I would gladly live with to have defeated Typhon. *But could the air just be a little cooler for my wedding day?*

"I feel like I'm going to erupt in fire," I said.

Stassi's eyes widened. "No spontaneous combustion on your wedding day."

I smiled. "Promise." My nerves weren't as sure of my promise and my hands shook.

"My understanding is that fiery feeling is normal for a demon coming into their power," Aunt B said, zipping up my dress and sparing a glance at Stassi. My aunts understood Stassi had been made aware of many of the celestial goings-on that most humans weren't, but they were still hesitant to say much in front of her.

"Especially the way I did. I get it, but it would be nice to not have my dress stuck to me on the way down the aisle."

She led me to the mirror and positioned me to look at my reflection. Stassi turned a fan toward me before she bent down to fluff the bottom of my skirt. Mother smiled at my reflection.

"You look beautiful," she said, placing the veil on my head.

"This is too much, isn't it? Too human and not enough demon or angel tradition," I said, my words coming out like vomit.

Mother fastened the lace into my updo and secured the tiara in place — a small one with rubies and diamonds. "It's the perfect nod to the part of Jax that is still human."

"We both wanted this," I said.

Mother squeezed my shoulders. "I know, and you look angelic."

Tears brimmed her eyes. She swiped the dampness away. "I do have one pin for your waist if you are okay with that."

"Of course, Mother."

"Stassi, will you hand me that red box?" Mother motioned to the box on the couch. Stassi passed the velvet case to her with a smile. Mother opened the box, and the pin had two halves. Hers and Father's symbol and mine and Jax's made of diamonds. "May I?"

I nodded, unable to get words past the knot in my throat. She pinned the emblem to the center of the embellished belt, and the entwined symbols fit perfectly where the midpoint had been blank as if intentionally holding space for this gift.

"It's perfect, Mother. Thank you." I reached out to hug her. She held me in a tight embrace for a moment.

"We should go before we both start crying. Your father is probably losing his mind."

I giggled. "You're right. He'll be pacing and could very well send someone to the dungeon."

Jophiel looped her arm through Aunt B's. "We'll go take our seats."

"See you there," I said. I inhaled a deep breath and let it out slowly. *One... Two... Three... I can do this.*

Mother and I wound through the corridors and stopped a short distance away from the main chapel door I'd enter through. Father was indeed pacing as we suspected in his black and red uniform of a suit.

"Lucifer?" Mother called to him. "Come take your daughter's arm."

He turned, and a proud smile lit up his face. "You look beautiful, Morena." He kissed my cheek. "And so do you." He turned to Mother and placed a soft kiss on her lips.

Mother ran her thumb over his lips to wipe away her red lipstick. "And you are still the most handsome man in the world."

A small sigh escaped my lips. That was the enduring and undying love I wanted to have with Jax.

Mother left us to take her place in the front pew. The invitations were limited. Our ceremony was meant to be for us. Another demon bonding ceremony would be held in Hell sometime later, but this was what we wanted. Today was about our love story, mine and Jax's.

I entered the chapel on my father's arm and immediately found Jax. He didn't wear any of the regalia typical of our ceremonies in Hell but instead wore a sleek black tux. He looked sexy as sin, and I imagined pealing his clothes from his body after he was my husband. *Husband.* The word fluttered in my stomach. His forehead was wrinkled and his handsome face was full of nerves that disappeared and softened. My gaze locked with his and everything and everyone else fell away. It was only me and him. His lips moved to form three words, words I struggled with at times but no longer. I mouthed *I love you* back to him. He was the most important thing to me. Father tugged my arm. "Ready?"

I looked up at him. "Ready."

The candles around the chapel all flamed to life. He'd once called those parlor tricks for those with lesser magic when I was a kid, despite how much I begged for him to do it. I peeked up at Father with a smile and whispered, "Nice touch."

"Those theatrics are just for you, my daughter."

Father guided me down the center aisle and held my hand out to Jax. He smiled, his eyes glistening as he accepted it in his.

"Who brings this woman to enter into marriage today?" The judge we'd hired, and that Father used his demon powers on to make sure the man thought ours was a normal wedding, asked. I'd requested the judge to change the traditional wording from 'gives' to 'brings' because no one was giving me to Jax except myself. I freely gave myself to him just as he did to me.

"Her mother and I do," Father said. He kissed my cheek and took the seat beside Mother.

Jax held my hand in his, and there was a bit of slickness in his palm. He was nervous too. I smiled up at him, and he leaned in close to my ear. "You look exquisite, and I can't wait to take that dress off you and be inside my wife."

I pressed my thighs together at the immediate arousal, and I should probably have some shame over my reaction in a chapel. We had souls, but we were demons too, so fuck the shame and guilt.

"Today, Jax and Rena have chosen to write their own vows," the judge said.

Jax and I faced each other. "Rena, when we were kids, you were my best friend, and I'm grateful you are still my best friend and so much more. My love for you has grown every day, and I promise to love you more each day as your husband. Forever yours. Forever loved."

I blinked back tears. "Jax, I can't imagine one day without you. You are my heaven, my hell, my Earth, and my dream. Everything in my life has led me back to you, and that is because we are the perfect fit together. My love for you goes beyond the realms of our existence and is infinite. There isn't anyone else I'd want to fall from Hell with, and I'm honored you chose to fall with me. I'm yours for all eternity."

The judge smiled, and I wondered what Father's magic had him thinking we'd said, but that didn't matter. I was staring at my husband. *My husband. We made it.* A sweet floral scent wafted around me that smelled like I imagined love did, and love was definitely looking back at me with big hazel eyes. "By the power vested in me by the state of New Mexico, I pronounce you man and wife."

White rose petals fell from above us, but that wasn't planned. I looked up, and they came from nowhere. My gaze landed on my aunts and uncles. The bashful smiles on their faces were so unusual the coy looks told me this was a gift from them, likely Aunt B's doing. They blessed my marriage.

"You may kiss the bride," the judge said, his voice quiet as if he was in awe of the flower petals.

Jax leaned in and brushed his lips across mine. He was gentle, deepening it only a little. He pulled back, and his cheeks were flushed red. "My wife."

I smiled up at him. "My husband."

After the Wedding

Our wedding present from my parents was to live among the humans. Fate willing and barring no more prophecies, we would have centuries if not millennia to live in all the places we wanted to explore together. Jax and I were bound together as the balance and the scale, and that, along with his jinn activated, meant he no longer would age. Gabriel was our messenger and would bring communications, especially if we were needed, but Mother and Father promised to visit often. I couldn't ignore callings to balance nor Jax for the scale, but we were free to live a very long life together.

I turned to my husband, who stared out over the ocean from the Greek island of Ithaca. The sunset was deep as if the sun could touch the ocean. I bent down and ran my hand through the water until it rippled.

"Perfect," Jax said, his voice warm like the temperature on the island.

I sighed. "Completely. I'm glad we started in Greece to rewrite memories."

Jax pulled me into his arms. "I wouldn't change anything." He brushed the hair from my face and cupped my cheeks. "Everything, the good and the... terrible all brought us to this point, and that is a life with you I couldn't imagine a few years ago. I wouldn't trade any of the pain, Rena, because I get to call you my wife for an eternity."

His sincerity shook me to the core. My heart swelled as if my chest couldn't contain the intense love. He was all the realms and more to me. "You are my everything, Jax. You are my eternity."

Jax rested his forehead to forehead with me and brushed his lips to mine in a gentle caress. I urged him on, deepening the kiss.

"Have me here on this beach." My voice was a breathless whisper, but I knew he could hear me.

He chuckled against my mouth. "Whatever my wife wants my wife gets."

Jax scooped me up, placed me gently on the blanket, and unbuttoned my shirt. My breath quickened in anticipation of his touch. He paused. "I love you, Rena, with every ounce of my essence I am yours."

Tears sprung to my eyes. "With all that I am and everything I have, I am yours, Jax. I love you beyond time and beyond measure."

His hands speared my hair, and his mouth found mine with a fierceness that sealed our eternal promise to each other.

EPILOGUE

Rena

5 Years Later

I sipped a cup of tea Jax made for me, taking in the sunrise from the porch of our house on the private island my parents gifted us. The pinkish-orange glow reflected on the pristine water, and I was thankful we enjoyed more mornings like this than not. Jax's connection to Uriel had faded, but mine had grown stronger with him and the other archangels. It was good to see Uriel and his family in the Elysian Fields. I could peek in on them from time to time, but the experience was different than the communication with the archangels in the realms I traversed. The archangels could be overwhelming with their constant chatter, but I'd learned to shut them out and shield the parts of my life I wanted to keep for Jax and me...like when we were here during our six-month reprieve. I'd make time to check in every couple of days, but for the most part, the angel connection was blocked from this space.

The door squeaked and banged. I turned to see Jax juggling a tray of bacon and a pot of what I assumed was more tea.

"Need some help?"

He chuckled. "You ask me that every day, and what do I always say?"

"No." I laughed.

"I hope you're hungry. I got a little carried away." He sat the tray down on our small table just big enough for the two of us to sit on either side.

I scanned over the contents and couldn't control my giggle. "What is all this?"

He pointed to each item. "Bacon, of course. Avocado toast. Boiled eggs. Pancakes, butter, and syrup."

"Are we expecting company?"

He took my hand in his and brushed his lips over them. "It's our anniversary."

I narrowed my eyes at him. "Are you feeling okay? Our anniversary isn't for another couple of months."

"Not our wedding anniversary. It's the anniversary of the day I knew I fell in love with you and began my journey to prove my worth to you." He rubbed his thumb over the palm of my hand.

My chest warmed as my heart expanded. He still found ways to make my heart melt. I rested my hand on his cheek. "You have always been worthy of me, Jax. I'm the one who had to become worthy of you."

He tugged my hand and pulled me around the table into his lap. His familiar warm demon scent mixed with the salt breeze coming off the water. The aroma was home to me. "I will never get enough of you...of this."

I peered at the blue-green waters of the ocean. "It really is beautiful here."

He pushed the hair out of my face and nuzzled my neck. "Nothing more beautiful."

"I was talking about the scenery." I giggled.

"So was I." He kissed the spot below my ear that instantly made me press my thighs together.

"Our six months here always go by so fast." I sighed.

"Mmm. Hmm." He hummed against my collarbone as his hand slid up my thigh.

"And you are not tired of splitting your time between here and Hell?"

"You are my home, Rena. Whether we are in Hell or here on our private island. No matter where we are, you are my personal paradise. Never doubt how much I love you." His mouth crushed mine, and I let him in like he was the sustenance I needed to survive.

I pulled back. "Thank you, Jax."

He brushed his lips against mine. "For what?"

"For knowing me and what I need, even when I might

not know myself. I love you for eternity and whatever is beyond that for us."

"I love you," he said. "And I think I know what you need now."

Jax scooped me up, and I threw my head back, laughing. "I think you do."

He paused in front of the door and turned toward the ocean. "The water looks inviting."

I wagged my eyebrows at him. "It does."

In a couple of months, we'd be back in Hell running things while Mother and Father took a vacation. They were never gone as long as we were. Father didn't want that to be our burden until the time came for me to fully ascend the throne. For now, I focused on the callings of the balance and those had become fewer over the years. I hoped that was a sign we were at or nearing a time of peace. Tonight, I planned to talk to Jax about starting a family. We'd wanted time for ourselves before we did, and I wasn't even sure we could. I wanted to try though, which meant research and probably a trip to the Library, and I didn't mind that at all these days. We could be complete with just us, but the thought of seeing a little Jax running around made me content.

"What are you thinking?" Jax pulled me from my thoughts.

"How happy I am with our life."

"Hmm." He tossed me into the ocean.

Jax," I yelled.

He yanked his shorts off and dove in after me.

"You still happy?" he asked, a huge smile on his face.

I wrapped my arms around his neck. "Eternally."

The End

ACKNOWLEDGMENTS

To my sister and my nieces, you are always there cheering me on, celebrating wins with me, and encouraging me when I need it. I'm so glad you are here for the journey whether attending events or bouncing ideas around with me or talking about my books with people you know. I'm so thankful for your constant support.

To my friend, Lizzie, thanks for making me get out of my head and out of the house at least once a week. Our shop talks and record browsing kept me sane during the final stages of getting this book done. Thanks for the hilarious moments that will likely end up in future books, but most of all, thank you for the encouragement.

To my beta readers, ARC readers, and fans, how you have continued to love Rena and Jax as much as I do made it the hardest to end the trilogy. Thank you for the emails, posts, and messages about what you connected within each story. I want to recognize those who actively seek out indie authors to support whether that is on booktok, or bookstagram, or any other platform. You help indie authors so much, and I appreciate you.

To my editors, Dawn and Lisa, thank you for making me think about the story and characters from different angles. You make me better with every note and comment, and I would not have made it this far without you.

To the judges who chose Fallen, Book 1 in the Falling From Hell series, as the paranormal category winner for the National Excellence in Story Telling contest, I thank you. I needed that news in a big way the day it arrived in my inbox.

ABOUT THE AUTHOR

Susan Person is an award-winning author in the paranormal and dark paranormal romance categories. Recently, she returned to college to pursue a degree in anthropology and graduated in 2021. Susan enjoys meeting writers and readers alike at conferences and events. She knew at an early age she wanted to write powerful heroines and fulfills that dream by writing badass empowered heroines who take charge in their paranormal worlds.

Susan grew up on a thoroughbred horse farm before moving to the big city of Dallas. She considers herself a Texan but is loyal to her home state of Arkansas. A lover of travel, she has visited several countries with many more to go on her list. She particularly loved dowsing at Stonehenge and seeing the Parthenon in Athens. The outdoors is a place where Susan finds inspiration and can often be found in a park, at the lake, or on a road trip. She especially loves the mountains. Furry animals hold a special place in her heart, and dogs tend to seek her out as a friend.

Connect with her at <u>susanperson.com</u>

instagram.com/susanwritespnr

tiktok.com/@susanwritespnr

facebook.com/susanwritespnr

goodreads.com/susanperson

bookbub.com/authors/susan-person

WANT TO LEARN MORE ABOUT SUSAN PERSON?

Scan the QR code below to see where you find more of Susan's book or see what reader events she is attending.

FALLEN, FFH BOOK 1

Winner of the paranormal category of the National Excellence in Story Telling contest!

REVERIE, FFH BOOK 2

The second book in the Falling From Hell series.

COMING SOON

A new romantasy series is coming soon. Join my newsletter to learn more!

Also by Susan Person

The Blood Moon Prophecy

Queen of Sacrifice, Book 1

Queen of Darkness Book 2

Queen of Moons Book 3

A Vampire Ice Age Series

In Blood & Ice, A Vampire Ice Age Series - Book 1

Reclamation In Ice, A Vampire Ice Age Series - Book 2

Book 3: TBA in 2025

Enchanted Rock Immortals World

Fae Undone, The Enchanted Rock Immortals Clan Fae 1

Fae Redone, The Enchanted Rock Immortals Clan Fae 2